THE STARR STING SCALE

Also by C.S. O'Cinneide

Petra's Ghost

The Candace Starr Series

The Starr Sting Scale

C.S. O'CINNEIDE

THE STARR STING SCALE

THE CANDACE STARR SERIES

DUNDURN
TORONTO

Publisher: Scott Fraser | Acquiring editor: Scott Fraser | Editor: Dominic Farrell
Cover designer: Laura Boyle
Cover illustration: Sanya Anwar
Printer: Marquis Book Printing Inc.

Library and Archives Canada Cataloguing in Publication

Title: The Starr sting scale / C.S. O'Cinneide.
Names: O'Cinneide, C. S., 1965- author.
Description: Series statement: The Candace Starr series.
Identifiers: Canadiana (print) 20190130741 | Canadiana (ebook) 2019013075X | ISBN 9781459744844 (softcover) | ISBN 9781459744851 (PDF) | ISBN 9781459744868 (EPUB)
Classification: LCC PS8629.C56 S73 2019 | DDC C813/.6—dc23

 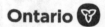

We acknowledge the support of the Canada Council for the Arts and the Ontario Arts Council for our publishing program. We also acknowledge the financial support of the Government of Ontario, through the Ontario Book Publishing Tax Credit and Ontario Creates, and the Government of Canada.

VISIT US AT

 dundurn.com | @dundurnpress | dundurnpress | dundurnpress

Dundurn
3 Church Street, Suite 500
Toronto, Ontario, Canada
M5E 1M2

For my daughters, strong female protagonists every one of them.

The Starr sting pain scale, developed by Christopher Starr, rates the overall pain of stings on a four-point scale. One is the lowest rating. Four is the highest. Everything in between still hurts.

CHAPTER 1

"I'M NOT SURE THAT I CAN HELP YOU."

"On the contrary. I'm quite certain that you can."

The well-kept blonde in her fifties bats her considerable lashes, quite a feat given the amount of Botox injected in her face. She sits opposite me, perched on a high bar stool at the back of the Algonquin, a dive we affectionately refer to as The Goon. *Affection* is perhaps too strong a word when talking about a dark, dank, seventies-wood-panelled hole that smells like stale beer and jism — the former odour compliments of the full-time barmaid, Lovely Linda, and the latter a result of the brisk part-time business she transacts in the men's toilet on request. I'm Candace Starr, a woman who gets paid for a different kind of service. I still fit in here. But the blonde is definitely out of place.

"A friend of mine sent me," she says, flicking a strand of straightened hair off her polished forehead. "She told me you assist in these matters. That you helped her with a rather difficult husband."

Difficult husbands are a specialty of mine. Rarely in my line of work do you run into a husband who isn't difficult in some way. They cheat, they lie, and occasionally they smack their women around. It's like the metal in a wedding ring creates a strange magnetic force within a guy's body that sets off his asshole switch. Maybe wives should insist on a wooden band.

"I'm retired," I tell her.

"You look a bit young for that."

"I'm older than you'd think." I've managed to keep my looks over the years despite my lifestyle. It's the Italian blood from my mother's side. That olive skin covers up a lot of hard living. The woman abandoned me on a median strip when I was three, but at least she left me with a good complexion and a figure that holds up. Everyone thinks I'm in my early twenties, but I've been on the wrong side of thirty for a few years now. I've got legs that go all the way up to my armpits — at an age when most women are starting to gather ass up from around their ankles.

"I can make it worth your while," she says, batting her eyes again. The Coach bag she's clutching costs more than a month's rent. I bet she can make it worth my while and then some. I'm impressed that she had the balls to come here. To track me down. Most society mavens like her would find a go-between to do this sort of dirty work. A gardener with connections, a boy toy with designs. This woman has made the effort herself to make sure the job gets done. I respect that.

"Stand up."

"I beg your pardon?" She blinks repeatedly. The smooth paralysis of her face doesn't allow for any other facial movement that denotes surprise. Or any other emotion.

"I said stand up."

She tentatively gets to her feet. I drop down from my own bar stool and come up behind her. She's tall in her Steve Madden boots, but I'm taller. At six foot three, there aren't many people I don't look down on. I pull back my curly mess of long, honey-brown hair and tie it up with a rubber band from my wrist. The blonde's hair is cut short in the back, revealing a shapely neck. I could snap it if I wanted to. I've done it before. Instead I reach around and dart my right hand inside her cool silk blouse. She gasps, but I'm in and out in a flash. After all, this isn't a cheap excuse to cop a feel. This is business.

"You can sit down now," I say, returning to my own seat. "Just had to make sure you weren't wearing a wire." I take a pull off the draft she bought me, my first drink of the day. "Now, tell me about the job. I'm not saying that I'll do it. I'm just letting you tell me about it."

She looks like she'd like to raise one of her finely shaped eyebrows at me but manages only to achieve a slight twitch in the corner of her right temple. I wonder if she gets those brows waxed or threaded, making a mental note to ask her later, before I lift her wallet. I'm not much into the girlie stuff, but even a woman like me needs to landscape. When the blonde goes to sit on the bar stool again, her high-heeled boots peel away from the sticky linoleum floor, making a sound like someone pulling a band-aid off fast.

"The job, as you call it, is simple," she says. "I want you to get rid of this young man." She pulls out from her purse one of those strips of four photos you get from a booth. Shit, does anyone use those anymore in the era of selfies? A tousle-haired youth grins out from each rectangular square. He sits next to a pretty, plump teenage girl with doe eyes and big tits.

"He's kinda young for you," I say. I've probably insulted her, but it's the truth. I know these middle-aged tantric-yoga girls can keep themselves up fairly well, but come on, she could be that kid's mother. He didn't even look old enough to be a difficult husband.

"Age is deceiving," she says. And I suppose it is after your third butt tuck. "But this person is not an associate of mine. Rather, he is an associate of my daughter."

I inspect the strip of photos again to get a better look at the teenage girl. The big hazel eyes, the slope of the neck. Definitely related.

"You want me to off your daughter's boyfriend?" I ask, incredulous. Taking out a target who doesn't even shave on a daily basis is pretty heartless, even for me.

"Boyfriend is not the right word for him," she says, sipping on the Diet Coke that Lovely Linda delivered on her way to the men's restroom with a friend. "He is a parasite. A barnacle affixed to the hull of society with no purpose or design. He smokes. He sells drugs. He sits in his basement and plays video games all day, and he fucks my daughter." She adjusts her ass a bit in the chair, as if remembering her own days of being fucked in a boyfriend's basement. "He's got to go."

"Maybe it's a phase," I say. "These things blow over."

"It's been two years," she says. "Nothing is blowing over except my daughter's chances of being accepted into a decent university."

"But c'mon, a kid?"

"That kid gave her a disease," she almost shouts, looking around the bar before she collects herself again. "He can't keep it in his pants. He can't keep down a job. He can't even manage to graduate high school. He is so lazy that he has to set an alarm to get up and binge drink, and his conversational skills consist of grunting in response to any inquiry while he grabs at his genitals." She takes a deep breath and continues. "He has no future and no prospects, and he clings to my daughter like a lemur on a high branch. I want him out of the picture."

I look hard at this flushed, badass woman, and then I look at the boy in the picture. He smiles back at me with his goofy photo-booth face. I can see a vape kit tucked into the front pocket of his jean jacket, a zit about to erupt on his chin. He has his whole life ahead of him. A string of doe-eyed girls in his future. Years of parties to crash, millions of brain cells to damage, along with half the people around him, as he lives out his days in a rented room over a run-down convenience store, falling into a sour-smelling bed drunk each night, only getting up to go to the bar, or to meet with disgruntled women of a certain age who need difficult men disposed of. Like my old man — or like me for that matter. I look back at the woman, who begs me with the same wide hazel eyes as her daughter.

"Ten thousand," I say, "delivered like I tell you." So much for retirement. "And you have to do exactly what I say." I finish off the beer in one go and motion Lovely Linda across the bar for another. She's back from the men's restroom.

"I'll arrange for it today." The mother opposite me blinks one last time from her glacial face, and the deal is sealed.

CHAPTER 2

"MOVE IT ALONG, BOYS."

The two punks are hunched over the magazine section practically feeling up the skin mags. I know them from the neighbourhood, a couple of meth heads. I'm watching the store for Majd, the owner. He gives me a break on the rent for covering the cash from time to time. There are benefits in living above an E-Zee Market. Although this is probably the only one.

"Free country," one of the punks retorts. They stay their ground. The other kid grabs a *Hustler* and slips it under his jacket. Jesus, what's the matter with these assholes? Haven't they ever heard of the internet? They got stuff on the deep web that'd make a hard-core porn star pee her pants.

"Make me," the little shit with the *Hustler* says. Then I remember. It was his girlfriend I saw in here a week ago, with her sweet but strung-out face all blown up. He'd beaten the crap out of her for reasons she couldn't remember but decided somehow she deserved. I'm going to enjoy this.

"I said to move it along." I get up from the stool I've been sitting on behind the counter, not happy to have been disturbed. I deliver my unhappiness to the kid by slamming him into the Slurpee machine while I twist his right arm behind his back in a way nature never intended.

"Holy shit, Candace, I was only fucking around." The punk whines my name with a nasal pitch. I think I may have broken his nose. If he got blood on the machine, I swear I'm going make him clean it up.

"Yeah, well, I think you'll realize that fucking around with me isn't highly recommended." I give the punk the bum's rush out the front door, where his meth-head buddy has already disappeared in a hurry. When his body hits the pavement, it sounds like a wet slap.

I close the door and return to my stool, picking up today's paper where Majd left it behind the counter. Another thing you can get off the internet, but I like the greasy feel of newsprint in my hands. Folding over the front page, I find a headline that gives me pause. I take a sip of the Jack Daniel's I've been nursing behind the cash. I'm an alcoholic but not a sloppy one. I can hold my liquor even though it's probably killing me. I'm still reading the article when the little bell jingles on the front door and a man I know but don't want to see walks in and approaches the counter.

"Long time no see, Candy."

The cop wears a rough overcoat on top of a cheap suit. He's a detective, so he doesn't have to dress in the usual getup. The sparse hair on his balding noggin has the consistency of dryer lint, and his face has that large-pored, flared-nostril look of a guy who spends more time smoking stogies and scarfing fried food than he does at the gym. Even sitting on the stool I tower over him, what with my height and being on the platform behind the cash. I know having to look up at me makes him uncomfortable, like most men. I barely glance over the top of my newspaper as I acknowledge the man. I hate it when people call me Candy.

"Detective Saunders," I say, returning to the article on the front page. He stands at the counter and waits for me to give him more of my attention. I fold the paper slowly and then look him in the eye. The two of us have history. "Can I help you?" If sarcasm were an Olympic event, I would have scored a ten out of ten from all the judges, even the Russians.

"I see you've been reading the paper," Saunders says, who always had a way of stating the obvious. Not the shiniest tool in the homicide division's box.

"I see you're still buying off the rack." Honestly, what do they pay these mugs? Even when my dad was on the skids, he wouldn't have been caught dead in this Hugo Boss knock-off. Then again, Dad was a sucker for upscale brand names. He had a Cellini Rolex watch that showed the lunar phases. I remember as a kid being fascinated by the silver moon that flashed from a deep blue circle punched with stars on its face. He wore that watch every day of his life, right up until he disappeared. The tug that finally fished him out of the harbour a week later claimed to have never found it on his bloated wrist.

The bell jingles again and a fairly tall Asian woman around my age walks in. She slides off a full-length smoky-grey raincoat and goes to stand beside Saunders.

"I don't think you've met Detective Malone," he says. The woman lifts an eyebrow at me in lieu of introduction. They're arched and well shaped, much like the rest of her.

"Malone?" I ask.

"Dad's from Kerry. Mom's from Canton," she says.

"Another Irish cop, imagine my surprise."

She smiles and pushes a strand of her angled, dark bob behind one ear. "Imagine how surprised you'll be if I charge you with the assault of that gentleman out there on the sidewalk."

I take a closer look. This detective is smarter than Saunders and much classier, with her tailored black slacks and crisp white button-down shirt, the type where the loss of one more button would make people take notice. Her well-worn army boots kind of ruin the look, though. I can see the label on the coat she has draped over her arm. London Fog. At least this one knows where to shop.

"I got no idea what you're talking about," I say, staring her down from my perch on the stool. She locks me with her jade-green eyes, not flinching. She isn't intimidated by my size, or possibly anything else. Where was a cop like her last week when that little meth head rearranged his girlfriend's face? He deserved to have his nose broken.

"Listen," Saunders says, interrupting our little standoff. Too bad, I was kind of enjoying it. "We don't care about that," he says.

"What is it that you care about then, Saunders?"

He grabs the newspaper off the counter where I'd left it and points at the front page.

"This kid. Tyler Brent. You know him?"

I look at the picture. The boy has the same goofy grin on his face that he had in the photo-booth snaps the blonde showed me at The Goon. I look back at Saunders. "No, can't say that I do."

"Well, that's funny, because we found him down by the river yesterday with a broken neck," Saunders says, putting the newspaper down.

"I'm not sure why that's funny but whatever gets your rocks off." I look at Detective Malone and give her what I hope is an endearing smirk. She just keeps those green eyes of hers trained on me like an emerald-infused laser beam.

"Looks a whole lot like your work," Saunders says, leaning on the counter. "Or Mike Starr's."

"That's interesting. But since my old man's been choking on cemetery dirt for five years now, you can probably take him off your most-wanted list." I'm secretly flattered by the comparison. My dad taught me everything I know.

"And you, Candy. You don't seem to be choking on much these days, except that time I sent you upstate for." Like I said, Saunders and I have history. He managed to nail me on conspiracy to commit murder a few years ago through dumb luck and a guilty wife who started singing like a scarlet tanager when the cops took her in for questioning. I served three years, mostly because the tanager flew off to South America and couldn't testify;

or at least that's what everybody thinks and I'm not about to correct them.

"You got me all wrong, Detective," I say, holding up my hands. "I'm not in the game anymore." And the truth is I haven't been for a while. Cooling my jets since prison, working at the E-Zee Market and keeping a low profile. I'm out of that racket. I am. I was.

"Really," says Detective Malone, interrupting Saunders this time. "So, you don't know anything about this kid or who might have snapped his neck so bad he could watch his own ass walk away?"

"Listen, anyone can do anything these days. Build a bomb, break a neck. They have instructional videos on YouTube for fuck's sake." I take a shot of the Jack and smile as I wipe my mouth with the back of my hand.

"Do you know anything, or don't you?" Malone says.

"I don't."

"You mind telling us where you were last night?" Saunders pauses to look up something in his tattered black notebook. "Between ten and midnight?" He looks up at me again, snapping the ratty cover shut with a flourish over his sloppy handwriting. Jesus, hasn't anyone heard of technology?

"Between ten and one," Malone says quietly before I can answer.

"What?" Saunders says, turning to look at her. He's annoyed.

"Between ten and one," she says. "The coroner extended the time of death window on account of the cold snap last night."

Saunders gets flustered, missing his pocket the first time he tries to put his little notebook away. "Between ten and one in the morning then," he says, looking up at me, his face turning red.

"Easy. I was here, watching the store."

"Anyone able to verify that?" he asks.

"I don't need anyone to verify it."

"What the hell does that mean?" Saunders says, still flustered.

"The security tapes," Malone says, pointing at the video camera on the wall. Definitely smarter than Saunders.

"I'm happy to give you the tapes," I say, grinning. My teeth are straight and almost eerily white. I take good care of my mouth. "When you bring back a warrant."

Saunders's face is starting to go the colour of the Caesar I drank for breakfast. He leans in on the counter, so close to me I can smell his crappy aftershave over the stink of his sweat. I feel sorry for Malone if she has to travel in the unmarked car with him. It's like being assaulted by a basket of rancid fruit.

Malone puts a hand on his shoulder, drawing him back. "She's right. We need a warrant." Saunders turns around and gives her a look that betrays his view on women in the police force.

"Let's get the fuck out of here. I've had enough of this bitch." He walks right past Malone and smacks the door open with the heel of his hand. It slams hard behind him. The little bell jingles so violently it almost falls off.

"I think your partner has a hot streak," I say, leaning back on the stool.

"He's not my partner."

"Really? You work alone?"

"Sometimes," she says. Malone looks over at the door and then back at me. "I caught the case. Saunders just came out here with me because he knows you."

She does an in-depth visual scan of me, no doubt taking in my faded State U T-shirt and the loose boy-friend jeans that actually came from an old boyfriend. I have boyfriends, despite my occasional flirtation with the ladies. I'm an equal opportunity employer when it comes to sex.

I can see Malone's eyes flick to the bottle of Jack with the shot glass next to the register and then back to me, with my tangle of hair falling over eyes that remain sharp as knives. She's trying to figure me out; anyone could tell her that's a waste of time. I'm an enigma.

"I've got a proposition to make," she says.

"I'm listening."

"This case is getting a lot of play in the media. A lot of concerned citizens worrying about their kids. *What's the world coming to?* That sort of thing."

"Uh-huh."

"A case like this could make or break a detective's career." She looks over her shoulder at the door again. "And Saunders is useless."

"I could have told you that." He may have nailed me on that conspiracy charge, but that cop has the IQ of a stick of furniture.

"I need someone to help me. Someone who knows the landscape. If you know what I mean." She trains those green eyes on me again. "I want you to work on this investigation with me." She's actually serious.

"Like an informant?" This woman doesn't know me very well. I may be a drunk and a criminal, but I'm no snitch.

"No," she says. "More like a partner."

"Are you kidding me? Why the hell would I do that?"

"Well, for starters, to avoid me busting you for that pistol you have stuck down your pants."

I stand up from the stool and look down at the slight bulge at the front of my jeans. I'd forgotten about the gun. "Why would I carry a gun in front?" I say, playing dumb.

"Because I'm guessing most men aren't expecting you to shoot them when you reach for your crotch." She's a salty one, despite the class act. But she's right; women don't expect it either. I had a special holster made and everything. "If your parole officer finds out you're in possession of a firearm, you'll be back in a prison jumpsuit. I don't imagine you'd want that." She's got me there. I look like shit in orange.

"And what will they say when I tell them you offered a convicted felon a job helping you investigate a homicide?" I can't imagine this is standard procedure. Then again, there is nothing standard about this woman.

She waits before she answers, rubs her lips together in the way some people do when they're holding back something they want to say. She cocks her head to the side and then finally spits it out.

"Your father's murder. We know who did it," she says.

I don't respond at first. Then I tear out from behind the counter and stand in front of this cop, looking down at the part of her smooth dark bob, so close I could do some spitting of my own. "What the fuck are you talking about?"

She puts her hand on her holster, but other than that she doesn't budge. She looks up at me and answers. "We know who murdered your father. And if you help me with this investigation, I'll tell you who it was." Only then does she step away, pulling out her card and dropping it on the counter. "We don't have enough to make it stick. But the guy is as guilty as sin. Trust me."

"I don't trust cops."

"Well, you better learn to make exceptions, Candace." She smiles. Her teeth are tiny and bright white. She takes care of her mouth, too. "Of course, those security tapes better check out. And we'll be pulling your bank records to make sure you haven't received any big chunks of cash lately. Wouldn't do to have you investigating your own crime, would it?" She goes to leave, the little bell jingling as she opens the door.

"Why?" I say, and she turns around, her hand still on the glass of the door. I can see her height from the colour-coded measuring sticker on the wall. Five foot eight. "Why the hell do you want to use someone like me to find a killer?"

She pauses and smiles again. "It takes one to know one," she says. "Think about it." Then she walks out the door.

I stand there for a while. I guess I'm in shock. My worn cowboy boots, the ones my dad used to call shit kickers, are rooted to the tile floor. I want to scream. I want to punch something. I want to chase after Malone and hold her face to the pavement until she tells me what she knows. But I don't do any of those things. I'm bereft, but I'm not stupid. I walk back behind the counter and take a swig of the Jack straight from the bottle. It burns going down, knocking me out of my paralysis, and gets me thinking straight. Some people get foggy with alcohol, but I get clearer. It numbs the other shit inside me, so I can focus. People often don't believe that a woman can be a functioning alcoholic. They obviously haven't been out to the suburbs where the McMansion soccer moms are pouring vodka on their cornflakes every morning.

I've tried to find out for years who took out my dad. It was hard, because I was on the inside when it happened, awaiting trial for the conspiracy charge. They let me out for his funeral. I remember dropping the earth on his coffin with my wrists pinned together in handcuffs. I tapped every connection I had to find out who was behind his death, both in prison and when I got out. But nobody was talking. And believe me, I can be quite convincing in getting people to chat.

I slip Malone's card into my pocket. I've got other things to take care of before I think about her offer. After another shot of the Jack, I get down to business.

It won't take much to doctor the security tapes. The time stamp has been busted for months. I can make a tape that'll say whatever date and time I want. I learned more working in the prison's AV department than how to keep a roomful of convicts from rioting after the second screening of *Miss Congeniality* in a month. And Majd won't talk. He grew up keeping his head down in Syria, where the government and rebels were busy annihilating each other, along with any civilians that rubbed them the wrong way. He knows when to keep his mouth shut.

My bank account, well, they can check that out all they want. All they'll find is ten bucks and a history of overdraft. I never took the blonde's money. Like I said, I'm out of the game.

That is, unless I find out who put the hit on my old man. Then I have one more play to make.

CHAPTER 3

"COME ON IN, CANDACE."

My uncle Rod's permission to enter his bungalow is redundant, since I already let myself in with my own key. Sometimes when I'm between places he lets me stay here. It's not much, but it's a decent couch to crash on. He's sitting on it now in the small living room, leaning forward, elbows on his knees. Coloured blurs on skates move impossibly fast across the flat screen bolted to the wall in front of him.

"Jesus H. Christ!" he shouts, slamming his fist on the coffee table. A pizza box falls off the side and onto the floor with the vibration, while a half-dozen empty beer bottles surprisingly remain standing. He has a Budweiser on the go in the fist that wasn't banging the table. "You'd think these fellas would know how to check a man when he's going for a breakaway down the ice, but they've all got their fingers up their arses."

Sometimes Uncle Rod gets mistaken for Irish, but he's Canadian. From Newfoundland. All the Newfies sound like that on account of being descended from famine-crazed Micks, he's told me. He flies home every year for the same two weeks to visit with those misplaced Irish, no longer starved for anything but steady jobs. The last time I saw my dad, he was visiting me upstate after taking him to the airport for such a visit. I didn't have Rod's aging mother's phone number in St. John's with me in prison, so I couldn't let him know what happened. When he flew back two weeks later, he waited for my dad for three hours before finally giving up and calling a taxi. Uncle Rod's not really my uncle, but he was my dad's best friend and the closest thing to family I've got.

I clear some newspapers off the seat beside him to sit down. Tyler Brent's face stares up at me as I move them aside.

"What period is it?"

"Second. Gagné's on the injured list with a concussion and it doesn't look good for the Habs, by God." Newfoundland doesn't have a hockey team, so Uncle Rod roots for the closest team in proximity, Montreal. He objects to French Canadians in principle, but he'd gouge an eye out before supporting the Toronto Maple Leafs.

As if responding to my uncle's prediction, Montreal loses the next faceoff. The Penguins' right wing zips down over the blue line and flicks his wrist to send a slap shot into the top right-hand corner of the Habs' net. Another goal for Pittsburgh.

"Shag it!" he says, grabbing the remote. He switches off the game. "I can't bear to watch those numbskulls lose to a bunch of fuckin' Yanks again." He passes me the Budweiser he was drinking. "No offence."

"None taken," I say, accepting the bottle and throwing back what's left of the beer mixed with my uncle's backwash. It's rare that we get to share such a moment. Rod only drinks when he watches hockey. The rest of the time he's dry. It's hard to believe he and my dad got along so well, considering. Then again, they were in the same business, often worked for the same organizations, preferring the trade of their own kind, fellow criminals, as opposed to freelancing like me.

Neither of them ever used guns or knives. I was allowed a pistol on account of being a girl, but it came with express instructions to only use it to threaten rather than kill. Weapons tell a story, Rod and my dad used to tell me. Where you've been. Who you are. Your gloved hands and the element of surprise never talk. Both men had been trained somewhere along the way on the ins and outs of using those hands to be more efficient than the most high-powered rifle. Dad in the military. Rod with some mercenary group. Neither would talk about it. They had a lot in common, even if one was drunk most of the time and the other sober.

"I had an interesting day."

"So tell me about it," Uncle Rod says, as he walks into the kitchen. There is a large rectangular pass-through to the living room, so he can still hear me. Down a small hallway beyond the kitchen are the bathroom and bedroom. There used to be two bedrooms, but Rod knocked the wall down between them to give himself more space. The back door and the cellar door are next to the fridge, where I can hear him rifling around for something to eat. I can see his arm, sinewy and strong despite middle age, holding the fridge's handle. Rod is thin and wiry, not a big guy like my dad was. You'd never guess what he's capable of, which often works in his favour. I once saw him stop a man's heart for good with one well-positioned sucker punch to the temple.

"I had a visit from Saunders," I tell him.

"That bastard," Rod says, as he grabs a disc of coral-coloured meat and slaps it into a frying pan. He turns on the gas for the one burner of the stove that still works and lights it with a match. Uncle Rod could probably afford a new stove. He makes good money at what he does. But at his age, and with the physical demands of the job, he's worried about what he'll do when he can't work anymore. Even criminals have to think about the state of their 401K.

"He brought another cop with him," I say. "Name of Malone. A woman. Asian. Sort of. They were asking me about this kid in the paper, Tyler Brent. Did you read about him?"

"I did," Uncle Rod says over the sizzle of the pseudo-meat. The scent of it wafts through the pass-through, a combination of black pepper, maple syrup, and dirty feet.

"Well, the funny thing is, I actually know something about it," I say, grabbing another beer from the old red-and-white cooler tucked beside the couch. We used it camping once, when Rod and Dad had taken a job to get rid of a park ranger. The ranger had busted a gang of bikers for running their motorcycles through the protected forest. In the process, he stumbled upon a banker tied to a tree being repeatedly whacked with a tire iron for underperforming stock portfolios. The banker survived the gang's wrath, but the star witness for the prosecution did not, once my father and Rod had completed their assignment. My dad said it was okay because the Park Ranger was taking bribes from people poaching black bears. I accepted this kind of logic as a child, the way most kids accept a half-assed explanation for why the sky is blue.

"I thought you were after retiring." Rod doesn't look up from the frying pan.

"I am." The spicy smell of the meat fills the little bungalow as I tell my uncle about the blonde's visit to The Goon. The details of her unique request to rid her daughter of a barnacle of a boyfriend. Then the visit from Saunders and Malone, asking about him and how he got his neck broken. Rod listens attentively while he flips the meat, not asking any questions, allowing me to get to the end. Always listen first, I'd been told growing up. It's how you end up knowing more than the other person, right from the get-go.

Uncle Rod slides a couple of pieces of the meat onto two mismatched plates and shoots out a good squirt of ketchup next to each round disc. Then he walks into the living room and serves the fried bologna, one for him, one for me. When he plunks the plate on the coffee table, one of the cupboard doors in the base of it pops open to reveal fifteen years of Stanley Cup playoffs on VHS. He taps it closed with his foot. Honestly, I don't know why he doesn't put those onto DVD. But he's a fucking fossil when it comes to technology. His VCR sits like a museum piece in a corner of the living room, so not of this era it could have dinosaur crap on it.

"You didn't tell them anything, of course," Uncle Rod says, handing me a knife and a fork.

"Of course not," I say, but I'm squirming a bit.

"Did you kill him?" my uncle asks, raising one bushy eyebrow.

"No," I say, staring down at my meat. "I'm retired."

"Maybe the blonde hired someone else," he suggests.

"Maybe." He waits to see if I say more. I don't.

Rod takes his own knife and fork and turns back to his dinner. "Then what's the interesting part?" he asks, cutting into his bologna. Being questioned about a crime you have some involvement in doesn't constitute much of a story to a man who's been suspected of more than a few murders in his time. Not half as many as he's actually committed, though.

"After Saunders left, the other detective, Malone, she made me an offer." I still haven't touched my own meal.

"What's that then?" Rod asks,

"She asked me to help her find who offed the kid." I watch him cut into the sweaty sandwich meat again, dip it in the ketchup. "And she'd tell me who killed Dad."

Rod's fork stops in mid-air, ketchup dripping back onto the plate. He looks straight ahead, like the TV is still on, but it isn't. "How the hell would she know that?" he says, turning to me, dropping the fork onto his plate.

"She says the cops know, but they don't have enough to make an arrest. You know yourself, Rod, we've done plenty of shit the cops know about but still can't pin on us." It takes a surprising amount of evidence to convict someone; the courts are too full and the cops are too busy to bother if they know they can't make a case. Innocent until proven guilty. Our saving grace.

"I don't know, Candace." He stands up and walks over to the bay window, clenching and unclenching his hands. Then he turns around. "I pulled in every marker I had to find the fucker who did in your father. And no one knew nothin'." I know I'm bringing up a sore subject for him. He's a man used to being in the know, particularly when it comes to murder. It must irk his professional sensibilities that a cop might know more about the subject of crime than he does.

"Do you think it could have been my mother?" I ask, trying to guide him away from the offence. "She and the old man used to scrap a lot, didn't they?" Perhaps it's the meeting with the blonde that has me thinking about mothers, because the idea that my mom might have rubbed out my dad has never occurred to me before. Their short-lived union was acrimonious and violent. One time she clocked my dad with the clothes iron, the only time I'm sure she ever picked it up.

"Don't be daft. That woman left you on a ride at the amusement park when you were four with nothin' but five bucks and a map to Burger King. We haven't seen hide nor hair of her since."

"I thought she abandoned me on a median strip on the highway when I was three?"

"Same difference," he says.

I leave it alone. Whatever the story, she didn't come back.

Rod returns to sit on the couch and takes one of my hands in his. They are still greasy from the bologna.

"Listen, darling, I just don't want you to get your hopes up on this. There's no guarantee this Malone is going to tell you anything. I never met a cop yet I'd trust as far as I could spit in a gale wind." He leans in to look directly in my eyes. "And you wouldn't help one of them, would you?"

"I would if I thought I could find out who slit my dad's throat and dumped him in the river." I take my hands out of his. I'm a little pissed at his reaction, although I don't know what I expected. "Wouldn't you?"

"I might," he says, picking up his fork again. "Then again, I'm not as close to this Tyler Brent business as you are. Where did you say you met with the mother? He takes a bite of bologna and chews on the soft meat before he swallows, as if it's even necessary.

"The Goon," I say.

"Were you seen?"

"Just by barflies and lowlifes." Uncle Rod nods his head. He knows the clientele of The Goon. It's not a stellar bunch. The fact that I'm perhaps both a barfly and a lowlife goes without saying. Then again, the blonde did stand out there. She could be remembered. And her association with me would be hard to explain.

Uncle Rod grabs the remote and turns the TV back on. His earlier disgust with the Habs has been soothed with the meal and a brief time out. Two of the players have dropped their gloves and are trying to tear each other's jerseys off in a strange kind of embrace. This is how men on skates fight — like they're slow dancing. It's hard to punch and stay upright on the ice at the same time. You need the guy you're trying to level to hold you up, even as you attempt to punch his lights out.

"I don't know, Candace Starr," my uncle says, not taking his eyes off the screen. "You could be asking for a peck of trouble."

"I could be," I say, picking up my knife and fork. The use of my surname invokes my father, as does the salty taste of the meat in my mouth. Fried bologna was a staple of my childhood. My dad learned to make it from Rod, and I couldn't get enough as a kid. I also couldn't get enough of trouble. And some things never change.

Although, in my experience, allegiances often do. Uncle Rod's reaction to my interesting day seems a little off, and Newfoundland isn't too far away for a man to fly back, take care of business, and then fly out again. Maybe I'll have to find his aging mother's number and give her a call. He may be the only family I've got, but in a clan of killers, weapons aren't the only ones capable of telling stories.

I eat my bologna and watch the black-and-white-striped referee pull apart the fighting players. They skate to their respective penalty boxes like spoiled children who aren't getting dessert. The partners' dance is over. At least for now.

CHAPTER 4

THE GUY AT THE LIQUOR STORE is attracting attention. He's spent the last fifteen minutes loading up his cart with bottles and six-packs, with no apparent rhyme or reason. Premium liquors like Hendrick's and Chivas Regal lie alongside cheap bourbon that would take the paint off a car. Organic light beer from a microbrewery jostles up against Black Death from Iceland. Right now he's clutching a forty-ouncer of Jack Daniel's in one hand while he reaches for a bottle of white wine with a large black high heel on the label called Girls' Night Out. He is not a discerning shopper. Neither is he a discerning dresser. He's forgotten to wear a shirt and his grey sweatpants look like he's pissed in them. Smell like it, too.

"Can I help you with anything, sir?" The smiling liquor store employee pretends nothing is wrong, but we all know differently, except the guy. He slurs something unintelligible and tucks the white wine with the high heel into his armpit. The smiling liquor store employee goes back to stocking shelves.

I turn away from the drama and go to the back of the store to look through the bargain bins. Tonight I need quantity over quality. I've got too much on my mind. I pick up a couple of dented boxes of no-name fortified wine, steering clear of the Thunderbird. That bum wine turns your tongue black. I'm on my way to the cash when the guy with the cart does a runner out the exit doors, moving surprisingly fast for a man who can barely stand up. He makes it about ten yards into the parking lot before he's tackled by two undercovers from the store. The bottles smash into pieces on the pavement.

"Candace?" A chubby but pretty middle-aged woman with a no-nonsense pageboy puts her hand gently on my elbow. That's almost the highest she can reach. It's Charlotte, Uncle Rod's petite on-again, off-again girl-friend. She's holding one of those little wire baskets with a bottle of the Girls' Night Out wine in it.

"Hi, Charlotte." I drop the two boxes of fortified wine on the rubber conveyor belt. They travel down toward the cashier like soldiers going to war.

Charlotte places her own purchase on the belt and moves ahead of me, dropping the shopping basket and opening her wallet. "I'll pay for these," she says, indi-cating my booze as well as hers. Charlotte's nice that way and has always had a soft spot for me. She's forever dropping by my place bringing food or gossip, a covert way to check in on my well-being. I've never under-stood it, liked or disliked her attentions. I'm missing the flip side of maternal instinct: the need to be mothered. That need is like music from a long time ago, and I've grown tone-deaf.

"Can I drive you home?" Charlotte asks.

"Sure." Least I can do is keep the old girl company in her Toyota hatchback, since she's financed the evening's entertainment. Plus, it's raining again. We walk out the automatic doors together and into the parking lot, careful to avoid the broken glass and the screaming, bleeding, alcohol-drenched drunk who is now in handcuffs. He must have fallen on the broken bottles when he got nabbed. A police cruiser has arrived.

"That was fast," Charlotte says, as we load the back of her car with the drinks.

"They probably called them as soon as he walked in the store," I reply, keeping my head down as I go to get in the passenger side of Charlotte's car, my unruly hair drawn across my face. I've had enough run-ins with the cops today.

We are turning out of the parking lot when the large fishing lure hanging from the rear-view mirror swings around and almost catches me in the cheek as I lean forward to adjust my seat belt. Charlotte's a nice enough woman but a lousy driver. The lure is shaped like a bottle of Screech, Newfoundland's infamous cheap, high-proof rum. It is a souvenir from the one and only time Rod took her home to meet his mother. A disaster of a trip. The two of them started bickering as soon as the plane was in the air. By the time they got to St. John's, they were no longer speaking to one another. Charlotte stayed in a motel and got a flight home to the States the next day. The mother never got introduced. Uncle Rod had brought the fishing lure home as a make-up gift. Charlotte embedded it in his hand first before accepting it. Still, it gets me thinking. I may as well ask.

"Did Dad and Uncle Rod ever fight?"

"What do you mean? With each other?" Charlotte narrowly misses a cyclist as she turns right. The rider falls off his bike and onto the curb, his spandexed legs tangled up in the frame. She doesn't even notice. The windshield wipers swish furiously back and forth, only one of them making contact with the glass. The road is a melting watercolour on my side of the glass. If Charlotte kills us in a head-on collision, at least I won't see it coming.

"Yeah." I make sure the seat belt is still fastened. "With each other."

"Rarely. They were cut from the same cloth, those two. Like brothers," she says.

"Brothers fight," I say. But it's true. I can't remember a cross word between my dad and Uncle Rod, although maybe they did their arguing out of earshot, an attempt to give me something resembling a stable childhood. Though they didn't seem to mind if I heard them beating some guy to death with a bag of oranges in the basement until it made juice. Or leaving me alone to toast marshmallows by the campfire in the dark while they went to break a park ranger's neck.

"There was the one time." Charlotte bites her lip, immediately ashamed of saying anything. "But that was a long time ago."

My interest is piqued. "What did they fight about?"

"Your mother." Charlotte switches into the right lane and clips the side mirror of a parked van.

"What about my mother?" Of all the things they might have argued about I hadn't thought my mother would be one of them. On that woman the two had always seemed to be in complete agreement. She was the "thieving wop" to both of them. They used this term to refer to her so often that as a child I thought it was all one word: *Feethingwop*. I thought it might be a cross between the boogie man and the tooth fairy.

"I shouldn't have said anything," she says, biting her lip again.

"Well, you did," I say, as Charlotte pulls into a parking space in front of the E-Zee Market and slams on the brakes. The booze smashes against the back of the rear seats. She doesn't look up from the steering wheel. The neon sign of the E-Zee Market sputters in the window. Majd really needs to get that fixed.

"Tell me, Charlotte."

She sighs in surrender. "Your mother was connected," she says. "Or her family was. She was estranged from them, though. Ran away with your dad when she got pregnant." She must be on an "out" with my uncle, or she wouldn't betray him like this. Nobody is ever allowed to talk to me about my mother.

"And?" I prompt. She's not getting away with only giving up half a story.

"When she disappeared, Rod was afraid there might be repercussions." Charlotte adjusts the rear-view mirror, like she's afraid we're being followed. The fishing-lure hooks dance back and forth.

"But she didn't disappear. She took off," I say.

"Some weren't so sure." She shifts in her seat, fiddling with the keys in the ignition, but she doesn't turn the car off. "I think they argued about that, too. What happened to her," she says.

"What *did* happen to her, Charlotte?"

Charlotte pops the hatchback with a button on the dash, the car still idling.

"Honestly, Candace, I just don't know."

★ ★ ★ ★ ★

Sitting in my apartment at midnight, with half of the last box of sickly sweet wine left, I decide it is too late to call Rod's aging mother in St. John's and ask whether he took off for a couple of days during his visit five years ago. But it is not too late to call the number on the card I hold in my hand. Usually, I have to go downstairs to the E-Zee Market and ask Majd to use the land line behind the counter. But I lifted Charlotte's phone from her purse today when she went to unload the booze. I'll give it back, though. I don't steal from people I know. Or at least from people I know who bring me cookies. I figure a cop's got to have voice mail to intercept late-night calls. I'll leave a message. But Malone surprises me by picking up on the first ring, despite the time. A keener.

"Malone here."

"I'll do it," I tell her.

Silence, and then finally, "Candace?"

"Who else?" She's quiet on the other end for a moment.

"There's going to be some ground rules," she says.

"Hmm."

"No breaking the law. No lying."

I agree, knowing this is, in itself, a lie.

"You give me Tyler Brent's killer, and I'll open up the file to you on your father's murder. No arrest, no file."

"What if I just promise to do my best?" I say in a saccharine-sweet voice, before polishing off the wine in my fruit jar.

"Then your best won't be good enough," Malone says.

She gives me an address. Tells me to ask for her at the front desk tomorrow at ten o'clock. I don't need to write it down. I'm good at remembering things.

"Of course, we're going to have to keep things on the down-low," she says. "We'll tell people you're a private investigator here to consult. A few people might know who you are, but for God's sake try not to draw attention to yourself."

I stand up to get another fruit-jar glass of wine and catch my reflection in the cracked full-length mirror nailed to the back of the door. It cuts off my head at the top. I'm wearing only a sports bra and shorts, so the gold five-pointed star tattoo on my flat stomach shows. A deep navel made for body shots at the centre winks like an indented wormhole. The kind Einstein wrote about, not the kind that actually houses worms. That would be gross. "I'm not a person who exactly blends into the wallpaper, Malone," I tell her.

"Well, you'll just have to practise your chameleon moves," she says.

I tap the little spigot on the box of wine, my shoulder pinning the phone to my ear. What's left of the crimson liquid spurts into the jam jar. It leaves red-tinged bubbles at the top. "I still don't get it, Malone. Why are you doing this? What's in it for you?"

"I told you, career advancement," she says. But there's a hesitation there that others wouldn't notice. My life has depended on having a fine-tuned ear for tells.

"I'll see you tomorrow, Malone." I hang up the phone and go stand at the one window in the room. It looks out on the street. Down below I can see into The Goon across the road. Inside a man with a familiar diagonal fade of tightly wound curls sits at the bar. He's a bounty hunter I like to roll when he's in town. Marcus Knight. Black guys like him rarely set foot in The Goon, it being strictly a hangout for white trash. Marcus is neither one of these.

I take in the shape of his sturdy shoulders and strong back from my apartment and think how I'd like to run my fingernails down them. But I need to get up early if I'm going to meet Malone. Well, early for me. Instead of joining him in the bar, I lie down on a mattress on the floor and study the stains on the ceiling while I finish off my drink. It's my usual form of meditation before I pass out.

I don't buy Malone's story about career advancement. Something's making her wet enough to risk involving a volatile entity like me, and whatever that is, it's way hotter than a promotion. I couldn't give a rat's ass what happened to my mother. But I'll do whatever it takes to find out what happened to my dad. Even help the cops find Tyler Brent's killer. Or at least make them believe that I have. Whatever it really is that Malone wants me for, I'll find that out, too.

And if she's screwing with me, she'll only live long enough to be sorry she did.

CHAPTER 5

BEFORE I LEAVE TO MEET MALONE the next morning, I use Charlotte's phone to call Rod's elderly mother, Agnes, in St. John's. Charlotte can afford the long-distance charges. She has a good job with the government in the Accountability Division. Other than looking for typos in their quarterly newsletter, I've never been sure what exactly she is accountable for. I'll leave the phone in her mailbox on the way to the address Malone gave me. It's in the same neighbourhood.

"I'm sorry we can't come to the phone right now. Please kindly leave a message." I love how she still uses the word "we" even though it's just her and her pet hedgehog, Boris. Women, particularly older ones, do this so you won't think they're alone; they don't know that most people who mean to do them harm don't give a shit anyway.

"Hi, Agnes, it's Candace. Mike Starr's daughter," I say after the old-school answering machine beeps. Then I clear my throat, at a rare loss for words. "Can you please give me a call when you get this message?" I leave the number of the E-Zee Market and repeat it twice, knowing I won't have the phone handy later. After I hang up I realize the old girl might think something is wrong with Rod or someone else close to her if I'm calling all the way from the States. So I call again and leave another message. I don't want to be on the hook for causing an old lady's heart attack in Canada. Especially one who sends me thick, hand-knit wool socks every Christmas that I never wear but make for excellent silencers. I use the gun for more than intimidation, but I don't tell Rod that.

"Where you going to today, Miss Candace?" Majd asks. He can see I've made an effort to look respectable, my hair tamed into submission and a smattering of makeup on my face. He is busy working on fixing some old speakers he found at the curb on garbage day, trying to coax them back into something he can hook up to the receiver that Lovely Linda gave him from The Goon when they replaced the sound system with digital.

"Nowhere," I say. And he accepts that. Majd is the most awesome Syrian refugee I know. He has the gratefulness of a person who knows what it's like to have nothing, and he cooks kick-ass samosas. He also isn't afraid to take the piss out of stereotypes.

"Look," Majd says, smiling, as he teases a red wire out with a pair of pliers from among the black ones sprouting from the speaker. "It's a bomb."

"Jesus, I wouldn't say that too loud."

"It doesn't matter," Majd says, going back to his work. "Misunderstanding people will think it just the same."

I would have said ignorant instead, but Majd is a class act. He knows not just what it is like to have nothing, but also what it is to be afraid. If I had his understanding and compassion I wouldn't have killed half so many people.

★ ★ ★ ★ ★

When I get to the front reception desk at the address on Baker Street, I'm an hour late. The woman at the semi-circular desk takes one look at me and asks for identification. She has ultra-Aryan blond hair that's poofed up and lacquered like a batch of hard cotton candy. I want to touch the surface and see if it is actually a bulletproof helmet issued to all police support staff.

"I don't have any," I tell her. Which at the moment is true, but in the larger sense is a load of horseshit, as I have about twelve different IDs at home stashed away in a large douche bag I ordered off the internet. People will search many things, but a women's douche is where most folks draw the line. Always hide your contraband in plain sight, my dad used to say, because that's where nobody looks.

"No ID, no entry," she says fiercely, standing at attention and snapping her high heels together like an underling of the Gestapo.

"I'm expected," I tell her.

"I doubt that."

"I doubt you've ever had a decent lay, but I'm still fucking expected."

The receptionist makes so much noise in reply that a bunch of people come around the corner, including Malone.

"You're late," she says.

I just shrug in my black leather jacket. Underneath it I'm wearing a T-shirt that says GIVE ME HEAD UNTIL I'M DEAD.

"C'mon," she says.

I walk past the front desk, but not before I give the pissed off receptionist the finger.

"So, what do I call you when we're in the cop shop? Ma'am? Detective? Sir?" I ask as Malone leads me down a tiled hallway that smells. Before this she made me go to the restroom and put my shirt on inside out so no one can read the sentiment. It doesn't even make sense, she said.

"You can call me Malone."

"If we're going to be working together I should know your first name, don't you think?" I try to sound coquettish. A word I would not be caught dead using in a sentence, but one I learned during my brief brush with university. "So, what is it? Your first name?"

"Chien-Shiung," she says.

"Chien-Shiung Malone?"

"Yes," she says, as she opens heavy double doors to a brightly lit room. She motions for me to go ahead of her.

"That's quite the handle," I say, as I step inside, and then I realize why the hallway smelled so bad. There are stiffs everywhere. We're in the fucking morgue.

"But you can call me Malone."

★ ★ ★ ★ ★

The morgue isn't the worst place I've been, but I don't like it. I have no problem with dead bodies, as you might expect, but the order freaks me out. The corpses filed like tax returns in metal drawers. The clean white sheets and ridiculous toe tags identifying the owner like a bag of candy corn from the bulk store. I think I have the opposite of OCD. I can't stand the idea of "a place for everything and everything in its place." Particularly when it comes to death, which is messy and undignified no matter how you slice it. The only place in my life where I demand perfection is my work. Which I suppose, to be fair, is the case with the forensic pathologist Malone is currently introducing me to.

"This is Dr. Peyton Kolberg," she tells me, motioning to the stupidly thin chick in a white coat. She looks like she hasn't seen a good meal in weeks. I guess working here could turn a person's stomach, or she's just one of those high-functioning anorexics. They're often high achievers. Nothing like puking up your breakfast in the morning to get you in the mood for taking on the world.

"Hi," I say. I don't put out my hand to shake hers. She might have been elbow deep in some skag hag's colon before this.

"Hello," she says. And then gets right to business. She walks over to a stainless-steel table and pulls back the white sheet. There lies Tyler Brent, face down, like he's just passed out from a three-day drunk. She didn't have to go to a drawer for him. He'd already had his file pulled.

"Young kid," I say. And he is. Although not an innocent, as I found out with a little digging. But I'll play those cards when and if I need them.

"As you can see the damage is to the C2 vertebra where it transected the cord." She runs one gloved finger along the back of the kid's misshapen neck. "Making the cause of death spinal shock." She continues with her bony finger down the middle of Tyler's back. "A break lower than that, at the C3 or C4, and he still would have died, but it would have been from asphyxiation."

"Why?" Malone asks. But I know. You break a guy's neck too far down and you paralyze just about everything, including his lungs. Then it takes about two minutes of gasping like a beached orca before he finally bites it. Way too far down and you only make him a quadriplegic, which at least makes it easier to overpower the target and get the job done, but is way too much work for the money. Dr. Kolberg explains all this to Malone, who obviously never needed to kill a guy in the men's toilet so quietly and efficiently that the district attorney taking a crap three stalls down doesn't notice.

"So, the person knew what they were doing?" Malone says, and while she doesn't look at me, I know she's thinking about it.

"Not necessarily," says Kolberg. "Come over here and I'll show you." She moves to the head of the table and pulls back some of the kid's long hair to show us the fleshy side of his neck. Malone moves closer. I stay where I am. I can see already what she's talking about. "See these ligature marks here and here," she says, pointing to the angry red lines that criss-cross at the side of his windpipe. "There is another term people use for a clean break of a C2 vertebra. The Hangman's Break."

"More like the Hangee's Break," I say. The doctor cracks an eerie smile. It freaks me out worse than the toe tags.

"But there was no evidence to support a suicide at the scene," Malone says. "No rope or anything he could stand on. Just the river down in the gorge below him and a grassy field where he was laying."

"That may be," says Kolberg, as she snaps off one of her latex gloves with a vengeance only a woman who will be eating celery sticks with salt for dinner can muster. "But make no mistake, this boy's been hanged."

"Shit," says Malone. "Anything else?"

"Two things," she says, using her still-gloved hand to pull the sheet farther down to display the boy's full body. His ass is white with bright angry pimples on it. Like I said, there is no dignity in death. On the back of one of his hairless calves is a tat that stretches from his ankle to his knee. Four disembodied white arms encircle the dark face of a wolf. It makes me a little queasy to see it, and I wish I had a shot of bourbon to wash the sight down with.

"You ever seen a tattoo like that before, Candace?" asks Malone.

"Nope, can't say that I have," I say, even though if she read my file, she'd know that I probably have. "We done here?"

Malone turns to the doctor. "You said there were two more things. What's the other one?"

"Oh yes," she says, replacing the sheet and taking off the other glove. Dr. Peyton Kolberg picks up a clipboard and scans the front of it until she finds what she's looking for. "He had about three beers in him, traces of THC, 50 mg of Valium, and a half a pound of gummy bears."

"Now that's my idea of a Saturday night," I say to no one in particular. No one in particular laughs. Especially not the dead boy on the table, tagged like a jumbo-sized bag of candy.

★ ★ ★ ★ ★

We're working through the contents of a clear plastic bag in an alcove off the evidence room when a petite Middle Eastern honey peers around the corner. "Hey, girl, I heard you were in the building." Malone stands up and gives the woman a hug. Female bonding. Never understood it.

"And who do we have here?" she says.

"Uh," Malone says, a bit uncomfortable. "This is Candace. The one I told you about. This is Detective Selena Patel."

"Hi," she says, taking me in, as I sit at the table with the last personal effects of Tyler Brent: a dime bag of weed and an almost-empty wallet that reeks of boy sweat. "So, you're the hitwoman," she says with just a touch of awe.

Malone shushes her.

"I prefer personal assassin," I say, not standing to greet her.

Selena smiles with her whole face. She's got those smoky good looks some Indian women have, where deep brown eyes appear outlined in kohl even when they're not. Her long, sleek, ebony hair is pulled back tightly in a functional ponytail.

"Like I said, Candace is helping me out with a case," Malone says and sits back down next to me again, as if I need a handler close by, which I probably do. She straddles the chair backward so she's still facing Selena.

"Don't know how much help I can be if the kid offed himself," I say, leafing through the wallet with latex gloves on. I pull out an expired student card, two rubbers, and, surprisingly, a pink dry-cleaning slip.

"We don't know that," Malone says, more for her friend's benefit than mine.

Just then, a blue-eyed Adonis with thick, wavy red hair walks up and stands beside Selena. His beard is angled in at the sides and fuller at the chin. Not one of those *Duck Dynasty* abominations that make a man's face look like a poorly kept pussy. He is serious *GQ* material and the red hair is a pleasant surprise on a guy pushing thirty. Many men lose that colour around the time their wisdom teeth come in. I'm not usually in favour of gingers, but I'd make an exception for this guy. When he enters the cramped alcove, Malone stands up abruptly and whacks her head on a shelving unit. Several stuffed three-ring binders fall to the floor at his feet like a sacrificial offering.

"Hi, Malone."

"Hi, Danny." Malone doesn't bend down to pick up the binders. Just stands there looking like an idiot. Someone has to give this girl a few pointers. Nobody says anything. I think about handing her one of the condoms, but something tells me she wouldn't appreciate the joke.

"Hi, I'm Danny Anderson," he says, breaking the awkward silence and extending his hand. I stand up to shake it and realize he's the exact same height as me, six foot three. I'm about to give him my own name and perhaps my phone number when Malone cuts in.

"This is Carrie," she says. "She's a private investigator I've brought in on a case."

"Does Carrie have a last name?" he says, still holding on to my hand.

"Fisher," Malone blurts out. We both look at her. Danny finally takes away his hand and gives Malone a questioning look.

"Listen, I hate to interrupt the little party you ladies have going on in here," he says then turns to his partner. "Selena, we better get going."

"Duty calls," Selena says, shrugging her slender shoulders. Next to Danny she looks even more petite. "You still on for tonight?" she asks Malone.

Malone nods. She starts to pick up the binders off the floor, returning them to the shelf.

"Okay, I'll see you at the rink at eight." Selena and Danny disappear around the corner. Malone finishes cleaning up the binders.

"Carrie Fisher? That's the best you could come up with?"

"I was afraid he'd recognize your real name."

"So you went with fucking Princess Leia?"

"It's all I could think of on the spot." She sits beside me at the evidence table.

"What's this about a rink?" I say as I hand her the rubbers to put back in the evidence bag, latex on latex in our slick powdered gloves.

"Selena and I play hockey together."

"No shit? Women's hockey?"

"Yeah." I think about what Uncle Rod would think of that. He's always said women play a better strategic game than men. Every time the Olympics roll around he enjoys watching the Canadian women's team beat the hockey pants off all the other countries' teams.

"Looks like you'd like that Danny for a bit of stick-handling," I say.

"Shut up, Starr."

"Okay, Malloy."

"It's Malone," she says.

"Whatever."

I could continue teasing her. It would be good sport. But instead I decide to make an observation to appear eager and smart instead of lazy and mouthy. Not too smart, just enough to look like I'm earning my keep, while I wait and watch and see what this ice hockey–playing detective is really shooting for by involving me in this case.

"Do you see anything out of the ordinary here, Malone?" I say.

"Yeah, the dry cleaning ticket. We'll have to go down and claim whatever he had there. See if it leads anywhere," Malone says.

"That's what you see, Malone. Now tell me what you don't see."

She feels around in the bag then stands up and grabs the evidence log. Standing in the entryway, she scans the information on the clipboard that came with Tyler Brent's meagre belongings.

"What seventeen-year-old kid hasn't got a phone practically stapled to him twenty-four hours a day?" I ask. Just like my dad didn't have his Rolex when they fished him out of the harbour, Tyler was missing what should have been his most prized possession.

"I can't believe I missed that," Malone says. "I thought they just had it held over with tech services, but you're right, he didn't have one on him." She scratches her bobbed head while thinking it over.

"I'm always right," I say, leaning back in the chair and taking off the gloves. My long legs stretch out so far they reach clear across the alcove to the opposite wall. "And now it's time to buy this girl a drink for it."

CHAPTER 6

MALONE DOESN'T BUY ME A DRINK, but she does throw me a burger in the back seat of the unmarked cop car after I bitch enough. There aren't any interior door handles, but I didn't want to ride in the front in case someone saw me. Besides, this way Malone has to keep opening the door to let me out like she's my chauffeur.

"I don't see why we couldn't have stopped for lunch," I say. I had been hoping for the famed liquid lunch of working professionals. Or maybe that's just an urban legend, like people stealing your kidneys at business conventions. Although I have seen it on *Mad Men*, the liquid lunch, not the kidney stealing. But the women on that show never do get to participate in the booze; they're mostly treated like pond scum around the office since it's the sixties. I suppose the show is a bit outdated for assessing the current corporate culture. Although when you look at the gender wage gap, you've got to wonder how fucking much.

"I told the parents we were coming," she says, pulling into the driveway of the tired looking but massive red-brick century home. "And I want to get over to the crime scene before it gets dark."

I want a Scotch served neat with a beer chaser, but I keep that to myself. There'll be time enough for some premium liquor this evening when I spend some of the cash I lifted from the skinny pathologist's purse. I found it in a desk drawer when she and Malone were reviewing the last of the autopsy report. At least her wallet wasn't anorexic.

There hadn't been much left to review. Nothing under Tyler's fingernails. No DNA to lift, or fibres to match, except the most minuscule threads of orange nylon they found embedded in his neck. No signs of a struggle either. But I could have told them all that.

Malone consults the rear-view mirror, brushing some of her long bangs out of her eyes. I'd thought her hair was almost black, but in this light I can see it's actually a rich dark brown with a tinge of red in it, the Irish ginger gene trying to punch its way out. Maybe that's why she's so hot for Danny Anderson: the sharing of their common Celtic DNA. Although he probably got his from the Scots instead of the Irish. She looks at her reflection and adopts a serious but approachable look, getting her compassionate cop face on. Then she gets out of the car and lets me out of the back seat. As I stand next to her, I see she comes up to my chin instead of my armpit. She wore her boots with a heel today.

"And you," she says. "Behave yourself."

"Malone, their kid just died. I may be a first-class bitch, but I think I can handle this." When she steps away, I pull a mickey of vodka out of the inner pocket of my leather jacket and take a good long swig, before wiping my mouth with a sleeve. I don't pretend to be anything I'm not, unless it suits me. There was a time I didn't need to drink, but things change. I embrace my alcoholism. Hell, I'd wrap my long legs around it and French kiss it if I could. Malone just looks at me and shakes her head.

We walk together up the scuffed wooden steps and ring the doorbell. I steady myself for meeting Tyler's parents, absentmindedly fingering the bottle in my pocket.

★ ★ ★ ★ ★

"He was a sensitive boy. A creative boy," Cynthia Winogrodzski-Brent says after explaining that they'll have to make it quick. They are expected at a march on City Hall to protest the sale of non–Fair Trade coffee from sandwich trucks. A person has to keep on going after all, for the important things, she told them.

She dresses like one of those Stevie Nicks wannabes, all batwings and fringe. Doesn't look that bad on her, but it's not my style. The place is crammed with antiques that have been in her family for years, along with far too many spider plants. If I were her, I would have dumped half this junk, along with the Polack surname, as soon as I got married. My great-grandfather was a Pole, but he had the sense to change Starekczyk to Starr as soon as he hit Ellis Island.

The father, Greg, wears red-framed owl glasses and stovepipe black jeans. A hipster. Both of them come from money and have never had to really work, it seems, although technically they run a small online business selling organic hemp clothing that makes people look like they're dressed in burlap bags. The rest of the time they busy themselves with causes of one kind or another, mostly environmental — which I can sort of admire, since the planet's on its way to hell in a fossil-fuelled handcart. The mother shows us a framed picture of her hugging a huge sequoia out west with her husband while chained and holding hands. I notice there are more pictures like these around the room than of their two kids, Tyler included.

"Of course, his given name was Tidal Wave," the father adds, putting an arm around his wife. "He was born right here in a saltwater birthing pool on the back porch. Remember the huge cascade the placenta made when it was delivered, Cyn? We still have it. Would you like to see it?"

I don't know whether he means the pool or the placenta, but thankfully Malone responds in the negative to both. The father goes to the kitchen to get some tea for his wife. He had asked if either of us wanted any, but Malone and I said no. It's probably that crappy herbal stuff anyway. The couple seems to have recovered from their earlier start when they saw the two of us at the door: an Asian woman with a gun and a wild-haired Amazon with a whiff of the street about her. I swear I saw the dad reach for a particularly pointy umbrella out of the stand, readying himself for attack.

Finally, after all the bullshit chit-chat, Malone gets down to business.

"Tell me, Mrs. Brent …" she begins.

"Ms. Winogrodzski-Brent," she interrupts.

"Oh yes, my apologies." I am dying to hear Malone say this ridiculous faux-feminist hyphenated name out loud with a straight face.

"But you can call me Cynthia." Damn.

"Cynthia," Malone says. "Is there anyone that Tyler didn't get along with, anyone who would want to do him harm?" The father has come back in the room with a mug of what looks like steaming yellow piss for his wife. Must be chamomile. I so called it.

"He was a free spirit," says the mother. "We raised him that way. I don't know why anyone would want to harm him." This time she actually looks a bit torn up. "He had dozens of friends."

"Can you give us some of their names? Maybe a friend he was out with last Saturday night?" Malone has her iPad virtual keyboard at the ready to record Tyler's many friends, but the mother looks like she's in Final Jeopardy! and can't figure out the answer in the form of a question.

"Well, there are just so many," she finally manages. "It's hard to keep tabs, to learn all of their names." Some mothers leave you on a median strip and some leave you with a succession of nannies while they go around the country hugging trees. Neither type is around enough to learn the names of your friends.

"If you give us his phone, maybe we could look up some of his contacts. Do you know where it is?" Smooth move, Malone, slipping that in there.

"I thought it was with the police," the mother says. "It's not here at the house. Tidal Wave always took his phone with him. We bought it for him for safety reasons, so he could call if he was in trouble." Yeah, right. I've seen kids send five hundred texts a day, upload to Snapchat and Instagram until they've got disjointed thumbs, but never have I seen one of them use the damn thing for an actual phone call.

"There's Lachlan Reid," the dad volunteers. And the mother shoots him a disapproving look. Malone picks up on it and raises an eyebrow.

"We didn't approve of that relationship," the mother says. "Not that we would ever try to control something as sacred as friendship. But he was a bad influence on our son." Impressive that she can't remember the kid's name but can still blame him for her son's less-than-stellar behaviour.

"Was he depressed?" I jump in, wanting to take the conversation down a different path.

"What do you mean?" the mother says, looking offended.

"I mean depressed. Lying around in his room, wearing black all the time, listening to Kurt Cobain on repeat."

"If our son was depressed, we would have gotten him the appropriate help. We do not believe in the stigma of mental illness," his mother replies stiffly. "But he was not depressed. He was planning on buying a motorcycle with his birthday money. He just needed to get his licence."

"Yeah, but listen, the Kurt Cobain …" I say.

"Any other friends you can remember?" Malone asks, shutting me down.

"First, I'd like to understand what your associate is insinuating," the mother demands.

"She has Tourette's," Malone says without missing a beat. I turn to her with my mouth open as she continues. "She can't help but blurt out obscenities and nonsense words during conversation. We hired her as part of an affirmative-action program for neurological disorders." For the first time in my life I find myself at a loss for an obscenity to blurt out, I am so stymied that Malone has seen fit to categorize me as brain-damaged.

"Oh, I see," Cynthia says, smoothing her skirt, giving me a kind, pitying smile. "Well, Greg and I have always been supporters of affirmative-action programs."

"Absolutely," Greg agrees, giving me the same sappy look. I swear, if the two of them reach over and give me a group hug, I'll vomit.

"So," Malone says, taking the floor again. "Any other friends you can remember?"

Cynthia continues to smooth her skirt. The father bites his lower lip.

"Well, of course there were girlfriends," the mother finally manages. I notice the plural. So does the father.

"I thought there was just Alice Corrigan," the dad says.

"There was another one," the mother says. "Jessica something. She showed up at the house one day looking for him."

"But he and Alice had been going out for a whole year," the owl-eyed dad says, really shocked for the first time since we arrived. If the guy was expecting fucking monogamy from a hormone-infested teenage boy with a free spirit, his jeans must be cutting off the circulation to his brain.

Malone takes down the additional names, entering them on the iPad. She needs to get to the hard questions. Shit or get off the pot. I decide to help her out a little with my Tourette's.

"What about his rap sheet?"

Malone elbows me discreetly in the gut. The father clears his throat. The mother chokes a bit on her chamomile.

"Maybe we'll have that tea after all," Malone says to the father.

"No," Cynthia says, grabbing her husband by his sweater vest and yanking him back down on the couch. "I am afraid you misunderstand my son," she says, only giving me a break because she thinks I'm disabled. Otherwise, she'd be bitch-slapping me right now.

"The thing is, Mr. and Mrs. Brent," Malone explains, trying to bring the focus back.

"Mr. and Ms. Winogrodzski-Brent," the father corrects her. "I took Cynthia's name as well when we partnered for life." Oh, for fuck's sake.

"Well, sir," Malone continues, "it's not like Tyler — I mean Tidal Wave — wasn't known to police." That's an understatement. I read the printout of Tyler's criminal record in the car. It filled a whole page and the kid wasn't even eighteen yet.

"Just the usual acting out, finding himself, experimenting," the mother says.

"We encouraged him to experiment. It is only through allowing a child from infancy to fully explore the world with no restrictions, that they can find true peace and understanding." The father sounds like he's repeating a cheesy Facebook post he read. I cannot get over this couple. I have seen infants operate. In my opinion, if you allow them to explore the world with no restrictions, the little buggers will find and drink the drain cleaner under the sink. Not that I have any real experience with kids.

"Well, there were some run-ins with drugs and an assault charge," Malone suggests, trying to tread carefully.

The mother and father sit there blankly, as if Malone is speaking a foreign language. Their united front of complete denial is impressive, even to a hard-ass like me.

"And we were called out here," Malone continues undaunted, consulting her notes even though I know she doesn't have to. "Let's see. Yes, I believe we came out last fall for a domestic disturbance."

"That was a misunderstanding," the dad says, bristling in his skinny jeans. Something has penetrated the united front.

"Your daughter, correct? She was eight years old at the time. Is her name Echo?" Jesus, where was this one's placenta delivered, in a storm drain?

"Do you have any children, officer?" the mother snaps, batwings fluttering. I hadn't thought about whether Malone might be married or a mother. I find myself interested in the answer.

"Detective," Malone corrects, still wearing her compassionate cop face, but I'm starting to see the impatient woman who threw my lunch at me in the car. "And no, I don't have any children."

"Well, if you did, you would know that sometimes children have scuffles, and sometimes things can get a little bit out of hand. But it's all part of the normal maturation and development of the human animal."

I need to move this thing along. None of us are getting any younger.

"This animal stuffed your daughter's head in the gas oven until she told him where her allowance was," I say.

Not long after that we leave. But not before we search Tyler's room. No phone.

I never do get any tea. I think it's because I have Tourette's.

★ ★ ★ ★ ★

"I want to go back to the scene. See if we missed anything. Tyler's phone. A rope."

"Do we have to?" I wish I never said anything about the phone. If Malone would just take the autopsy at face value, we could forget all this and call it a suicide. Then I can get the information about my dad and get the hell out of this whole fucked-up situation.

"Yes," Malone says. "We do."

"C'mon, the kid was obviously mentally unbalanced, growing up in a house with those two wack jobs. How could he not be? He did some weed, downed some Valium, and then reflected on the futility of the human condition until a rope presented itself. Case closed."

Malone pulls into a parking lot bordering Riverside Park, opens up the back door of the unmarked, and lets me out again like a kid imprisoned by the child lock. I can't believe we've been at this for hours. This is way too much like work. She pierces me with those green eyes as I get out. They appear to be throwing sparks.

"Quit the crap, Candace."

★ ★ ★ ★ ★

We walk down an embankment and then over to an open grassy piece marked off with police tape. You can hear the river running fairly high in the deep gorge below. Early spring run-off. The water is about a hundred feet down and twice as far across.

"Hey, Malone." A tubby older cop is removing the tape. He has long sideburns like Roy Orbison.

"Hey, Doug. How are things?" Malone appears nervous. She also appears to be trying to hide me behind her. But I'm not easy to hide unless I want to be hidden.

"Oh, you know, can't complain, and if I do, who the hell would listen, right?" I step out from behind Malone and the guy sees me. His friendly smile collapses like a used tissue in the rain.

"Oh, yeah, this is …" Malone begins.

"I know who she is," he says then spits on the ground. "What the fuck is she doing here?"

"I had some questions. Thought if I brought her here she might find her answers better." Malone is lying again. I am impressed by this side of her.

"We both know that's bullshit, Malone." He walks over and hands her a big wad of sticky yellow tape. "But I'm three months from early retirement and I don't give a shit. Just keep her away from me." He walks past us and over the embankment. Malone throws the tape on the ground once he's gone. Then she starts pulling out her equipment, gloves, evidence bags, and a pair of tweezers. I remember now that I forgot to ask the blonde in The Goon that day who did her eyebrows. Maybe I could ask Malone. She looks like she knows where to wax.

"What's his problem?" I ask instead, once I figure the fat cop with the bad attitude is out of earshot.

"Doug Wolfe?"

I'd caught the first name earlier. The last name reminds me of the tattoo on Tyler Brent's calf, the floating arms framing the face and the snarling black muzzle. "Yeah, Wolfe. Guess he isn't big on introductions," I say.

"He didn't like your dad much," Malone admits. A lot of cops didn't.

"A bit of a lackey job for a guy who's been on the force since the time of Christ," I say. "What did he do, fuck the wrong man's wife or something?"

"Something like that." She hands me a pair of gloves and a flashlight. It's getting late, so we move quickly.

"What are you expecting to find here that the dozen cops who combed through this place last night didn't?" I ask after a few minutes of beating the bushes.

"I told you, a phone, for one thing." Malone lifts up a rock and shines her beam underneath. All she finds are some blind earthworms writhing in the light.

"And what, a smoking noose for the other? So we can finally say the kid killed himself in a drug-aided fit of teenage angst and go the hell home?"

"You know as well as I do that dead men don't remove their own nooses," Malone says.

"Maybe someone found him afterward and took it off."

"Peyton says it must have been removed almost immediately after death to have left so little bruising."

"Peyton?"

"The pathologist."

"Oh yeah," I say and gently squeeze the thick wad of bills in my front pocket. "Maybe it was a suicide pact. Somebody helped him and then went and drowned themselves in the river."

"He doesn't seem the type."

"They never do."

"Besides, there's nothing around here he could have hanged himself on anyway," she says, waving her arms around at the grass and low-lying brush. "The body's been moved. That points to murder, not suicide."

"You never know."

"Listen, Candace. I'm getting tired of you trying to find ways to get out of actually solving what the hell happened to this kid. If you aren't interested in the terms of our agreement, you can just go." She puts her hands on her hips, like she's a fifties housewife scolding a ruffian. If she shakes her finger at me, I'll cram her flashlight up her ass.

But I want to find out what happened to my father, so I turn around and pretend to look some more. Maybe she'll give me an A for effort and I can finally get to The Goon for that Scotch.

After ten more minutes of poking around in the bushes with flashlights, she finally notices it. Then again, it's getting dark, and it is around a bend in the river, and at least a hundred yards away, so maybe she isn't a total loss as a detective.

"What's that?" Malone points at a thin line that crosses from a small shack on the other side of the river across the gorge. I squint like I'm thinking about it.

"I don't know," I say, hoping to hell she'll let it go.

"It's a zip line," Malone says, walking toward the dirt platform embedded on the edge of our side of the gorge. It's the landing spot for thrill-seekers who pay to sail high above the river rapids and pretend to be Tarzan.

She reaches out and pulls a sturdy lanyard attached to a pulley on the static line toward her. Earlier it had blended in with the grey rocks of the gorge and what was left of the cloudy day.

"Hey, Candace, guess what I found?"

"Shit," I say. I hope the orange fibres left behind on the lanyard are negligible, but I'm guessing they're still going to tie me to this cop until we solve this case, just like someone tied Tyler Brent's neck in a noose before they pushed him across the river on the zip line.

Looks like Malone is going to miss her hockey game.

CHAPTER 7

THAT NIGHT I TIE ONE ON at The Goon, after finishing a bottle of Johnny Walker at home with my new friend Shannon, who I met at the liquor store. I had hoped I might spend the night with Marcus. But apparently he hasn't been into The Goon all day. Probably on the road back to wherever he came from, with whoever he's been tracking stuffed in the trunk like a bag of empties waiting to be returned. You wouldn't think I'd get along with someone who makes his money capturing wayward criminals, but I appreciate men with strong hands and a good sense of how a woman's body works. Marcus Knight has both, with six-pack abs to sweeten the deal. I could use some of that right now. But for the time being, Shannon has a taut enough belly that's made for body shots, much like my own. I prefer men for sex, but I'll take a woman if that's what's handy. Shannon is currently proving the shotworthiness of her midsection to half a dozen guys at one end of the bar while I talk to the old-timer at the other.

He isn't the first old man I've pulled aside tonight, the ones of a certain age who frequent the fringes of places like this. After what Charlotte said when she drove me home, I need to talk to someone old enough to have known my mother back in the day. Hopefully one with enough brain cells still intact to remember what may or may not have happened to her. These older ones, they sit off to the side, their faces cast down to hide their rheumy eyes, looking up only to pay the waitress for watered-down draft with their stack of pennies. This guy's different from the grey-haired sad sacks I've been grilling up until now. Roberto is his name. He wears a white fedora with a black band and shines his shoes so you can see yourself in them. Each night he comes into The Goon and asks for two shots of grappa. One he drinks quick and the other he nurses throughout the evening at the bar while he makes gentleman-talk with Lovely Linda. At nine o'clock, he tips his hat, leaves Linda a dollar tip and walks home. He's not a big guy. Even sitting at the bar I register that he is at least a foot shorter than me. His polished patent leathers dangle from the bar stool like a kid's.

"Yes, I knew your mother," Roberto says, ignoring the boys in the background slurping B-52s from Shannon's belly. "And also her family."

"Her family?" Somehow I had never pictured the "thieving wop" with a family. I think my dad said both her parents died in a boating accident when she was ten, or was it a bowling accident? In any case, he made me think he was my only relative, and I took him at his word.

"The Scarpellos were an old Italian family." Roberto takes a tiny sip of the grappa, barely wetting his lips. "The oldest kind. Sicilian."

Even after a bottle of Johnny Walker, I know what that means. "She was *La Cosa Nostra*?" Just like Charlotte said. She was connected. I can't believe it. I'm going to dig my father out of his grave and slap him for not telling me. The mob doesn't have any real pull where we are. The Daybreak Boys, an MC run out of Pittsburg, controls the girls and the drugs here, along with the firepower that goes with them. The Daybreak Boys are vicious bastards: less of a motorcycle club and more a fraternity of psychopaths.

"Not her, her grandfather. El Mafioso. Like the son, her father. Although he and his wife got blown up in their Cadillac one day on the way to mass." *Neither bowling or in a boat*, I think to myself. My mother did have family, and none of them ever tried to find me. Maybe they didn't know I existed.

"Do you think they knew about me?" I say, silently ordering a grappa for myself.

"I don't think so at first. They lost track of your mother after they excommunicated her for marrying your father. El Protestante." These Roman Catholic mob families kill me. They don't excommunicate you for torturing someone with a wet towel and a pair of battery cables, but fuck a Protestant and you're out.

"They looked for your father after they hear she disappeared. But he can be a hard man to find." We did move around a lot after mom did her runner. But I figured we were trying to lose the law, not the Mob.

"I think perhaps they find him when you went on trial for that …" He waves one well-manicured hand in dismissal. "That unfortunate business with the wife whose husband died."

My name was in the papers. My picture. I've been told I look like my mother. They probably put two and two together.

"But why did they want to find my father so bad? He didn't know where she was. You'd think they'd be ecstatic that she dumped him." She also dumped me, I'm thinking, but I don't say that, at the risk of sounding like I give a shit.

"They look for your father not because your mother 'dumped him,' as you say, but because they think he may have dumped her."

"What do you mean?" But this is something Charlotte already hinted at.

"Like at the bottom of the lake."

"So they were after my dad because they thought he killed my mother?" Just then Shannon comes back, throws her drunken arms around me, and slips me the tongue. I yank her off but don't let go of her shirt. I may want that tongue later.

"They are not the only ones who think it, Candace Starr." He downs the last sip of his grappa. "Or the only ones who think *La Cosa Nostra* finally did find Mike Starr after all those years." He smiles. "Your mother, Angela, she was a beautiful woman. Not as tall as you but still very similar." He steps off the bar stool and tips his hat. "Goodnight, ladies."

The little guy sails through the chaos of The Goon like a ship with a white fedora sail. Shannon burps loudly in my ear and then whispers in it. I throw back a last shot and take her roughly onto my lap, kissing her long and deep on her sloppy, full lips. The guys at the bar stare.

"What are you looking at?" I snarl. They turn in unison back to the bar. They know me, and of me, and huddle together trying to make themselves small.

I take Shannon back to my apartment above the E-Zee Market to lose myself for a while in the salty slickness of skin on skin. I won't sleep much tonight after what the old man has said, so I might as well not be alone. And like I said, I'm a girl who knows how to make use of what's handy.

★ ★ ★ ★ ★

The next morning, a protesting Majd unlocks the door of my apartment for Malone, who stands in the open doorway looking like a storm about to hit. She's pissed, mostly because it isn't morning. It's noon. Shannon is passed out across me on the mattress, starkers, her tramp-stamped ass in the air. We make a fleshy *X* on the bed.

"You were supposed to meet me at nine," Malone roars. My head is not appreciative. I give Shannon a nudge and she rolls off me with a groan. Then I stand up full frontal and ask Malone to hand me the long T-shirt hanging off a bare-bulb lamp at the door. She does. Majd runs down the stairs and back to the safety of his cash register. I pull the T-shirt over my head and give Shannon a light boot with my foot.

"Get up, girl, the fuzz is here."

She groans again. I start collecting her clothes, dumping them on top of her as she lies there comatose. She doesn't really come fully awake until the end of a pointy stiletto catches her on an outstretched forearm.

"Okay, okay, already." She gathers her shit and disappears into the can to get dressed.

"You can't pull this crap with me, Candace," Malone says, looking at me all serious while I stand there in a T-shirt that just barely skirts my bush.

"Keep your voice down," I say. "Some of us have well-earned hangovers here." I bend over to pick up yesterday's panties from the floor and pull them on. Then I grab a pair of clean jeans from a basket in the corner. Charlotte had come by yesterday while I was out and done some of my laundry, even ironed my underwear, making them too stiff to wear. She's trying to buy my silence to Rod about what she told me, using Tide and loving starch. Not only did I miss her visit yesterday but also the phone call from Rod's dear old mother in St. John's. Majd is going to get the wrong idea with all these maternal types checking in on me and start to think I actually have a heart or something.

"We made a deal, Candace," Malone says. She's not letting it go.

"Tell me, Malone. Why do you care so much? Sounds to me like Tyler Brent was a real piece of work. I mean, he tried to gas an eight-year-old for her piggy bank." I grab a Mason jar from the kitchen counter that runs down one side of the one-room apartment and fill it with water from the sink. Leaning against the fridge, I gulp it down. The water tastes like it's been run through a rusty washing machine before hitting the pipes. Then I start brushing my teeth. Like I said, I take care of my mouth.

"That's not all he did. You didn't see the whole file," Malone says with a sigh as she comes through the doorway. She takes in the Formica table covered with empty beer and wine bottles then moves a few aside so she can lean on it without getting her London Fog dirty. "Seems to me that child will be sleeping a whole lot sounder now that her brother's not around."

"If you knew all that shit, why didn't you pull the kid in long ago?"

"As you know, Candace, knowing something and making it stick can be two different things. If they weren't, you'd be doing consecutive life terms right now." Clever comeback. And reasonably true.

"Whatever," I say, dumping the Mason jar in the sink with the other dirty glasses. "But say what you will. As bad as I was, I never stuck a kid's head in an oven."

"Yet," Malone says.

Shannon comes out of the washroom dressed in the clothes she wore the night before. She gives me a kiss before she leaves.

"Call me?"

"Don't have a phone," I tell her. I really do prefer men. Fewer complications.

"Oh," she says, glancing self-consciously at Malone. "Well, I guess I'll see you around then."

"Yeah, see you around," I say, but I've already turned to face the long mirror on the door. With all the rolling around last night, my thick curly hair is almost as wide as it is long. I grab a hair band and wrestle it into a messy bun. By the time I turn around, Shannon's gone.

"I didn't know you were into women," Malone says.

"I'm into everything," I say, pulling my black Converse high-tops on, snagging my leather jacket from behind the door. "But right now I have to go see a friend."

"What?" Malone grabs my arm before I can leave. I stop and look down at her hand, each finger white-tipped with a half-moon French manicure.

"You don't want to do that." I keep my voice as level as I can.

"What are you going to do, Candace, break my neck right here? Majd is downstairs and half a dozen witnesses saw me come up here. You take out a cop, you're up for some serious downtime." She's right that I'd probably get caught if I did anything. But she's wrong if she thinks that would stop me.

"I just need to see a friend," I say slowly, emphasizing each word. Then I remove her hand from my arm and try to soften my tone a little. I'll get more out of this fly with molasses than with my usual vinegar. "I promise I'll meet you in an hour, Malone. At The Goon. I just really need to take care of something first."

She shakes her bobbed head as if she can't believe she's going along with the plan of a hustler like me. I can't believe that she is either. But she has stipulations.

"Not at The Goon," she says. "I think we've seen what happens when you get yourself too close to a bar. I'll meet you at The Tulip, the luncheonette on Main. It's down the street from Tyler's school. I've set up an interview with the principal."

"Fine," I say and take off out the door. Malone can let herself out.

"What about those security tapes?" she shouts down the stairwell at me.

"Ask Majd. He has them," I call up over my shoulder. I took care of those tapes before I even met Malone at the morgue yesterday. I've got my priorities straight.

Once outside, I start walking toward Rod's place. Fresh-smelling laundry or not, I'm not keeping my mouth shut about what I've been told. And Uncle Rod better come as clean as my underwear did.

★ ★ ★ ★ ★

He's on the roof of his bungalow cleaning out the eaves-troughs when I walk up the lawn, grab a good-sized rock from the garden, and throw it at him. It hits him square on the right shin.

"Jaysus! What did you do that for?"

"That's for lying to me," I holler up at Uncle Rod. Then I grab the garden gnome I gave him for his fiftieth birthday and smash it on the front steps.

"Oh, for God's sake, what's gotten into you, Candace? I was going to buy that little fella his own wheelbarrow and all." He goes to get on the ladder to climb down and talk to me, but I pull it away and it falls sideways onto the driveway with a clatter.

Rod stands at the edge of the roof, pulls out a smoke, and lights it. "All right, so what's got your knickers in a twist?"

I stand below him and look up, but it's not that far. If I had a step ladder, I could grab him by the ankles and pull him down. "My mother's family was *La Cosa Nostra*."

Rod blows out the smoke in his lungs. "And so what if they were?"

"So what if they were?"

"Your dad and I thought it was best you didn't know too much about Angela. That woman was a disappointment, Candace. To all concerned."

"So much of a disappointment that dad put her six feet under?"

This surprises him, and he chokes halfway through an inhalation. Rod only smokes when he's doing outdoor work. He says it makes the fresh air smell sweeter. "Who told you that?"

"Never mind who told me that," I spit. "Is it true?"

"Why don't you bring that ladder back over here? I can climb on down and we'll discuss it."

"No."

"Oh, come now, Candace."

"I'm not bringing it over until you tell me. Did Dad have anything to do with my mother disappearing?"

"Well, that would be both a yes and a no, kiddo." He holds the cigarette with his thumb and forefinger, like a joint. He says it's because he only had his dad's hand-rolleds as a kid to pilfer from. If they weren't held tightly at one end, you'd inhale a grainy mouthful of shag tobacco when you took a drag.

"What the fuck are you talking about?"

"He didn't kill her, if that's what you're thinking. Although she sure did her best to murder him before she left. Came at him with a grapefruit knife when he was at breakfast and carved up his face a fair bit."

"A grapefruit knife?"

"She wasn't an exceptionally cordial girl, our Angela. But what she lacked in manners, she made up for with passion."

"Huh?"

He sighs in exasperation, like he did when Charlotte stuck him with the Screech fishing lure. It must have hurt like hell, but like most pain Rod just found it inconvenient. "Your father was after having an affair with Shelley Wolfe. Angela found out and just about blew one of her tits over it. After he managed to get the grapefruit knife away from her, she packed her bags and left town. None of us seen her since."

Where had I heard the name Wolfe before? Then I remember.

"Shelley Wolfe," I say, trying to sound all nonchalant. "She any relation to Detective Doug Wolfe?"

"Now how do you know that?" Rod's eyes narrow for a second then he recalls he's the one on the roof and not in a position to ask questions. "Shelley was his wife. Wolfe found the two of them in bed together when he came home early from a night shift. Your dad was outrunning more than a grapefruit knife after that caper." He laughs, and I picture my dad taking off out a bedroom window in nothing but his skivvies, trying to dodge the meaty arms of that cuckolded cop.

"Wolfe ever catch him?"

"Can't exactly arrest a man for screwing your wife better than you. Although I'm sure more than one man has tried." He throws down the spent smoke and puts it out on one of the asphalt shingles with his boot. "Now how's about you bring that ladder over and we can talk about this over a nice cup o' tea."

"I can't believe you and Dad never told me any of this." Didn't those two lugs realize that if a kid is given no logical reason for the heavily fucked-up behaviour of a parent, they just take the weight of the blame themselves? My mother hadn't left because of me. Whether she left me on a highway median or a Ferris wheel or playing happily on the floor of my room, she left because she hated my father, not because she hated me. That is, if you believe she left at all and wasn't buried in a shallow grave with a snapped neck, after being disarmed of the grapefruit knife. Uncle Rod lied to me or, at the very least, hid the lightness I could have gotten from the truth. And I'm not sure yet whether he's still keeping me in the dark.

"One more thing, Rod." He folds his arms. He's getting impatient now. Normally making Rod Jessome impatient is a dangerous pastime, but I'm practically family. "Do you think the Mob had anything to do with Dad's death? You know, payback for screwing over their daughter." Or possibly murdering her.

Rod shakes his head. "I've got friends in the Scarpello clan, Candace. Believe me, they were happy your father took that woman off their hands. She was nuttier than a squirrel in a shit factory." This is just one of his back-home sayings that make absolutely no sense at all. It's a Newfoundland thing. Like fried bologna. I think he makes half of them up. I start down the sidewalk, the ladder still in the driveway.

"See you later, Rod."

"Oh, come now, Candace, don't be like that," Rod pleads from the roof.

But I'm going to be like that. And then some.

CHAPTER 8

MALONE IS WAITING OUTSIDE of The Tulip when I arrive, claiming we don't have time to stop for lunch. Again. She shoves half a gyro in my hand and I eat it while we walk to Brassnose Academy, the high school Tyler attended.

"Brassnose? Are you kidding me? Like brown nose?"

"It's named after some college in England."

"It's named after some kid I punched out in sixth grade."

"Come on, Candace."

It's only a block, she says. No point parking again. In between bites and me licking the tzatziki off my lips, she fills me in on what she's found out since last night.

"I contacted Daisy Chain Adventures, the outfit that runs the zip line in the summer. They came to open the door to the shack on the other side of the gorge that houses the launch deck. But they needn't have bothered."

"How come?"

"The lock was already busted."

"I guess that's what happens to shacks," I say.

"They just do it up to look like a shack," says Malone. "Makes it seem more of an authentic jungle experience when they side it with bleached-out wooden boards. Underneath those boards it's a one-room cement bunker built into the ridge with high windows and a wooden deck you step off for the ride. You can't get to the launch deck without going through the shack. The door lock is actually pretty sophisticated. They didn't want people breaking in and playing with the equipment."

"But somebody did."

"That's right," Malone admits, then goes on. "We found two sets of footprints in the dust on the floor inside. They only run the zip line from June to September. It's been sitting empty for months." She hands me a bottle of water to share and I drink the whole thing and hand it back. Malone stares at the empty bottle for a second then throws it in a recycling bin at a bus stop.

"One of the prints is a match for Tyler's size-ten skater shoes. The other set was smaller with a point, you know, like a high heel, around a woman's size seven. There weren't any prints leading away from the scene, but then again, it's rained since we found him." I swallow a piece of lamb or beef or whatever mystery meat they stuffed in the gyro and keep walking. Malone steps in front of me, forcing me to stop.

"What size are your feet, Candace?" We both look down at my black high-tops. The same brand and size I've worn since I was twelve, when my dad told me not to worry, that a girl grew into her feet, just like a puppy.

"Go ahead, Malone, try to match me to the fucking forensics. My feet wouldn't fit in a size seven if you chopped off all my toes and fed them to the sharks."

She doesn't have to take my word for it. She can see my feet are several sizes bigger than hers. I am often forced to order my footwear off the internet. It's hard to find thigh-high PVC dominatrix boots in a size twelve at your local JCPenney.

"So, you think it's a woman?"

"No, Candace, I think it's a cross-dressing homicidal maniac with freakishly small feet."

We start walking again.

"Do you know anyone in the industry who fits that description?" Malone finally asks after a half a minute of saying nothing. Too bad: with my hangover, I'd really been enjoying the silence.

"What description? The owner of a size-seven high heel?" I finish off the last of the gyro, wipe my face with the napkin it came with, and shove it in Malone's coat pocket. I can feel her bristle when I reach in. "That's not a description, that's goddamn Cinderella."

"It appears a woman was with him before he died, and you know people in the business. There aren't many females."

"What business?" I say, messing with her.

"The business of dispatching two-timing Tidal Waves with a noose and a bottle of Valium."

"Listen, Malone, no professional in their right mind is going to truss up a target on a zip line. We've got our artistic pride, for Christ's sake." Uncle Rod used to say there should be a union, or at the very least a guild, which is like a union but it doesn't go on strike or make people disappear like Jimmy Hoffa. "Did you discover anything besides a couple of dance steps in the dust?" I ask her.

Malone waits for a moment and then she reaches into her purse for a small blue notebook. She must have got caught without her iPad.

"Whoever was in there took a couple of harnesses." She consults her notes. "A sit and a chest harness, along with some of those fasteners." She squints at her own writing, trying to decipher it. "Carabiners," she finally says, putting the notebook away. "The chest harness was orange. The owner gave me a duplicate, so we can try to match the fibres against what we found on Tyler's body, and the lab ..."

"I still say it was suicide, Malone. The kid broke in and —"

"No," she says, cutting me off. "It wasn't."

We've reached the front door of the school. The two of us start up the multiple steps to the stone-columned entranceway. An insignia is carved into the marble archway: Brassnose Academy, *Provehito in altum*. Something tells me the kids from the hood don't go here.

"Peyton says with the amount of Valium in that kid's blood he couldn't have tied his own shoelaces, let alone a noose to a zip line lanyard. He probably wouldn't even have been able to stand up without assistance."

"Who's Peyton?"

"The pathologist!" she screams at me.

I am beginning to love messing with Malone. When those jade eyes spark with the thwarted desire to throttle me, I can't help but smile.

★ ★ ★ ★

Principal Cutter sits behind a huge mahogany desk that bears the scuff marks of a hundred kids' sneakers on the side facing us. He's a squat, pasty-looking guy with stick-out ears. A full head of hair, the colour courtesy of Grecian Formula, is about all he has going for him in the looks department. Malone and I sit in two hard chairs that appear to have been designed for toddlers. The room is so hot the back of my neck is starting to sweat, despite my upswept hair. On the walls are pictures of Cutter forcibly smiling at students who are accepting awards or shaking hands with him at graduation. I have been in my fair share of principals' offices, and they are all the same. Intimidation mixed with a mandatory air of accessibility.

"I'm sorry, what did you say your name was again?" Cutter has been eyeing me since we came in. He's not buying Malone's claim that I'm a PI on retainer. He knows a troublemaker when he sees one, having made a career in trying to rein them in.

"Candace," I say. I hope he doesn't have access to my permanent record. While containing surprisingly good grades, it also has a suspension file several inches thick.

"We want to hear about Tyler Brent, Mr. Cutter," Malone says, jumping in. She's taken off her London Fog in the heat and rolled up her shirt sleeves. Her forearms are sleek and tanned.

"Yes, a terrible business. We are all very upset and shocked here at the Academy." Cutter looks about as shocked as an old-hand whore asked for change.

"What can you tell us about him?" Malone says.

"Well, as you know, school records are confidential."

"He's dead," I say. "I don't think he cares much now whether we know if he was flunking English or not."

"It would really help with our investigation," Malone says, putting on her best winning smile. But Cutter is impenetrable to Malone's charms.

"I would have to get permission from the parents first, and of course the board, which doesn't meet until the middle of next month."

"That's a shame," says Malone. "It would be just terrible if something were to happen to another student." She sits back in the toddler chair and steeples her fingers in front of her. "And if we could have prevented it, you know, with the information, it would be such a shame. The press tends to jump on that kind of thing. I'd hate for the school to be painted as not co-operating — you know how lousy the press can be — or even held responsible for the second death of a student."

Cutter keeps his poker face, but there is a slight twitch to it ever since Malone said the word *press*.

"Of course, I could give you my personal reflections on the student, just unofficially, without consulting his file. Would that be considered sufficiently co-operating?" He gives us much the same smile that he wears in the pictures on the wall, just as forced, but dripping with a whole lot more "fuck you."

"I believe that it would," Malone says, unable to hide her satisfaction. She picks up her iPad to take notes. "What kind of student was he?"

Cutter sighs and looks out the window, letting his guard down with the weariness only a person who has worked with the cesspool of adolescence for decades can muster. "The kind that doesn't grace the school with his presence all that much." He turns and faces us again. "I don't think I ever saw him before one in the afternoon, if I did at all." He pours himself a glass of water from a pitcher and takes a sip, not offering either of us anything as we sweat in his overheated office; a pound of flesh extracted for daring to breach his inner sanctum. "We had a special protocol in place for when he was here. If he became agitated. The staff had strict instructions not to engage with him."

"Agitated?" I say.

"Yes, agitated," Cutter repeats.

"In what way would he become agitated?" Malone asks.

"In the way where he would throw a math compass across the room, almost impaling a physics teacher's neck."

"Oh," I say. "That kind of agitated."

"Listen, I don't know what to tell you. The boy was lazy, violent, and so full of self-entitlement he expected the ground to cough up cash for allowing him to walk on it." He takes a long drink from his glass. I'm starting to wonder whether that pitcher only contains water. "I never understood what Alice Corrigan saw in him. She was a good student, a nice girl, before she got involved with him. After that ..."

"This is the girlfriend," Malone says. The girlfriend, as opposed to the other girlfriend.

"Yes. At first, I thought it was just a passing thing. A chance to walk on the wild side. A lot of girls like to get a taste of that when they're young." *And some girls swallow it whole*, I think, but keep my mouth shut for fear Malone will elbow me in the gut again. Plus, she warned me after the meeting with the parents. No more Tourette's.

"But then, it was as if she became obsessed with him. Talking him down from all his various dramas, following him around like an abused puppy. It was like she couldn't breathe without him. A teacher caught her cutting class one day on her way to see him at home. When he told her to go back to class, she threw herself on the ground, kicking and screaming, crying hysterically that Tyler needed her. We had to sedate her in the nurse's office. Apparently, Tyler had texted her to bring him a submarine sandwich. That young man knew the control he had over her, and he used it to his best advantage."

"What did her parents think about that?" Malone asks. And I think about what the blonde said in The Goon that day. How the kid gave her daughter a disease. How he was ruining her chances for a good university. Sounds like he might have been ruining more than that.

"I am not at liberty to discuss that," Cutter says.

"Can we talk with Alice?" Malone asks, and the principal bristles again.

"Not without the express permission and presence of her parents. In any case, she is not in school today."

"Not in school?"

"No. Understandably."

"Yes. Understandably," Malone says. But I don't think she can understand any better than me why a girl would mourn the death of a boy who used her as his own personal Uber Eats. "What about Lachlan Reid?" she asks, switching tacks to inquire after Tyler's friend, the bad influence his parents told us about.

"Lachlan Reid is also absent today," Principal Cutter says, drumming his fingers on the green blotter of his mahogany desk. His hands are chubby and small, like a child's.

"His attendance record much like Tyler's?"

"Birds of a feather," Cutter says. "But Lachlan is absent today for a separate reason."

"And that reason would be …?" Malone leads.

"Suspension," he spits out after a moment's hesitation, abruptly quitting his impatient finger tapping. He uses his chubby little hand to grab the tumbler of water and down what's left in one gulp, as if finishing the drink will also bring an end to the conversation. He's tired of protecting students' rights and just wants to get rid of us.

"What did he do?" Malone asks.

"He got in a fight last Friday." Cutter pours himself another drink of water from the pitcher, coming to accept, perhaps, that we aren't quite done with him. Malone and I sit sweltering in the overheated office, coming to accept that the pitcher probably doesn't have water in it.

"Who with?"

"With Tyler Brent." He spits out the boy's name like he spit out the suspension. "Lachlan was hurt quite badly; maliciously, you might say. An ambulance had to be called."

"It sounds to me like you didn't like Tyler Brent very much," Malone says.

He turns to her at first looking defiant, and then he sighs and starts rubbing his temples, standing down. I think this man may have once really believed in the importance of educating young people, but a guaranteed pension and nine hundred pubescent ingrates a year passing through his doors beat it out of him.

"Listen, I don't want to speak ill of the dead, but that kid frightened the hell out of us," Cutter says. "I'm not completely surprised he met with a violent end. And while I would never wish tragedy on a young person with their whole lives ahead of them ..."

"You think he deserved it," I say.

Cutter sighs again. "I think," he says, taking another sip of the water-that-is-vodka, "that I have been doing this job for far too long."

★ ★ ★ ★ ★

Apparently, while we cannot look at Tyler Brent's file, we can look in his locker. Lockers are school property and the administration can cut the locks off anytime and have a look inside. So much for individual rights.

Malone and I take out Tyler's textbooks one by one, flipping through the pages with our gloved fingers. I really should invest in whatever company supplies the police force with latex. They go through more of these gloves in a day than my dad used to go through shot glasses.

"Here's something," I say, and point to a drawing on the back of a history book. It depicts an oversized dick with matching droopy balls. "It's the fifth one I found. I thought maybe it represents a trend."

"Excellent detective work," Malone says, starting to go through the notebooks, which have nothing in them, not even grotesque dicks. Just blank pages, wishing someone would write on them. "You've cracked the case."

"I didn't think you were one for sarcasm, Malone."

"I didn't think you were one to find badly drawn phalluses something to remark on."

"Listen, Malone," I say, picking up *Our World: A Connected Community of Life* off the floor. "Do you have a problem with me?"

"I just can't believe you're telling me you have no idea who would have been at that zip line shack with Tyler. You know everyone. That's why I brought you in on this case. If you're holding back on me, Candace, I swear I'll ..."

"You'll what?" I say, raising one eyebrow. But she just lets out a sigh of exasperation and goes back to the notebooks. She pulls out the last binder, along with a rotting banana, from the bottom of the locker. That's everything. No phone.

When I flip to the back of *Our World,* expecting to find more genitals, I discover something else: a slip of red-lined paper from a notebook. This one even has writing on it. But I don't think it's Tyler's.

"You know, Malone, I think you'll find that murders are rarely the result of professionals." I hold up the note from Alice Corrigan, hastily written on both sides in leaky purple pen. Or maybe her tears made the smudges. I dangle it in front of Malone. "Something tells me that in this case, you should probably be looking a hell of a lot closer to home."

★ ★ ★ ★ ★

"I'll just stay here in the car."

"Like hell you will." Malone turns around from the front seat, looking at me through the metal mesh. We're in the driveway of Alice Corrigan's neat, ranch-style house with way too many begonias in the front garden for my taste. Next to us is a Mercedes AMG, gleaming in the sun.

"I don't see how I can be any help with talking to this girl."

"You'll provide a distinct perspective," Malone says.

"And what the fuck would that be?" I say, blowing a piece of hair out of my face.

"The appreciation of what would drive a seventeen-year-old girl to threaten to cut off her boyfriend's scrotum with a Bowie knife if she caught him cheating."

"C'mon, Malone, you never been in love?" The letter had been quite graphic. It seems that Alice had caught wind that there might be someone else mowing her grass and she wasn't at all interested in sharing the lawn care. There was the usual "If I can't have you, nobody can," but shit, everyone says that. It's like "It's not you, it's me" and "I swear, I never saw those boxer shorts/that garter belt/that used cock ring before." Something you just say in the moment.

"Love's not like that," Malone says, leaning back in her seat and closing her eyes. I don't think she slept at all last night. Probably worked through it, looking in to the zip line thing. She's starting to lose her enthusiasm.

"Isn't it?" Most of the love I've seen, from my parents to the meth head and his girlfriend, has convinced me that love is just that. A big, explosive fucked-up mess of the human condition to be avoided at all costs.

"No," Malone says, her eyes still closed.

"Are you married?" I really don't want to go into the Corrigans' house and risk seeing the blonde again. I'll do anything to stall, even lullaby Malone to sleep with small talk.

"I was engaged once," she says.

"And?" I say. I use an open question to keep her talking.

"It was good. For a while. Until it wasn't."

"Why?" I lean forward, so I can talk quietly right behind her ear. She has her hair tucked behind it, and I can see a tasteful pearl stud in the lobe through the mesh. A second piercing above the pearl is long grown over.

"I don't think he found me exciting enough."

"You're a homicide detective, Malone."

"Yeah, go figure." She smiles but doesn't open her eyes. I can see her tired face in the rear-view. People say a smile isn't real unless you can see it in the eyes, but Malone's still looks like the real thing. It makes me want to smile myself. Infectious, that's what they call that kind of smile Malone has, like it's a disease. "My mom liked him," she says, carrying on with the story but not the smile. "He was Chinese. Came from a good family. But he wanted different things in life than me. Designer labels, designer babies, everything brand name or brand new."

"And what did you want?" Before I was just trying to avoid going inside the Corrigans' house, but now I actually want to know.

"Someone to sit with at the end of the night. Someone to come home to. Someone to look at the screwed-up world with me from a distance, so we can stand apart from it. A perfect biosphere of two."

"That's pretty deep, Malone." It really is.

"Yeah," she says. "I guess he didn't think so." She opens her eyes, rubbing them with her fists.

"What happened?"

"One of my sorority sisters went down on him when she was visiting from Pennsylvania. I wasn't going to believe her until I found her lipstick on his foreskin."

"A brand-name lipstick, I'm guessing?"

She just shakes her head and gets out of the car, opening the back door for me.

"Time to go, Candace. And this time, try to keep your mouth shut."

Damn, these cops just never fucking sleep.

★ ★ ★ ★ ★

The dark-haired guy standing in the double doorway of the Corrigans' house has an arrogant three-piece suit and an attitude to match.

"Good evening, I'm Detective Malone." She holds up her badge, but he doesn't allow her to get any further with the introductions.

"I know who you are," he says, stepping onto the front stoop and closing the doors behind him. "I'm Alex Lopez, the Corrigans' attorney." He hands Malone a card. "I'm afraid the family cannot be disturbed today."

"We just want to ask a few questions," Malone says through gritted teeth. The only people cops hate more than criminals are lawyers.

"Well, I'm afraid you'll have to wait," Lopez says. "The Corrigans have had quite a shock. They're concerned for their daughter's emotional state." I bet they are. If she needed to be sedated when she couldn't bring Tyler a sub, I can't imagine how fucked up she is over this.

"This is a murder investigation. It's critical we speak to Alice Corrigan about her knowledge of the deceased." Wow, that sounds straight out of a cop textbook. I wonder if Malone drew dicks in hers.

"I understand the seriousness of the crime. But without a subpoena or an arrest warrant, my client isn't obliged to talk to you."

"Can you at least tell us if Alice Corrigan is at home?" Malone asks, clearly exasperated. She looks like Uncle Rod when a restaurant serves him halibut and he knows that it's cod. Newfoundlanders are serious about their fish. And Malone is seriously looking like she wants to grab Lopez by the narrow lapels and shake him until his twenty-four-karat-gold tie clip falls off.

"No, I cannot confirm or deny that anyone is at home," says Lopez, adjusting his skinny, polka-dot tie. But I see the curtain moving behind the window and the quick retreat of a blond head.

"Fine," says Malone tightly. "We'll be back with a subpoena."

Lopez watches us walk back toward the driveway. "And make sure you don't get any fingerprints on my

Mercedes. I just had it handwashed and detailed," he says before he slams the double doors shut.

"Where were your wisecracks this time, Candace?" Malone unlocks the car using the remote.

"You told me to keep my mouth shut."

I climb in the back of the car. Malone opens the driver's door as hard as she can into the dick-of-a-lawyer's AMG. Not once but twice.

"Didn't think you had it in you, Malone," I say, leaning toward the front seat. She knocks me back against the upholstery when she pulls out of the drive.

"I have more in me than you'll ever know, Candace," she says, taking off down the street quite a few nickels over the speed limit.

I'm starting to think I'd like to know more about what lives inside Malone. But that might involve getting closer to a cop. And experience has taught me that's more dangerous than a speeding car.

CHAPTER 9

WE CALLED IT A DAY after the run-in with the Corrigans' lawyer. Malone was exhausted. She dropped me off in front of the E-Zee Market and went home.

I tried calling Rod's mother again but got a busy signal. Who the hell doesn't have call waiting these days? Those Canadians probably still use tin cans with a string between them to communicate over the Arctic tundra.

After that I went upstairs and took a few Aspirin before climbing into bed with some sangria. I watched *Fried Green Tomatoes* on TV then fell asleep with my cheek on the bottle. I'm a sucker for chick flicks, the one thing I had to myself growing up surrounded by men. I was too embarrassed to ask my dad to rent them at the video store. This was back when you actually had to go out of the house to pick up a movie. Now you can just park your ass in an armchair and be infused with a steady IV drip of Netflix. I was afraid Uncle Rod and my dad would make fun of me for wanting to watch an airheaded bimbo go to law school or the diary of a woman with more hang-ups than decent underwear. So

I fed my guilty pleasure, closeted in my room, with the old movies they showed on TV. *Beaches. When Harry Met Sally. Pretty Woman.* I learned about being female from these movies, and it somehow both comforted and confused the hell out of me. Female friendships were rooted in jealousy, orgasms were fake, and the hookers in Hollywood looked a whole lot better than the saggy-titted wrecks with the sores on their lips I saw outside my bedroom window. I lived vicariously through these celluloid women I didn't understand. I would have told Richard Gere to get stuffed if he wanted to get his sex for free by making me his girl. Business is business, after all, no matter how much of a Cinderella complex you have.

The next morning Malone knocks before she comes inside my apartment. I'm in the corner, lifting weights. I finish a final bench press and then hook the barbell back into its brace.

Malone sits down next to the Formica table on the only chair in the room. It has ripped yellow vinyl that catches your butt cheeks if you sit on it naked, and it wobbles a bit. I stay on the weight bench and take a slug of green-tea Kombucha straight from the bottle.

"I hadn't pegged you as a fitness nut," she says.

"Picked up the habit in prison," I tell her, downing the rest of the sweetened drink that's supposed to help with the ulcer I think I may be developing.

"I thought the only thing you lifted was a bottle," she says, looking at the empty bottle of pre-mixed sangria on the bed.

"I'm not a total fucking cliché, you know."

"Adopt any other healthy habits in prison?" she asks, raising that eyebrow again. I really have to remember to ask her where she gets them done. But I know what she's hinting at. Whether I dried out on the inside. Alcohol had been harder to get than drugs in lock-up, but I had friends. Moreover, I had people who owed me. Something I've found to be much more lucrative than friends.

"I run," she says. "Do you?" She probably can't imagine me keeping my physique without any kind of cardio.

"Some people like to run, Malone," I say, standing up. I grab a towel to wipe off the sweat. "And some people like to run after things."

She stares at me, not getting it.

"Like a ball, Malone."

"Really?" she says, tilting her head, her bob grazing one shoulder. "I didn't see you as a team player."

"I actually used to play on the women's floor-hockey team in the pen."

"I'm glad to see incarceration got you involved in such wholesome activities."

I pull off my tank top and wipe the beads of sweat clinging to the gold star on my stomach. "You kidding? We had more injuries in a season than they did during a two-day prison riot." While I search for a clean T-shirt, I catch Malone eyeing my tat.

"You're a Sneetch," she says.

"I'm a what?" I say, thinking she just called me a squealer.

"The star," she says. "On your belly. It's like the Dr. Seuss story with the Sneetches."

I narrow my eyes at her. I'm not getting it.

"You know, some Sneetches had stars on their bellies and some didn't."

Then I remember the animated special from when I was a kid. "Some had stars upon thars," I say, remembering. That kind of repetitive schtick was the old doctor's calling card in all his stories.

"That's right. The ones that didn't have them had them put on, and when the original star-bellied Sneetches found out, they had theirs taken off. To differentiate themselves."

"This is not a status symbol, Malone."

"Then what is it?"

"A statement," I say, finally finding a clean white T-shirt. I pull it down over my star, thinking now that if everyone got one, I'd probably have mine taken off, too. I get my jacket and keys, and Malone joins me at the door.

"Maybe you'd like to try out for my hockey team," she says. "Since you have so much experience."

"Ha," I laugh. "No fucking way."

"Not with a fox?" Malone quotes, as we walk out into the hallway. "Not in a box?"

"Not with a Sneetch tied around my forehead and a Who crammed up my ass," I tell her, locking the door.

But the truth is, I can't skate.

★ ★ ★ ★ ★

We drive to Lachlan Reid's house. It's not nearly as posh as the Corrigans' or the Winogrodzski-Brents'. Lachlan lives in a row of rundown townhouses in a small co-op complex. It must be at the very outer limits of the catchment area for Brassnose Academy, a tip of the hat to social equality by elitists in search of token poor people for display at school events. When we ring the doorbell, it makes a strangled sound. The father answers in a yellowed wife-beater paired with pilled soccer pants. He takes one look at Malone's badge and motions us up to Lachlan's bedroom.

"Would you like to be present while we question your son?" Malone asks.

"No need," says Mr. Reid, returning to the couch and the beer he's nursing while watching *Jerry Springer*. I'd like to join him, but I don't think Malone would approve.

We knock on Lachlan's door, but he doesn't respond. Then Malone announces herself and what she's come about, and we hear some scuffling and shuffling before a sheepish-looking boy with long, sandy-brown hair hanging down over his forehead opens the door. Even with the hair, I can see that one of his eyes is black and swollen shut.

"This is about Tyler," he says to Malone then looks up at me and does a double take. He steps away from the door and we go inside. There's only one chair, in front of the kid's computer. He sits down in it and Malone takes a seat on the bed. I remain standing, taking in the posters on the wall. Black Sabbath and Iron Maiden mostly. Jesus, can't this generation develop some of their own rock heroes? I also take in the tat on the kid's leg. He's wearing red basketball shorts. Malone sees it, too.

"That's an interesting tattoo you have," Malone says, indicating the wolf face framed by white arms. "Same as Tyler Brent's."

"Yeah, well, we were friends." His phone buzzes with a notification from where it sits on the desk next to the computer. He ignores it. A considerable feat for a kid his age.

"With friends like that, you should probably make sure your health insurance is paid up," Malone says, indicating the well-purpled shiner.

"That was nothing," Lachlan says, shaking his head so the hair falls in front of his eyes again.

"That nothing got you suspended."

"Got Tyler suspended, too," the kid says, sniffing.

Malone keeps the iPad in her purse, trying to put the boy at ease. *This is a dialogue, not an interrogation* and all that bullshit. "What was the fight about, Lachlan?" she asks him with her best 'I'm only here to help' face. Malone has a lot of faces.

"Nothing." Everything is nothing with this kid.

"Listen, buddy, your friend's tits-up in the morgue and you guys were whaling on each other the day before. You better answer the detective's questions if you want this to go the right way." I can do the bad cop thing. I've seen it in action enough times. Malone gives me a nasty look. Doesn't she understand she's supposed to be the good cop?

"I don't know what happened to Tyler," he says, fingering a loose thread from the hem of his shorts.

"Well, we've seen Tyler, Lachlan," Malone says. That makes him pay attention. He looks up from the thread.

"And while he didn't look so good, he didn't seem to have any marks on him from a fight."

"Did that make you angry? Getting a beating from your buddy? You decide you want to give him a scare. Then you snap and go a bit psycho and kill him?"

"I'm not the fucking psycho!" Lachlan shouts at me. He doesn't seem to know enough to be afraid of me, this kid. I'm just another ineffectual adult in his life hassling him.

Malone tries to calm things down. "Now, now, let's not get overheated here."

Lachlan still has his one good eye trained on me. He lifts up his white shirt, exposing his stomach. There's an angry red *T* on it that's just starting to scab over. "Tyler did this. He was the fucking psycho." He pulls the shirt back down and crosses his arms on his chest, looking away again.

"Tyler did that?" Malone says quietly.

"Yeah," the kid says. "He was going to carve his whole fucking name there if the fucking gym teacher didn't come along." Someone needs to tell this kid to get a new adjective.

"What were you fighting about, Lachlan?" Malone asks again. "She's right, you know," nodding her head at me. "It doesn't look good that you and Tyler had a fight the day before he got killed. A district attorney could make a lot out of that. Maybe even enough for a trial."

"I didn't do anything to Tyler. I never saw him again after that." His lip is beginning to tremble. I almost feel sorry for the kid.

"Then tell us what the fight was about," Malone says gently, all good cop to my bad. She's finally getting into her role.

Lachlan's good eye is starting to tear up. The swollen-shut one only oozes. He wipes both of them, along with his nose, with the back of his arm. "It was about Alice," he says.

"What about Alice?"

"He was two-timing her with Jessica Mendler."

"And she asked you to exact some justice for her?" I ask, trying to cast suspicion on the kid in front of me. It's not inconceivable that Alice would attempt to get a boy like Lachlan to do some rough stuff for her, given the graphic content of her letter. Pretty young girls can convince boys to do some ridiculous shit for them. Young men aren't just led around by their dicks at that age, they're enslaved by them.

"No, it was nothing like that," Lachlan says, reaching for a bag of frozen peas off the bed and putting it on his eye. But it was something like that. Unbelievably, Malone catches on before I do.

"Jessica was your girl," Malone says. "That's why you were angry at Tyler."

"We weren't going out or anything," he says, adjusting the peas. "But he knew I liked her." The last sentence is said with a vengeance that almost makes me think he did kill Tyler.

"Where were you on Saturday night, Lachlan? Between around ten and one the next morning."

"Why don't you ask Alice's mom where she was?" he says defiantly. "She had more fights with Tyler than I ever did. One day she went over to his house and threw his Xbox out the window."

"I've seen that woman in the society pages," Malone says. "She couldn't snap a twig, let alone somebody's neck." I guess she's not going to let Lachlan know about the hanging bit. That's the kind of evidence a cop holds back to try to trip a perp up later.

"She could have gotten someone else to do it," he says, looking down as he speaks to Malone. I can't tell if he's got something to hide or he's staring at her boobs. Like I said, that age group is totally driven by hormones.

"Where were you, Lachlan?" Malone asks again.

Whatever he was fixated on before, it loses his attention. He looks up at Malone's face. "I was here."

"Anyone able to vouch for that?" asks Malone.

"My dad," he says. Although the guy probably never got up off the couch once, I'm thinking, to confirm his son was at home.

"Anyone else?" I ask.

He looks lost for a moment then thinks of something. He drops the bag of peas back on the bed and turns back to the computer. After a few keystrokes, a website comes up on the monitor. It features a hulk of a man standing over a reclining woman, her breasts so huge she'd fall over if she tried to get up. Lachlan pulls up an avatar on the screen of a horned Viking warrior. The name under it says "Thorald."

"Thorald? What kind of dumb screen name is that?" I say.

"Thor was taken," he says. "But that's me. And I was questing with my legion."

"Your what?"

"Online, playing the game," he says, "with my team." He indicates some of the other characters standing around his avatar, a slinky chick with elfin ears and a three-hundred-pound horned pig bull wearing a bra. "I was online from after school until three in the morning." I'm glad to see the younger generation is getting so much exercise these days. He must have burned at least a hundred calories with all that mouse clicking. No wonder they're all so goddamn fat.

"Could have been anyone using your handle," I say. And that makes the kid collapse a bit. "But my dad ..." he says.

"Listen, Lachlan, we'll talk to your dad," Malone says. "Anything else you want to tell me? Stuff you and Tyler got into? Maybe someone he pissed off enough who'd want to hurt him?" She's looking at the tattoo on his leg, piecing something together. But the kid clams up.

"I want a lawyer," he says and turns back to the computer to start up the game.

★ ★ ★ ★ ★

"The kid's going to lose it when your techies take his computer," I say from the back of the unmarked. "He won't know what to do with himself. Might have to actually go outside or something."

Malone just says, "Hmmm."

"Hey, where are we going now?" I hope not back to see the Corrigans. I need to find a way to get out of that somehow.

"We're going to pick up Tyler's dry cleaning," she says, holding up the pink pick-up slip. "Then we're going to the station. I want to look up that tattoo. See if it means anything."

We pull into a strip mall and walk into Langley's Dry Clean and Laundromat. The broad behind the counter has a face so lined I'm thinking she could use a good steaming herself. Malone hands her the slip and the woman brings back a black leather jacket draped in plastic.

"Nice jacket," I say, as we walk out the door after paying. Malone didn't even identify herself as the police. They don't care whose stuff it is. If you got a little slip and fifty bucks , you can walk away with a five-hundred-dollar jacket, which is what I'm thinking this beauty must have set Tyler back when he got it. Except it looks like he cut the arms off, ruining the damn thing.

Malone throws it in the trunk and we're off again. I slip down as low as I can in the seat when we park at the cop shop. I even put on my shades. I keep them handy in my inner breast pocket, next to my mickey.

"Oh, don't be such a wuss," Malone says, letting me out of the car.

"Did you just call me a wuss?"

"Sorry."

"Put the handcuffs on."

"C'mon, Candace."

"That's Carrie Fisher to you, and I said put the hand-cuffs on." I'm not letting anyone see me walk into a cop shop unless it looks like it's against my will.

Malone pulls the cuffs off her belt loop and snaps them on my wrists.

"I can't believe you're making me do this," she says, as we do the perp walk over to the front door of the station. Malone has the dry-cleaned jacket over one arm as she leads me with the other.

"I think you'll find a girl like me can't be too careful, Malone."

"I think a girl like you left careful behind a long time ago."

★ ★ ★ ★ ★

Once we're inside, Malone removes the cuffs, and I push my sunglasses up onto my head. We walk through the hall to the back where her cubicle is. I see Saunders through an office window as I pass by and lower my shades again. Luckily, he's busy losing it on some chubby guy sitting at his desk. I can't hear what Saunders is saying, but the look on his face says it all. It isn't until he goes over to close the blinds that the guy in the chair turns around, and I see it's Doug Wolfe, the cop whose wife my dad was banging. I hide my face with my hand and hurry up beside Malone. Her desk is on its own against a window; a high partition separates it from the rest of the floor. I sit down on the window ledge at first, but people walking by can still see my head. I take the extra chair instead. Malone throws Tyler's leather jacket, still in the dry-cleaning bag, over the cubicle wall along with her own coat, and then she sits down at her locked-in laptop, booting it up.

"Tell me, Malone, did you know my mom's family was in the business?"

"I may have heard something like that," she says, still looking at the screen.

"You think they were the ones who took out my dad?"

"I doubt it," she says, typing away. "We kept an eye out for the Scarpellos when you went on trial. To see if they might show up in town. But our intel told us that they never even crossed the state line." So much for my loving extended family taking an interest.

"What about Doug Wolfe?" I say, thinking of Saunders and him going at it just now.

"What about him?" Malone says. Now she's clicking on pictures in some sort of database. She must sense me looking over her shoulder because she angles the screen away.

"My dad was doing his wife."

Malone turns around in her chair. "How did you hear about that?"

"I have my own intel, Malone."

She shakes her head and turns back to the computer. "Doug Wolfe was on a training course at Quantico when your dad disappeared. All week."

"Quantico's not that far away. He could have driven all night. Taken care of my dad and gotten back without anyone knowing."

"They checked it out, Candace. I've seen the file. No one found anything to suggest that." She continues her clicking then types something else into the keyboard. "But the suspicion of it followed him around like a bad stink afterward. That's why he got put on shit detail."

"So, you're saying it could have been him."

"No, Candace, I'm not. And quit trying to figure this out yourself. I told you I'd give you the information when we crack this case and not before."

"But it sounds like the guy had a pretty good motive."

"You're pissing in the wind, Candace."

"Nice language," I say. Malone ignores me. I content myself with looking around her cubicle. A couple of photos of her and her friends in their hockey uniforms. Some sort of citation for conduct above and beyond. There's a green button stuck into the fabric wall that says BECAUSE I'M IRISH with a cartoon of a frothy mug of beer. It impales one of those little red-and-gold envelopes you get money in at Chinese New Year.

"I knew it!" Malone says, sitting back in her chair in triumph. She turns the laptop around to show me what she's found. A photo of the wolf tattoo with the arms fills the screen. The one we'd seen on both Tyler and Lachlan.

"It's a gang tattoo," she says, narrowing her eyes at me.

"Is it?" I say, looking bored. "I don't know what kind of gang would have those two kids in it. Sure they're not just wannabes?"

"Let's go," she says, turning off the laptop.

"Where? I was just getting comfortable."

"To see Selena," she says, grabbing her coat. "She's in vice." I don't get up.

"Well, come on, Candace."

"Aren't you forgetting something?" I hold out my wrists.

"Oh, for God's sake." She puts the handcuffs back on again, and we're off to find out more about the Daybreak Boys, the motorcycle gang that were my father's best customers when he was alive.

CHAPTER 10

THE BUILDING WHERE SELENA works looks more like a place you'd go to meet your broker than a cop shop. Malone and I go in the back door with keypad access and walk up the stairs to the second floor. We enter a bright room full of desks, no cubicle walls, and floor-to-ceiling windows on all sides. A dozen or so plainclothes are typing away desperately on their laptops, as if they're going to catch criminals through their computer screens instead of out on the streets where they live. A familiar tousled redhead looks up and recognizes us.

"Hi, Malone," Danny says, smiling. Malone is suddenly rooted to a spot on the cheap office carpet. She smiles back, patting her hair.

"Hi, Danny," she says.

"And you've brought your friend with you. Nice to see you again, Carrie." He. leans back in his chair, legs stretched out. They're almost as long as mine.

"Hi," I say, rubbing my wrists where the handcuffs had pinched before Malone had removed them in the stairwell.

We stand there for a minute looking like a couple of idiots, Malone flipping her hair and me trying not to look like the criminal I am.

"You looking for Selena?" Danny finally asks.

"Yes," Malone coughs out. "Is she around?"

"I think she's in the break room getting some java," he says.

Malone turns to me. "I'll be right back. Don't go anywhere." She walks down a hallway toward the other end of the floor.

"So, I hear you're a PI," Danny says, looking me up and down.

"Yeah," I say.

"Well, you must be good if Malone brought you in. She's pretty independent. Where do you work?"

"J&B Associates," I say, using my dad's favourite whisky as a cover.

"Haven't heard of them."

"We're new in town."

He reaches over and grabs a travel mug but doesn't take a sip. He's wearing a white golf shirt that strains a little over the pecs. His forearms are smooth and taut, like a sailor's. I used to run contraband with a guy on the west coast with arms like that. They feel good wrapped around a woman's body, like a fleshy vice that pulls you in.

"Well, if you're new to the city, maybe I could show you around a bit," he says. "We all go to The Sip Club for trivia nights on Thursdays. You should come tonight." Trivia night. Next thing he'll be asking me to go steady at the malt shop. What a Disneyesque world these people live in.

"C'mon, Carrie," Malone says tersely from behind me. I didn't hear her creep up. That's not like me.

★ ★ ★ ★

We're in an interrogation room with Selena. The walls have more scuff marks than Principal Cutter's desk. I look around for wet telephone books. The cops sometimes use the drenched, heavy pages to beat confessions out of people. It hurts like hell but leaves no bruises. I don't think they even print those damn things anymore, though.

"The Daybreak Boys, well, well," Selena says. "They're a nasty piece of work."

They are. I once saw one of them beat a guy senseless then douse him in motor oil and light a match.

"What can you tell me about them?" Malone says.

"Well, they're a puppet gang for one of the larger syndicates. Half of those guys don't even ride motorcycles anymore. They just keep up the club's business side of things and let the smaller MCs do their work on the ground."

"MC stands for motorcycle club," Malone says to me.

"I know." Does she think I just came up Lake Erie on a tricycle, for Christ's sake?

"It keeps the head honchos out of jail, farming the rough stuff out to puppets like the Daybreak Boys. Even they outsource a lot of their hits. No one wants to get their hands dirty these days, except with drugs and girls. And they still do their own enforcement. They like being violent, but they try to leave the killing to professionals."

Tell that to the guy doused in motor oil. But Malone still gives me a sideways glance.

"Around here they run most of the massage parlours, moving the girls from place to place. Mostly Eastern Europeans. They also do a good business in illegal firearms and some extortion. But their main focus is drugs. We busted one of their meth labs last year. They'd gotten the recipe from a former Mob chemist. But he didn't live long enough to get caught in the sting. Word is they're into opioids now: fentanyl, carfentanil, and that new stuff, W-18, that's a hundred times stronger than fentanyl."

"Isn't fentanyl strong enough to kill a fucking gorilla?" I ask. Even I'm surprised. Who the fuck needs something a hundred times stronger? Next thing you know they'll have something that makes a junkie explode as soon as he looks at it. Doesn't make much sense, depleting your client demographic like that.

"It's what sells these days," she says. "And while the Daybreak Boys take their orders from higher up, they keep enough pathetic underlings to run their stuff on the streets. I'm thinking this is where your two young men might fit in."

"More outsourcing," Malone says.

"It's not just for conglomerates anymore," Selena says. "Being affiliated with the larger MC gives this local gang access to powerful friends and family members in the top echelon. They mix in legitimate circles. Political. Judicial. You name it. That's how the Daybreak Boys get away with it. They let the stooges do their street-level work and then ride down the street on their hogs with teddy bears raising money for the Children's Hospital, trying to convince the public they're just a harmless bunch of goons in leathers. But make no mistake, these guys are a vicious lot. They've got their tentacles in everywhere."

"I didn't know they had such reach," Malone says.

"They don't call it *connected* for nothing. Organized crime is its own LinkedIn," Selena says.

"Are these kids on your radar?" Malone asks.

"I don't think so. They're too young to be members. It takes years of grovelling at the feet of these animals before they invite you to become one of the pack. I saw the photos you sent me, and their tats aren't even official, just cheap imitations. The wolf's snout isn't symmetrical, and there are four arms surrounding it, not the usual five. But we might have been monitoring them as known associates. I can ask Danny if you want."

Malone colours a bit.

"Or you could do the asking, if you prefer."

"No, that's okay," she says. "Anything else we should know?"

"They've got a clubhouse down on Regent Street, with fortifications better than a state prison. Except it's for keeping people out, not in. You'd need a tank to get in there."

Malone types the address into her iPad then flips it back in its case. "Thanks, Selena. I really appreciate all this."

"Honestly, Chien-Shiung, these Daybreak Boys are a scary bunch. I'd steer clear of them if you can. It's hard to believe they'd even bother with this Tyler

Brent kid. They might give him the beating of his life if he was dealing for them and made the wrong move, but taking the time to order a hit would be a bit over the top."

"Maybe if he pissed them off enough," Malone says. Tyler was good at pissing people off.

"Maybe," Selena says. "But it would have to be pretty bad for them to risk taking the heat for killing a minor who wasn't even a member. Those guys are usually too busy killing each other to involve the greater public. Plus, hanging a kid from a zip line seems a little too creative and personal for a professional hit." I shoot Malone a look.

"Could have been trying to make it look like an amateur," she says, ignoring me and my look.

A guy pops his head in the door of the interrogation room. He needs it to interview a perp who tried to rob a bank with a banana and a pointed stick. They're bringing in a psych consult.

We walk out the door and past the would-be bandit. He's been disarmed of the pointed stick but is currently taking a healthy bite of the other weapon. The arresting officer must have peeled it. He wouldn't have been able to with his wrists cuffed like that. I'm surprised they're letting him eat it. I would have thought it was evidence.

"Just watch yourself, Chien-Shiung," Selena says, taking Malone's hands in hers before we exit into the stairwell. Danny is no longer at his desk. Maybe he's gone to interrogate a suicide bomber who tried to blow up a post office with an apple.

"I will," Malone says.

But she doesn't know what she's talking about. Her friend is right. The Daybreak Boys have their fingers in a lot of dirty little pies. And one of the dirtiest is the police force.

★ ★ ★ ★ ★

We're back in the unmarked. Malone hasn't got the subpoena yet to question Alice Corrigan. The family's lawyer, Lopez, had called to say he was getting a psych eval of Alice. It would state she's not emotionally fit enough to withstand questioning yet. You can get a psychiatrist to say anything for the right price. My defense attorney brought in a doctor who claimed I was "emotionally and psychologically scarred" from the abandonment of my mother and a childhood exposed to criminals. All I ever said in that stupid shrink's office was "Where the fuck is the couch?" In any case, we can't talk to Alice, so we're off to see girlfriend number two, Jessica Mendler.

"So how long have you known Danny?"

"A couple of years," Malone says. "Ever since Selena was assigned to vice. He's a good guy."

"I noticed."

"I didn't mean that."

"The hell you didn't. You just look at that piece of candied ginger and your head starts spinning."

She doesn't say anything, but I can feel the heat of her blush from the back seat.

"And what about Selena? Seems you've known her awhile."

"We met up at the academy, in training," she says. "Two visible minorities banding together, I guess." She's more comfortable discussing her friend than the candied ginger. "With that and being women, we had two strikes against us from the old boys' network." She glances at me in the back. "I suppose you don't meet many women in your line of work either, Candace."

"I told you, I'm retired."

"Sure," she says. "Still, it must have been hard."

"I've never been into that feminist bullshit," I say. "If that's what you mean."

"I hate it when strong women say that. Feminism just means that women should be considered equal to men. Are you telling me you don't believe that?"

"No."

"Really?" she says, pulling into the driveway of a better house than Lachlan Reid's, but quite a bit lower on the status scale than Alice Corrigan's.

"Yeah," I say. "I think we're better."

★ ★ ★ ★ ★

Jessica Mendler looks nothing like "the other woman" as we sit at the kitchen table with her and her mother, an older and even more fade-into-the-wallpaper version of her daughter.

"I don't know anything about what happened to Tyler," she says. Her eyes are red from crying. Honestly, what kind of hold did this jerk have on young girls?

"Where were you on Saturday night, Jessica?" Malone asks.

"I was here," she says, nodding to her mother, who looks like she'd like to hide under the table until we've left. That's when I notice that her eyes are red, too, and one's a little green around the edge, the last bit of healing left from a bruise.

"She was," she says, like an afterthought.

"Was anyone else here?" Malone asks. Jessica looks at her mother for an answer.

"My husband," she says. "He was here, I think."

"You don't sound too sure."

"He's been working some nights. Doing shifts for Hawk Security. He's had trouble getting steady work since he came back from Afghanistan." She picks at the end of a yellow dishtowel she has in her hands, pulling on the threads.

"So he's in the military," Malone says.

"Not anymore." Then the mother shuts down again. Malone turns her attention back to Jessica.

"Lachlan told us you were involved with Tyler," Malone says.

"Yeah," she says. "Sort of."

"Can you define 'sort of' for us, Jessica?"

"We went out a few times."

"Where?"

"Mostly the park," Jessica says. Then she realizes she's made a slip. She's been told that Tyler's body was found in Riverside Park. But there are a lot of parks, a result of forward-thinking urban planners who didn't take into account their current use as a place for junkies to get together and dispose of needles.

"What park?" Malone asks.

"I don't remember." Well, at least she said the right thing there.

"Did you go anywhere else with him, like to a movie, or maybe out for pizza?" Malone is trying to get a handle on Tyler's usual haunts. Unfortunately, her idea of teenage dating behaviour has come out of an *Archie* comic.

"Did you go to any parties with him?" I ask. The mother picks more furiously at the dishtowel.

"No," she says, looking into her lap. "He usually went to those with someone else."

"Alice Corrigan," says Malone.

"Yes," Jessica says. "He said he was going to break up with her. That she was way too possessive." I'd expected her to say this with a little more gusto. Usually the piece on the side loves their day in court to justify their actions. But she just says the words like she's playing a broken telephone game between her true feelings and what comes out of her mouth.

"Did Alice ever threaten you?" Malone asks.

"She said something to me once," Jessica says. "But that was after."

"After what, Jessica?"

She gives her mother a worried look. The mother worries back. The dishtowel may not make it.

"After we stopped seeing each other," Jessica says. But I know that's not it. When you encounter a girl like Jessica, you know there is a Before and an After, and the lightning strike in between them has a far more lasting impact than losing the attention of a two-timing loser like Tyler Brent. But if Malone realizes this, she decides to leave it for now.

"And what did she say to you, Jessica?" Malone presses.

"Just to leave him alone. I told her I wasn't seeing him anymore. But she didn't believe me."

"Do you know Lachlan Reid?" asks Malone.

"Yes," Jessica says.

"Did you know that Tyler and Lachlan had a fight at school the day before he died? It was about you," she says.

The girl looks up, surprised for a second. "Who said that?"

"Lachlan did."

She nods then goes back to staring at the table. "I haven't been to school much lately."

"Do you know anyone who might have wanted to hurt Tyler?"

Jessica doesn't answer. The mother stares down at the dishtowel then folds her hands on top of it. They are red and chapped, like she works in a laundry.

"Lachlan was angry at Tyler, Jessica. Do you know anyone else who might have been angry at him?"

"No," she says. But her shifting eyes say yes.

"Did you know he was involved with a gang? Maybe you saw them around, motorcycle guys? Maybe you even got to meet some of them. Took a ride on one of their bikes. That can be exciting for a young girl."

"Tyler was not a nice boy," the mother blurts out. The dish towel flutters to the ground.

"Don't, Mom."

The mother goes quiet again.

"I went with Tyler once to their clubhouse," Jessica says meekly. And then the tears start to spill. Something finally breaks free in the mother and she gets up from the chair and goes to stand beside her daughter, holding her head to her apron. They cling to each other like a couple of *Titanic* steerage passengers.

But Malone doesn't seem to notice. She's busy getting her iPad out to take notes and doesn't look up when she asks, "Where was that, Jessica? Do you have an address? Do you think you'd recognize any of the people there if I were to show you a few pictures?"

Shit, Malone, I think. *You're just not getting this*. I don't want to ask, but someone has to.

"What happened at the clubhouse, Jessica?" For once, I try not to sound like the sarcastic bitch I am.

"Tyler was not a nice boy," the mother says again. And then she's crying as well. The two of them hold each other at the kitchen table, sobbing. The yellow dishtowel on the floor is too frayed to dry up that many tears.

★ ★ ★ ★ ★

"Is there anyone this kid didn't screw over?" Malone says. "I didn't even know him, and I'd like to break his neck myself."

"I wouldn't say that too loud, Malone. Could prove intent."

"Yeah," she says, "But I didn't learn that he'd brought a sixteen-year-old girl to the Daybreak Boys to be gang-raped until after he was dead. It must have been some sort of initiation. But I can't do anything if she refuses to go on the record."

"Uh-huh." I'd heard about the initiation thing in some of the other gangs. But my father said it wasn't done in the MCs.

"We need to talk to Mr. Mendler. What happened to his daughter would make any father go ballistic," Malone says. I could point out that judging by the bruises on Mrs. Mendler, going ballistic is probably something Mr. Mendler is already in the habit of doing.

"Hmm," I say instead, downing a drink that came with a cherry on a plastic sword and motioning the waitress for two more. Malone has decided to let me near a bar again after all. But it's her kind of place, one of those low-tabled martini bars where young, motivated professionals hang out, hoping to meet more of their species. Malone's paying, or I wouldn't have set foot in a place that charges eight bucks a drink. Despite being from a different social gene pool than the usual patron, I still fit in. Hot women are the best kind of currency. They are accepted in more places than American Express.

"You've been pretty quiet since we left the Mendlers' house," she says, sipping on her chocolatini. Honestly, there's chocolate and there's booze, and no one in their right mind should have them together.

"You ever think maybe the father would be justified?" I say, looking around for the waitress. I catch her eye and she jumps, starts hurrying the guy mixing drinks at the bar. "Maybe the kid did deserve it, like the principal said."

"He didn't actually say that. Besides, no one deserves to die at seventeen," Malone says, but not with great conviction.

"Even a no-account punk who takes his girlfriend along to be a gang's plastic toy for the evening?"

"We'll have to check out Mendler's alibi," she says, ignoring my question, as she tucks her iPad in her purse. "See if he was working. I'll call Hawk Security in the morning. If the girl was too freaked out to report it to the police, her dad might have not been able to let it go."

The waitress brings over two more drinks. I down one and hand the empty glass back. I tell her to keep them coming.

"My dad didn't," I say, surprising both Malone and myself.

"Your dad?"

"Yeah, when I was in university."

"You were in university?"

"You're beginning to sound like a goddamn parrot, Malone. Yes, I was at university," I say. "For a while."

"What happened?" Malone asks.

"It's a long story," I say, biting the cherry off the sword of my current drink. It feels sharp on my tongue. "But basically I woke up in the hospital with multiple contusions and ripped up downstairs. I also had a concussion so bad I couldn't lay down new memories for three weeks."

"Oh my God, Candace. Did they ever find out who did it?"

"I couldn't remember anything. I was probably unconscious for the whole thing. That's the only way they could have got to me. And it was 'they'; the cops did a rape kit. For all the good that fucking did." The waitress brings another drink and I give her another empty glass.

"Didn't they have any leads? Did nobody see anything?"

"I was walking home from a party. I didn't drink as much in those days and I needed the air. I was young, you know? Plus, the party was full of smokers. Which I hate. If you're going to kill yourself, do it with something that doesn't make your mouth taste like the inside of a Turkish prison."

"And they assaulted you," she says. "On the way home."

"I guess so. My dad and my uncle Rod did their own research." I pause to allow Malone to consider the kind of research two men for whom *kneecap* is a verb might have conducted. "But no one seemed to know anything. Could have been a gang, like the girl. Could have been frat boys. Whoever it was, no one was talking, despite my dad's persuasion. I finally called him off before he broke the legs of half the freshman class."

"What happened after that?"

"Uncle Rod's girlfriend, Charlotte, took care of me after I got out of the hospital. But since it was three weeks before I could even remember what I had for breakfast that day, I wasn't exactly able to keep up with my studies. I lost the year. Never went back."

"And the police never found them." She says it as a statement rather than a question. Malone knows how hard it is for the police to find people sometimes.

"I wasn't exactly co-operative. I was just a kid." I remember the questions, which bore into every detail of my life. They'd had a heyday when they realized whose daughter they were dealing with. More interested in that than the fact that some group of psychos had left bite marks on my nipples. "I'm not a big fan of cops," I say.

This has a bit of sting to it, and Malone takes a considerable sip of her own drink.

"You should let me look into it," she suggests quietly.

"Leave it, Malone."

"There could have been something they missed. I could make a few calls. I could —"

"Leave it," I say more strongly before I down the last of my drink. "I don't need saving, Malone. I'm happy with my life. I'm not some sad sack on a talk show. Shit like this doesn't define me."

"What does?" she asks.

"I do."

I leave the bar, but remember the name of another. The night is still young, even if I'm not. I haven't had the luxury of being young in a long, long time.

CHAPTER 11

"HI, MARCUS."

It's late by the time I make it to The Goon. I had one other stop to make before here. A well-muscled familiar figure sits down next to me as Linda announces last call.

"Hi, Candace," Marcus says. He smells of Old Spice and pipe tobacco. A combination that I enjoy, despite how much I hate smokers. His dark skin seems to shine in the beige and grey drabness of The Goon.

"Whatcha in town for?" I ask. More like *who's* he in town for.

"I'm looking for a young lady who came home from a Mexican all-inclusive with cocaine stuffed in the applicators of her tampons," Marcus says. "She had four jumbo packs in her suitcase." He motions to Lovely Linda for two whiskeys. She serves mine on ice and his neat. "Her bail bondsman got a little premenstrual himself when she skipped out on him."

"Do you think you'll find her?"

"I'm not the kind of man to leave a lady behind." His dark-brown eyes are heavy lidded, with long lashes like a girl. Fuck-me eyes, like young Elvis, before the drugs swelled up his face.

"No," I say, smiling. "You're not."

The Goon is almost empty now. Linda has stayed open mostly for me. She works behind the bar, replacing glasses, going to each draft spigot and turning the key on the tap lock. When she thinks no one's looking she adds a bit of water to the cheaper liquors to make them last longer. The usual end-of-night stuff. At four o'clock this morning, long after she's gone, a cleaning service run by Dutch immigrants will clean the piss off the walls in the men's restroom and empty those disgusting paper bags in the women's cubicles. Then they'll vacuum the dirt and greasy onion-ring crumbs off the carpet and bring in a steam cleaner if someone puked before making it to the can. They are dive-bar cleaning fairies, working in the dead of night to make The Goon presentable for the first customers who bang on the door at ten in the morning. No matter how many urinal pucks and air fresheners they use, the place will still smell like stale beer and the sweat of the disenfranchised.

"What are you up to these days, Candace?"

I take a sip of the whiskey, rolling it around in my mouth first, the amber bite of it reassuring my mouth, making it looser.

"You wouldn't believe me if I told you."

But I do tell him. Marcus Knight is not quite a civilian or a criminal, making him an excellent confidant. He also knows how to keep things to himself. I don't think anyone knows that he's my bro with benefits.

I tell him about Tyler Brent and the blonde who wanted me to take him out. I tell him about Malone and her proposition and the Daybreak Boys. I tell him about the cuckolded cop, and my mother's connections, and how one of them might have put my dad in the harbour five years ago. I even tell him about Uncle Rod and how he reacted when I told him Malone knew who was behind my father's death.

"Come on, Candace," he says, his strong but amazingly gentle hand wrapped around the whiskey glass. "Rod's a straight-up guy. He's been around since you were born. He even went after those bastards after the trouble you had at college." Yes, he knows about that, too. He and Malone are the only ones I ever told outside of my dysfunctional little non-family of Rod, Charlotte, and my dad. Like I said, he's a guy I can talk to.

"You never know," I say.

"You don't trust him?" he asks, rubbing one of those remarkable hands along the back of his neck.

"I don't trust anyone," I say, finishing off the whiskey.

"Even me?" He puts his hand on the small of my back. I can feel the heat of it as he slips it up inside my leather jacket.

"Even you, Marcus."

I pull away from the warmth of that hand and step off the bar stool, giving him a lingering kiss on the cheek before I walk away. Then I step into the cool night.

There are times a woman needs to be with someone, and there are times when she needs to be alone.

Trust me.

★ ★ ★ ★ ★

The street is misty and deserted when the heavy oak door of The Goon closes behind me. A cold rain has started up. I'm not a fan of spring. It's just a soggy, slightly warmer version of winter in the city, shivery and wet until one day it's hot as hell and that's summer. I zip up my leather jacket and pull my hoodie up over my hair. Even a few drops on my mop of hair makes the whole thing explode like an airbag.

The E-Zee Market is closed. The neon sign is still on, making buzzing noises like a mosquito getting fried by one of those electric zappers. By this time on a weekday, Majd is sleeping in his small apartment attached to the back room. I've been in there, once. He showed me pictures of his family in happier times. His brothers smiling for the camera, along with his dad in front of some cartoonish backdrop that must have been the Syrian version of Disneyland. His mother was smiling, too, not knowing that three-quarters of her family would be gone in just a few short years. It made you want to walk into the photo and warn them. Tell them to turn in their all-day ride passes for a one-way ticket out of the country that would soon turn on them like a rabid dog.

I cross the street, the hand in my pocket hiding the sharp ends of my keys, sticking out between the knuckles. When I get to the door beside the E-Zee Market that leads to the stairwell to my apartment, I pull them out and slip the door key in the lock.

That's when I hear the car. Not a completely outrageous occurrence at this time of night. But when I hear the door open behind me, I get ready. Put the cold metal of the keys back in my fist.

"Candace Starr?" a voice calls out.

I turn around. A large man, even by my standards, is holding the door of a Lincoln Continental open for a grey-haired gentleman who now stands on the sidewalk. He is dressed impeccably but has one wonky eye that makes it hard to know where he's looking. I'm not sure if he's addressing me or the Popsicle Pete in the E-Zee Market window to my left. I decide it's me.

"Who wants to know?" I ask, keeping my fist with the keys hidden behind my back.

"Please," says the gentleman. He's not totally grey. Closer up I can see he's actually what they call salt and pepper, a hair colour that looks good on men of any age. He's wearing a three-quarter-length camel coat that stands out in the dark street like a beige-wool beacon. The rain is making dark splotches on his shoulders. "We only wish to talk," he says, the one eye still roving wildly.

The big man at the car door places a hand inside his own coat, a less expensive version of his employer's in a much darker colour. He doesn't pull anything out, though. Just wants me to know he has more than his considerable bulk backing him up.

"I'm not much of a talker," I say.

The old man smiles. "Then perhaps you would like to listen." He steps away from the car door and gestures with an open arm, like he's a footman guiding me into a pumpkin coach on its way to the ball. I realize I don't have much choice. It's either get inside or deal with the ugly stepsister holding the door. I walk over, get into the black sedan, and slide along the leather seat in the back to the far side. The gentleman in the camel coat gets in beside me, and the big guy closes the door. Then he plants his burly carcass next to the driver. The car pulls away from the curb. As we drive off, I can see Marcus through the window of The Goon, still seated at the bar.

The old guy leans forward and whispers something to the driver, who nods and makes a left onto one of the streets that lead to the highway out of town.

"So, Candace Starr," he says, turning to face me in the back seat, though his eye is turned elsewhere. "We have heard a great deal about you."

"All of it's true," I say, fingering the keys in my pocket. I haven't got my gun. I've been hiding it under the extra lotto tickets in a drawer behind the cash at the E-Zee Market ever since Malone caught me with it. I've tried to get Majd to keep a gun behind the cash anyway. He's been robbed before. But he said he had enough of lethal weapons back in Syria.

The old man smiles. "I don't doubt that it is." I'm sure he doesn't; that's why he brought Magilla Gorilla with him.

"So," I say. "You know my name. What's yours?"

"My name is not important, Miss Starr," he says. "Not for this conversation." I'm concerned about what he means by *conversation*. Will this just be a short convo with a large lead pipe or a deeper version of pillow talk that ends with me sleeping with the fishes?

"I'm listening," I say, staring out the rain-streaked window. It blurs the streetlights of the highway as we pull onto the ramp.

"I understand you have been asking questions about a certain family," he says. "And that family does not take kindly to being discussed."

The Scarpellos. Shit. I decide to see if my lineage will buy me any sway.

"My mother was a Scarpello," I say.

"Yes, you take after her," he says. "Although not quite as ..."

"Batshit crazy?" I suggest.

His roaming eye goes still for a moment. "I was going to say 'dark,' Miss Starr," he says. My mother's hair was jet black compared to my honey brown. "But since you mention it, Angela was a concern. A somewhat erratic woman. *Una pazza*." A crazy woman. I'd learned that word from the Italian guys who used to hang out at the pool hall. Dad and Uncle Rod liked to shoot a few games together back in the day. They'd let me sit on a stool as a kid and move the marker along the scoreboard as they sunk the coloured balls. I used to love twisting the end of a pool cue into those little square, indented pieces of chalk. It made a squeaky sound, like a toy. Maybe the old guy's wandering eyeball is the result of having a pool cue stuck in it. I saw my fair share of fights in the pool hall. When one broke out, my father would move me from the stool and put me up on the counter of the waitresses' station. I was given a hot pot of coffee to hold at the ready, with instructions to pour it on any brawler who got too close.

"More like *puttana pazza*," I say, using another Italian phrase I picked up.

The old guy narrows his good eye at me in disapproval. "Don't refer to your mother that way, Miss Starr. A parent should be treated with respect."

"She didn't show me much respect when she left me on the side of the highway," I say, looking through the rain at the passing median, wondering not for the first time whether that was the place I'd last seen her. Then again, Rod's inconsistencies on the details of my abandonment make me wonder if the whole thing was just a story for my benefit. Family lore passed down to cover up something either more mundane or more sinister.

"That aside, it is important in families to remain loyal. Your mother was not good at this. She didn't understand the importance of family."

"Tell me about it." We're crossing the bridge now, and I'm a little concerned it might be our destination. Then I remember they installed steel veils along the sides last year. A bid to stop the suicides that took place at least once a month. One guy had tried just the same, but he ended up too far over to hit the parkway below. Instead he landed with a thud on a high-school playing field that bordered the freeway, where a bunch of senior girls were playing soccer. He was conscious when they called 911. Poor bastard, he probably thought he'd died and gone to heaven when he saw all those bare teenage girls' legs huddled around him.

"The situation is this, Miss Starr. The head of the Scarpello family is in his declining years. He is not a well man."

"Sorry to hear that."

"Thank you for your concern." He leans forward again to whisper something in the driver's ear. "We are also concerned. Tell me, have you heard from your mother over the years?"

"No."

"It would seem strange, for a mother, to not at least check in on her daughter, even the once. Perhaps when you were on trial?" So they *had* noticed. I knew Malone's intel wasn't to be trusted. The cops don't know their dons from their Black Donnellys around here.

"I've never heard from her," I say. The driver takes an exit ramp, slowing down as he comes around the curve in the slippery rain.

"Perhaps you have heard of her whereabouts? We wonder whether she may have started a new family. There could be siblings of yours that have reached out to you, maybe a brother?" I've never thought about the possibility of my mother having other children. It seemed to me that when you have the maternal instinct of a gnat you would do something bright like having your tubes tied or your uterus yanked out. It would be cool to have a brother. Then it occurs to me why the old man is asking.

"You're worried about when the old don dies," I say. "About who's going to take over." They don't care about me. I haven't got the right equipment between my legs to stake a claim in their all-male hierarchy, but a brother would be different.

"Our succession plans are well thought out, Miss Starr. It is important to have continuity of leadership in an organization such as ours." He clears his throat, holding one heavily knuckled hand up to his mouth. "We wouldn't want anyone causing undue stress or turmoil when the time comes."

We're moving through an underpass that runs under the highway we were travelling on before. When we stop at the lights, a sleeping kid on a bench gets up and tries to walk over to the car with his squeegee. The thug in the front passenger seat lets down his tinted window and exposes his bulging chest. The kid goes back to the bench and crawls into his soggy sleeping bag.

"Listen, I don't know where my mother is, and I don't care."

"Then why have you been asking questions about her?"

Lying, in my experience, is usually the best policy. In this case, though, it doesn't seem like a wise course of action. Plus, his eye is really freaking me out. It makes for a stunning interrogation technique. I must tell Malone about it.

"I'm trying to find out who killed my father," I say. "I wondered whether my mother had been involved." I don't tell him that I also wondered whether the Scarpello family had been involved. Truth is the most useful when you only use half of it.

"Ah, Mike Starr," the old man says. "Another misplaced loyalty of your mother's."

"At least he stuck around to raise me." I'm pissed that I have to defend my father to this condescending wise guy. But I won't tolerate any trash talk about my dad if that's where this is going.

"Regardless, he was not an appropriate choice for your mother. She disrespected the family's wishes by marrying him. As she disrespected most of their wishes."

"Did you know my father?" I ask.

"I met him once," he says. "Shortly after your mother announced she was with child. Normally, the family would have gathered around at such a time. Raised the child as part of our community and perhaps taken the father to task for …" He pauses, looking for a polite phrase. "Taking liberties," he says. "But in this case, your mother was already showing signs of instability. We thought it best for her to leave with him and sever ties permanently." I wonder what lengths the Scarpellos might have gone to in order to disassociate themselves. Murder, in my experience, is the most reliable and permanent severer of ties.

"Why didn't you kill her?" I ask, getting to the point.

"She was carrying a man's child," he says, looking horrified. "This would be a sin."

I like how we keep talking about this child as if it weren't me. As if I'm something hypothetical like a butterfly that might flap its wings and cause chaos somewhere, or maybe just attract other bastard butterflies.

"Then we heard that you were born, and we were not as concerned."

Yeah, you sexist bastard, because I wasn't a boy who might come back and bite you all in your patriarchal asses.

"We like to keep track of our family members, even the estranged ones, but your mother has been elusive in that respect. Rather strange for a woman who was always attracting attention. You are sure you have heard nothing from her all this time?"

"I'm sure." We're cruising back into the neighbourhood now. I recognize the streets. The driver pulls up in front of a boarded-up warehouse about two blocks from the E-Zee Market; I can see the faulty neon of the sign flickering in the window off in the distance. The bodyguard or enforcer or whatever he is gets out of the car and opens up my door onto the street.

"You will contact us, Miss Starr, if you hear anything from your mother, won't you? The old man's health, as I said, is failing, and that is a time when you wish your family to be present, even those who have caused you distress in the past. Mortality has a way of breaking down these boundaries, wouldn't you say?"

I don't say anything. Just get out of the car. I look at the guy holding the door, but he doesn't look at me. Just stares straight ahead. I half expect him to cover his eyes with his hands like one of those "see no evil" monkeys. Maybe that's what happened to the old man's eye. It saw too much evil, and now it's trying to do a runner.

The bodyguard shuts my door and gets back in the car. As the Lincoln snakes around the corner, I wait and listen for the sound of the engine to fade away. Then I lift my hoodie back up and start walking home as the rain turns into a downpour. My hair's going to frizz like a bitch tomorrow.

I think over the conversation in the car as I dodge the puddles on the sidewalk — my shit kickers don't do well in water. It doesn't sound like the Scarpello family gave a shit about my father. They only cared that my mother might try to stir up trouble with an heir to the family throne. And if they didn't give a shit, they probably didn't wait over two decades to slit his throat.

I think about this in the pouring rain, with my keys held white-knuckled in my pocket. For all the old man said about family, he was full of crap. Words, especially polite ones, are just the weights people tie on to actions to drown the truth of them. But those actions, they float to the surface over time. The Scarpello clan had over thirty years to claim Angela Starr's daughter as one of their own. That and the fact that they'd left me alive, and with two eyes, meant they never gave a shit about me either.

CHAPTER 12

THE NEXT MORNING I'm woken up by Majd knocking on the door. His raps are so soft, I think it's rats scurrying in the walls again, but eventually I catch on and go open the door.

"Call for you, Miss Candace."

I throw on a pink silk kimono that a trans gal gave to me before she kicked me to the curb for selling weed out of her apartment. It has a black-and-white crane painted on the back. I lost the tie a long time ago, so I hold it closed with my hand. I wonder if it's the old guy from last night calling to give me a contact number in case I hear anything about my mother. He'd driven away last night without telling me how to reach him if I did. I guess the Mob doesn't give out business cards.

"Hello," I say. The E-Zee Market phone is bolted to the wall, old school, like all the things in this neighbourhood that showed up and were never able to leave.

"Hello, is that you, Candace?" Rod's mother sounds just like I imagine the grandma did in *Little Red Riding Hood*. It's the one book I remember my mother reading aloud, and it used to terrify me — the nasty wolf dressing up as an old lady in that creepy frilled cap with the nightdress. I still can picture the saliva dripping from his pointy canine teeth as he tries to pull one over on the little girl with her basket of goodies. *All the better to see you with, my dear.*

"Yes, it is, Agnes. How are you?"

"Oh, as best as can be expected. My sciatica is acting up on account of the change in weather, and Sylvia Patterson just got carted off to the Terrace." The Terrace is the Victoria Terrace Retirement Home in St. John's. Agnes has told me that she'll fetch her long-dead husband's rifle from where it's bolted under the kitchen table and go down shooting before she'll let anyone take her to one of those places. Rod says the only way she's leaving her robin's egg–blue row house on Franklyn Avenue is in a box. "Did you get the socks I sent?"

"I did," I say. I might have felt guilty about using one of them to strain the booze out of a broken bottle on Valentine's Day if I were the feeling-guilty type.

We chat for a bit. I don't want to appear obvious. I know how to put a person at ease despite my often abrasive manner. Allowing themselves to be lulled into a false sense of security has been the downfall of many of my targets.

"Listen, Agnes, I've been thinking about making a trip this fall," I say. "Out to Newfoundland."

"Oh, we'd love to see you, dearie. It's been years. I'd hardly know you, except for the pictures Rod brings me." I squirm a bit in the silk kimono. Maybe I'm capable of feeling guilty after all. "The last time you came you were in love with that Cinnamon group or whatever they're called, bopping around the living room with your CDs."

"The Spice Girls," I say, holding my hand over the receiver in case someone hears us.

"Oh yes, you wanted to be the one that none of the other girls liked."

"Sporty Spice."

"Ah yes, such a cute little urchin you were." I was twelve and already six foot. I may have been an urchin, but I wasn't little. And I'll wipe the smile off any man's face who ever refers to me as cute.

"The thing is, do you remember when I was working on that cruise ship for Disney five years ago?" We hadn't told Agnes I was in the slammer. Uncle Rod made me send her Mickey Mouse postcards from jail, telling her how much fun I was having playing Sleeping Beauty at breakfast for the kids. Luckily, she was way too far-sighted to be able to read a postmark. Rod was always trying to protect Agnes from the lives we led. He didn't tell her my father died until two years after we buried him. He said it was a fishing accident, something that apparently happens regularly in Newfoundland and no one asks questions about.

"Oh yes, I remember. I was so happy getting your sunny postcards. We had a piece of weather that year. Made my bunions scream, I'm telling you."

"Yes, well, anyway, I think Uncle Rod flew back early that year on a charter. I wanted to book a flight, and he said the service was really good. I thought I might book my flight with the same airline." Oh, I'm lying so shame-facedly to this old lady, I could be the wolf in the fucking fairy tale myself. "Uncle Rod couldn't remember the name when I asked him, so I thought you might remember."

"Oh honey, it was a few years back. I don't think I'd remember something like that. Have a hard time remembering where I put my dentures these days." She laughs and almost chokes a bit, as if her dentures might have started to fall out with the force of it. "But I don't remember Roddy ever leaving early. He always books the two weeks then plants his fanny on the chesterfield until it's time to go again. All his old buddies come to visit him here, and sometimes we even have a Céilí. When he comes from away, he likes to stay put."

So much for my idea of Rod flying back to take out my dad and then back to Newfoundland. He's got his mother and The Irish Rovers to vouch for his whereabouts.

"You'd love our Céilís," Agnes continues. "So much wonderful music. Maybe I could even ask one of the girls to play that 'Want to See' song you like so much on the accordion."

"Wannabe," I say, once again cupping my hand to the phone. I can never allow this woman to talk to anyone I know.

"Come in the summer to see us, sweetheart. Or anytime. Just make sure when you come that the nor'easters are done their storming. We'll have a wonderful time."

★ ★ ★ ★ ★

Charlotte is pulling up in her hatchback when I walk out of the E-Zee Market half an hour later. She dents a mailbox as she parallel parks, straddling the curb. I pretend I don't see her, but her little legs manage to catch up to me. She's huffing and puffing as she calls out my name.

"Candace!"

I can no longer pretend I don't hear her. I stop and let her catch up.

"Hi, Charlotte. Thanks for the laundry."

"Don't you 'Hi, Charlotte' me, young lady," she says. "I was just over at Rod's and he practically slammed the door in my face. Told me you came asking about your mother and left him on a roof. He was up there for two hours before he went around the side and tried to raise Mrs. Boddis at her bedroom window. He gave her a terrible start. She thought he was a peeper."

"Relax, Charlotte, I got my information from an old-timer at the bar. You're in the clear." I don't tell her about last night. She's wound up enough already. I wonder briefly if Roberto was the one who blabbed to the Scarpellos but then dismiss the idea. He's got too much class. Probably one of the less reputable types I interviewed that evening. Or someone who was listening. I must have really tied one on because I'm usually pretty wise to big ears. I make a mental note to watch for those who might need to have their lobes stapled next time I'm at the bar.

"But I was the one who put the idea in your head. Rod's going to know it was me." She looks really worried, yanking hard on her purse strap worn diagonally across her matronly chest.

"You tell him from me that it was the old-timer at the bar who filled me in. Tell him I'll back that up if he wants to ask me. You didn't admit to him what you said, did you?" There's only one thing more stupid than getting caught for a crime, and that's admitting to it.

"No, I didn't," she says. She's starting to let up on the purse strap, but there's still a furrow in the brow of her usually smooth dumpling face. I remember that face fretting over me in the hospital bed after I was attacked by that pack of bastards. Charlotte had plumped pillows and offered endless cups of tea I didn't drink, hoping that kindness might magically erase the marks on my body, along with its violation. The marks disappeared over time; the violation ended up needing something stronger than tea. "Promise you'll tell him it wasn't me who told you about your mother?"

"I promise, Charlotte."

She bites her lip. It's not enough. Rod must really be in what Agnes calls "a pressure." Charlotte hasn't waited all these years putting up with him in hopes of being made an honest woman to lose her chance over me and my ladder antics.

"Maybe you could come over and explain right now. I could drive you," she says, turning to indicate her car that a postie is now inspecting suspiciously, getting out a pen from his bag to take down her licence plate.

"What the hell are you doing?" she yells, flying back toward the parked vehicle. She has all but forgotten her tiff with Uncle Rod, faced with the possibility of another moving violation that might jeopardize her driver's licence. A document some DMV examiner had awarded her while obviously on crack. Her purse smacks on her hip as she runs threateningly toward the postie, menopause fuelling her road rage.

As I stand on the street corner and watch the altercation unfold, a minivan with two empty car seats in the back slows down beside me. The man inside holds his hand up to his mouth and makes a rude gesture with his tongue through his fingers. I turn around and start walking again. Sometimes I hate this damn neighbourhood.

After a few blocks, I slip down an alleyway and climb a fence to get in the back of a condemned building that nobody ever seems to get around to tearing down. I wedge myself through a gap in a boarded-up main-floor window. It is surrounded by a graffiti artist's lousy attempt to draw the Incredible Hulk's arm holding a can of aerosol paint. I enter through the crook of his acid-green elbow.

Charlotte isn't the only one who can be convinced to cough up intel, as Malone likes to call it. I have my sources. And this time I want information not on my mother but on what two boys so young they still had placenta behind their ears were doing mixed up with the Daybreak Boys. Malone wants me to find a killer, and no matter what rage-fuelled monsters I have to go through, I'm going to find one.

★ ★ ★ ★ ★

I find Rory working on a laptop in his squat on the third floor of the building. A stained bedsheet he's hung up in the window makes the room look even more drab and dusty. The only solid light comes from the glow of his screen and the greenish-lit aquarium that houses his turtle, Bubba. He has everything hooked up to a massive battery he charges at the laundromat once a day. Rory makes his money writing research papers for spoiled students with more money than brains. He steals his internet from the dilapidated library next door, where the only patrons are the bag ladies who sleep in between the shelves during the day. I've told him before there's better money in writing mommy porn, tame S&M erotica for bored housewives. I know a guy who writes that stuff and publishes it online for ninety-nine cents a pop. He now flies to Iceland for the weekend with his girl on the thirty K he makes each month. I tried my hand at it once. You'd think I'd be good at commercial fiction, since it's basically just writing down lies for cash, but it turns out it's a little bit more than that.

When Rory looks up from his laptop and sees me, he walks over to give a hug. I tolerate it as best I can, given I'm not much of a hugger. Rory had a bad smack habit a few years back, and my dad helped him dry out. Locked him in the basement at Rod's and refused to let him out until he was over the worst of it. Threatened him with a quick death if he ever touched the stuff again. Even with my dad gone, he's stayed straight. He loved the man for his help, and, by extension, me. Even if he did break every nail he had trying to scratch his way out through that cellar door.

"How you doing, Candace?"

"Good enough for rock 'n' roll," I say. But he can tell I've got more on my mind than that. "I wanted to ask you a few questions."

"I don't know if I'll have the answers," he says, eyeing me suspiciously.

"Then you can find someone who does."

Rory still has a hand in the game, supplying dope and coke to those who need it. Or guns, if their needs are more sophisticated. He's the best type of guy to consult when looking for reliable information, able to navigate these filthy inner circles with his compass still straight and sober. He makes enough cash to afford something better than the squat, but he's lived in these sorts of places most of his adult life and this squat has become his safe space. When he swore off his addiction it seems he needed to swear off most other creature comforts as well. He's like a priest holed up in his monastic cell.

"I want some information on the Daybreak Boys," I tell him.

"Shit, Candace. Can't you get that information yourself?" Rory knows my dad used to work for the gang, providing the professional hits they needed to distance themselves from. But I don't want to talk to them about Tyler and Lachlan. They'd end up asking too many questions of their own.

"Not this time," I say.

Rory walks over to the aquarium, pinches some flakes from a canister, and drops them in for the turtle. Bubba swims nervously from one end to the other, his head bobbing back and forth, smashing at the glass. That turtle has never been the same since he got caught in the filter. "Okay," he says, turning back to me. "What do you want to know?"

"There's a couple of kids I think might have been involved with them."

"Prospects?" Rory asks.

I remember the leather jacket with the arms cut off that Malone and I picked up at the dry cleaners. "Maybe," I say. "Although they could have just been dealing to their friends at the high school for them."

"The Daybreak Boys are cooking some pretty mean stuff for the average high-school kid."

"Yeah, I know the whole fentanyl thing. And that W-18 that's a hundred times stronger."

"More than that," Rory says. Bubba knocks his skinny turtle head more insistently on the glass.

"What the hell can be more than that?"

"They're selling smack again."

"Big deal." Heroin is hardly something the Daybreak Boys are unfamiliar with. They're the ones who got Rory hooked on it in the first place.

"Laced with W-18."

"Jesus Christ."

There seems to be no end to the drug world's creative development of shit that can kill you.

"These kids, what're their names?" asks Rory, putting the canister away. It has a picture of a red banana on it. Charlotte once went on a diet that consisted of only this colour of banana and green beans. The inside of her refrigerator looked like a Christmas decoration experiment gone terribly wrong.

"Tyler Brent and Lachlan Reid," I say. Bubba flips himself over, flailing in the tank. Rory reaches into the aquarium and sets him right again. When he pulls his arm out it's covered in red banana flakes.

"Isn't one of those kids dead?" I guess Rory reads the papers, too.

"Do you know anything about them or not?" I say.

"What's your interest?" He grabs a dingy cloth and towels off his arm.

"You know I can't tell you that."

"No, I suppose you can't." He walks over and sits in an armchair that bleeds stuffing, pulls out a cigarette, and lights it. Tobacco is his only remaining addiction. "I can't say I've heard the names in my travels. Other than the one kid's murder."

"But you can make inquiries," I say, taking a step toward him. He can tell I'm serious. It makes him curious and just a bit frightened.

"Okay, Candace. I'll do my best," he says. I can see the yellow nicotine stains on his fingers, next to the school ring he got when he made valedictorian. That was before the Daybreak Boys introduced him to smack. My dad had hidden the ring from him so he wouldn't hawk it, given it back when he got clean. It's important to protect your past, he'd said. I watch as the tarry smoke of the cigarette wafts across the airless room toward me.

"Make sure that you do, Rory."

I leave him with Bubba and the laptop, taking a deep breath of fresh air when I get outside. Cigarettes mixed with untapped potential always make me sick.

CHAPTER 13

"WHAT TOOK YOU SO LONG?"

"I didn't know this was like a day job, Malone." When I came home after seeing Rory, there was a message to call Malone waiting at the E-Zee Market for me. I called her back and agreed to meet her on the corner of Summerton and Pine. Every street in this city is named after either a dead upper-class twit or a tree.

As usual, I am riding in the back of the unmarked. I'm late because I had to pluck my eyebrows before I left. They've gotten a bit unruly lately. I've had a guy break my arm and never made a sound, but yanking those goddamn little hairs from between my eyes makes me blubber like a baby.

Malone grits her teeth behind the wheel. I can see her in the rear-view mirror.

"What are we in such a hurry for anyway?" I say. "Tyler Brent isn't any more dead than he was yesterday."

"The first few days of an investigation are critical, Candace."

"Yeah, I may have heard that."

"And I finally got a subpoena to take Alice Corrigan in for an oral deposition. We need to go pick her up." Shit. I knew I shouldn't have called Malone back.

When we pull up in the Corrigans' driveway, the Mercedes AMG is still there, with the well-earned ding on the passenger side. It must be nice to have the cash to keep a hound like Lopez on retainer.

The blonde answers the door. Her eyes flutter for a moment at the sight of me, and then her face resumes its usual paralysis. Not just because of the Botox. This is one badass woman, as I said before. She can play it cool with the best of the icy-hearted.

Lopez and a man I assume is the husband sit on the couch with the blonde. We take a seat across the glass-and-chrome coffee table from them. I get the wingback chair with the embroidered satin upholstery. Malone gets a less comfortable Louis XVI knock-off. There is potpourri in a bowl on one of the end tables next to a ceramic Royal Doulton tart holding up her skirts.

"I'm Detective Malone, and this is my associate Ms. Fisher."

"This is Kristina and Greg Corrigan," Lopez says, indicating his fellow couch mates.

The blonde smiles and pours some lemon-infused Perrier into a tumbler of ice, not even looking up. Her husband consults his watch as if late for a meeting, which he probably is. Malone hands the subpoena to Alex Lopez. He spends a fair bit of time reading it before he hands it back to her.

"I'm afraid Alice isn't available for a deposition. She's still extremely fragile, as we already told you."

"Fragile or not, Mr. Lopez, we have a subpoena."

"And I have a letter from Dr. Stephen Love stating that she is both suicidal and suffering from severe anxiety." Dr. Love? Is this guy for real? But he hands Malone an envelope with embossed lettering on it. She puts it down on the coffee table without even opening it.

"We sympathize with the young lady's emotional state," Malone says, nodding to the parents. "But we need to talk to her."

"Well, I'm afraid that you can't," Lopez says, adjusting his tie. He and Malone are in a pissing match. I wait to see whose yellow stream will reach across the coffee table first. I'm thinking it'll be Malone for the win when she stands and looks up the circular staircase to the bedrooms. "Well, maybe I'll just have to go and get her myself."

"Oh, for God's sake," the father says, glancing at his watch again. "Alice isn't here."

The blonde looks at him like he just blurted out the brand of her favourite vibrator. Lopez adjusts the crease in his dress pants.

"Her parents and her doctor thought it best for Alice to recover somewhere with fewer disruptions," the lawyer says, taking back control of the conversation.

"Where is she, Lopez?" Malone says, sitting down again, not even bothering with the niceties any longer.

"She is staying with her maternal grandmother for an indeterminate amount of time," he says.

"Well, then I would ask that you provide us with that address," Malone says, the terse tone of her voice making it clear she's not really asking.

"I could, but I don't think it would do you much good."

"Maybe you'll let me be the judge of that," Malone tells him.

The blonde, Kristina, takes a sip of Perrier and grimaces from the tartness of the lemon. Or perhaps it's something else. "Alice left yesterday on a plane for Madrid. My mother has a home on the southern coast of Spain; she retired there some years back with my father. It's the best place for our daughter right now."

"Madrid?" Malone says, not believing what she's hearing. But I'm not that surprised. Kristina has rock-hard balls.

"I have a copy of her itinerary here." Lopez pulls yet another envelope from his briefcase. With all this useless fucking paper we could make Peter Pan party hats for all of us.

"She left at eleven yesterday morning," Kristina says. The day after we first tried to talk to Alice and right around the time Lachlan Reid was showing us the bloody *T* carved into his gut. These people don't waste time.

"You can confirm with the airline, if you wish," the lawyer says. Malone is now clearly standing in a puddle of the lawyer's urine. "But Mr. and Mrs. Corrigan would be happy to answer any questions you may have."

Kristina's face goes blank, her version of welcoming. The father, Greg, looks impatient.

"Fine," Malone says, knowing this shit they're pulling is anything but fine.

★ ★ ★ ★ ★

We didn't get much out of the parents. Yes, their daughter was in "some kind" of a relationship with Tyler Brent. No, they didn't realize he had another girlfriend, but Kristina thought that Alice was about to break up with him anyway. She was a girl with more important priorities. *Yeah*, I think, *like carving up Tyler's nuts.*

They didn't know Jessica Mendler or her parents. They didn't travel in the same circles. I bet they didn't. They also made it quite clear that their daughter didn't involve herself with gangs or even with boys who might. Preposterous, Kristina Corrigan said, defending Tyler for probably the first time ever, if only to prevent his character from contaminating the family name. Malone spent a long time digging into that angle, asking for known associates, but she's wasting her breath. After about fifteen minutes of dicking around, which is about as neutered as Malone's subpoena, the father says he's late for a meeting.

"Can you tell me where Alice was last Saturday night?" Malone asks, checking off that box before we go.

"Well, of course, she was here with both of us," Kristina says, indicating her husband, who's already risen from the couch and has an ear glued to his phone. "Saturday is family game night. I believe we played *Life*." I remember playing that game as a kid, little pink and blue pegs in the cars representing all the family members. I always made my blue-peg husband sit in the back. Something tells me that most seventeen-year-old girls don't stay home on a Saturday to play *The Game of Life*. They're too busy living it.

The lawyer leads us to the door. It's not exactly a voluntary parade. I notice Alice's school picture in the hallway and am struck again how much her hazel eyes look like her mother's.

"I don't suppose you know anything, Detective Malone, about some damage sustained to my car?"

"No, I don't," she says, her eyes sparking again. I guess it's not just me who has that effect on her. "Have you filed a report?"

"No, I haven't," he says. "But believe me, I will." Then he slams the Corrigans' door in our faces. If I didn't want to get away from this house so badly, I'd go back in and strangle him with his designer skinny tie. But at least the blonde kept her head about her. She's no singing scarlet tanager.

"I can't believe the nerve of that asshole," Malone says as we get in the car. She watches her door this time as she opens it. Kristina Corrigan stands guard in the upstairs window, watching us.

"Even if Alice isn't guilty of something, they're sure making it look like she is," Malone says, looking over her shoulder as she puts the car in reverse. "Although it's hard to believe a girl of that age could have done something so cold-blooded." She pulls out of the driveway.

I see Kristina Corrigan snap the heavy brocade curtains closed across the window, knowing that cold blood can be inherited just as easily as eye colour.

★ ★ ★ ★ ★

There really isn't that much to do but paperwork now. Malone has to go back to the office and work on something that might compel the Corrigans to put their daughter on a plane back to the States. Later she'll supervise the removal of Lachlan Reid's computer. The warrant for that just came through. She's also trying to get a hold of the security company that Jessica Mendler's father works for, to verify his alibi.

She drops me where she picked me up, and I start walking over to Rod's, taking a few nips from the silver-plated flask I lifted from the liquor store last night. Usually, I don't bite the hand that feeds me, but it was just so damn shiny, I couldn't resist. I thought originally that I'd give it to Uncle Rod as a peace offering, but the weight of it feels too good in my hand. I'll tell him I called his mother. That'll make him happy. I'll even tell him I was talking about visiting the old lady. Better he hears it from me. And less suspicious.

I knock and wait for him to answer the door, assuming he's still steamed about the ladder. He greets me at the door with the look of a man forced to stay on a roof for two hours after it started to rain. Then he lets me in. The look mixed with the access says he'll probably forgive me, but he's going to make me suffer first. Charlotte is in the kitchen making meatloaf that she's currently testing for doneness with an oven-mitted thumb. I guess the two of them made up.

"Hi, Charlotte."

"Hi, Candace," she says so icily I think the damn meat might freeze in the pan. She shoves the meatloaf back into the oven and turns up the temperature.

"Well, well, well, the prodigal Scarpello returns," Rod says, all snarky. He's definitely not going to make this easy.

"Don't call me that."

"Don't leave me on the fucking roof again."

"I won't." I don't tell him I'm sorry. Not my style.

"Honestly, Candace, don't ever try that bullshit again. Not with the likes of me. Sure, if you were anyone else, you'd be eating cod tongue through a straw."

"I was upset."

"As upset as Mrs. Boddis next door, who thought I was after seeing her in her girdle?"

"Nobody wears girdles anymore, Uncle Rod."

"Well, then her Spank, or whatever you call it."

"Spanx," Charlotte corrects him, leaning into the pass-through from the kitchen. Rod glares at her, and she beats a hasty retreat.

"Whatever the case, it was a start for the old girl. I felt like a goddamn pervert."

"I called Agnes today," I tell him.

"My mother?" he asks, surprised. The mention of her softens him a little, but he's still suspicious. "Why were you after calling her?"

"I was thinking of maybe visiting her. The next time you go back home."

Rod smiles and his whole face changes. "Ah, she would be right tickled if you did that, wouldn't she, Charlotte?"

Charlotte mumbles from the kitchen, quite possibly remembering her own visit to Newfoundland and what happened afterward. I can still see the scar from the fishing lure hook at the base of one of Rod's fingers. It's shaped like a little white sailboat.

"She said her sciatica is acting up," I tell him, further trying to placate him with my recounting of the old woman's afflictions.

"Ah, that would be the weather," he says. What is it with meteorology and these Newfies? They'd blame AIDS and 9/11 on the goddamn change of seasons if they could.

He walks over to the couch. The coils inside squeak as he sits down. Not because he's heavy but because the couch is probably older than his mother.

"You still working with that cop?" he asks.

"A bit."

"Still think she's going to tell you who killed Mike?"

"I don't know."

"Then you're a bigger fool than I took you for." He motions for me to sit beside him. I hesitate just long enough to preserve my ego and then plunk my ass down beside him.

"I'm serious, Candace, you're playing with fire here. Anyone finds out you've been running with this Malone, you're going to find yourself on the outside looking in, with only me willing to watch your back. And I can't always be around."

I remember looking in through the office window from the outside and seeing the two detectives arguing at the cop shop.

"I saw Saunders yesterday," I say. "And that guy, Wolfe. The one whose wife Dad was making it with." Charlotte begins banging pots nervously in the kitchen.

"You see, this is what I'm talking about, Candace. All this police fraternization. It can't lead to no good."

"What do you think of Wolfe for it?"

"For what?"

"For killing Dad."

"That fat fuck couldn't have killed anyone. He couldn't fight his way out of a dog's vest with two cut peckers and a licence." Now he's definitely just making shit up.

"You know as well as I do that you don't need physical ability or strength, just the element of surprise. Isn't that what you and Dad always used to say?"

"Well, I'd be surprised as hell if that useless copper ever put one over on your dad. Besides, that whole thing with Doug Wolfe was years ago, Candace. If the man was going to slit your father's throat, he would have done it when he found Mike's face buried in his wife's muff."

"Rod," Charlotte scolds from the kitchen.

He rolls his eyes.

"Why don't you stay for dinner, Candace?" she says, coming around the corner wiping her hands on a dish towel. Looks like I'm forgiven.

I calculate how many drinks I can afford at The Goon tonight and how long it'll take me to drink them. I guess I have the time. "Okay," I say, "just let me wash my hands." Rory was touching me with his turtle hands earlier. You don't know what kind of deadly bacteria those amphibious buggers are carrying on them.

When I walk past Rod's bedroom, I see it on the dresser. He doesn't usually leave his door open, but Charlotte's probably been in there fetching his dirty laundry. I walk out to the living room again with the Diamondback pistol dangling from one finger.

"What the hell is this, Rod?" He looks at the slim gun, so small it's half the weight of most compact models but just as deadly. Charlotte does an about-face and retreats to the kitchen.

"I thought you and Dad never carried pieces."

"I'm holding it for a friend," he says.

"C'mon, Rod. That didn't work when you and Dad caught me with a joint at fifteen, and it won't work now."

"Seriously, I'm holding it for John Castleman. The cops are after searching his place, and he's not allowed to own a weapon on account of the terrorism charge."

"What terrorism charge?" John Castleman is a two-bit hustler with no greater political affiliations than the occasional room at the Y.

"He and a few lads got some dynamite a few years back and blew up a pumpkin patch out on Post Road."

"He's a squash terrorist?"

"Took out a scarecrow and all."

"Let's eat," says Charlotte, dropping a burnt offering on the round dining table. It looks more loaf than meat.

Rod walks up and takes the gun gently from my hands, putting it in the cabinet under the coffee table with his Stanley Cup playoff tapes.

"C'mon, girl, you could never leave well enough alone. Forget about Wolfe and this Malone and have some supper with us."

I think about Dad showing me his Rolex with the moon face, pointing at the stars. And his bloated empty wrist when I saw him in the morgue. That's the problem with a girl like me. I can't leave alone some of the things that I should.

And what's more, I can't bring myself to forget them.

★ ★ ★ ★ ★

When I get back to my apartment, there's an envelope from Malone pushed under the door. More useless paper for party hats.

Lachlan Reid is missing. If you know anything, you better call me now.

Shit. I told her not to take away his computer — that it would give him worse withdrawal than Rory had gone through in Rod's basement.

I bring the paper over to the stove. Light one end of it with the burner then dump it in the sink. It crinkles and writhes like that guy the Daybreak Boys set on fire with motor oil.

This is getting way too involved. I thought it would be a slam dunk at the beginning. Play along with Malone. Pretend like I was trying to help. Wait for Tyler Brent to be written off as death by misadventure and collect my just reward. But if she didn't buy the idea of a suicide pact before, she sure as hell wouldn't now with Lachlan missing. I look out the window at The Goon, wondering if Marcus might be there. He's good at tracking people; he used to do it as a Marine, running down terrorist cells overseas. If he could find Osama bin Laden, he'd be a good candidate to search for a snot-nosed kid who had his video games taken away. I might suggest it to Malone. More playing at helping.

But like Uncle Rod said, what's the guarantee that Malone is even going to deliver the goods on my father? What's with her anyway, involving me in all this? I know I'm taking risks here, but so is she. And I still haven't figured out why. It can't just be to find out who offed a useless waste of space like Tyler Brent. And after how many days of riding around with Malone in the back of that cop car, I'm no closer to finding out what happened to my dad or his watch. Rod may be in the clear now, but I still don't know about Wolfe. And while I've learned way more about my mother than I ever wanted to know, the Mob doesn't look like they cared enough to kill him, and Malone says they weren't in town anyway. That's if she and the rest of the police force would even have been capable of tracking the Scarpellos' movements. She can't even find Tyler Brent's phone, let alone assure me that one of *La Cosa Nostra* didn't slip in and arrange a hit while the cops had their fingers up their asses. The Mob has more plants than a fucking conservatory. It would have been easy to get a bent cop inside the force to make sure nobody saw anyone they didn't want them to see.

All this is making my head hurt. I turn the TV on, pour myself a drink, and pop a few Aspirin. I still have a few wobbly-pop vodka coolers from when Shannon came over. It's rare for liquor to last this long in my fridge. I must be getting soft on my hard drinking these days.

How to Lose a Guy in 10 Days is on the late show. That Kate Hudson was more believable in *Glee*. A chick that looks like her couldn't lose a guy if she put him in a maze blindfolded. Malone and I could teach her a trick or two. We've lost two guys in the last week. But, then again, I'm an expert at making people disappear.

CHAPTER 14

THE NEXT MORNING around eleven Majd knocks at my door again, this time with a hell of a lot more force. Malone's on the blower. I think he's losing his patience with being my full-time receptionist. The sun streaming through the window makes me want to bury my head under the pillow until it's dark again.

"You're starting to interfere with my beauty sleep, Malone," I say once I get downstairs to the phone. This time I pulled on a sweatshirt and a pair of booty shorts. Majd is still recovering from the last time, when my kimono fell open.

"Did you get my note?" she asks.

"Yes, I got your fucking note. And you got to quit coming around here. People are going to start noticing." I don't need some squealer across the street at The Goon telling everyone I've got a cop hanging around with me. Talk like that can be unhealthy for a girl like me.

"So, do you know anything about Lachlan Reid's disappearance?" The bell jingles and the two meth heads I tossed from the store last Sunday walk in.

They take one look at me and walk right back out. Smart boys.

"I get that you think I'm some kind of criminal mastermind, Malone, but my expertise doesn't extend to finding kids on the side of milk cartons."

"This is not a kid on a milk carton, Candace. This is Tyler Brent's best friend. His father said he hasn't seen him since the day we interviewed him."

"Probably running scared. Or at an all-night rave. Jesus, Malone. Seventeen-year-olds make a career out of not coming home and worrying the shit out of their parents. Don't you see the shares on Facebook?"

"For a person without a phone or a computer, you seem to know a lot about what goes on online," she says.

"I worked taking travel agency bookings on the inside. Better than the laundry. There was a fair bit of downtime between taking people's credit card information."

"They let you take people's credit card numbers?" Malone is horrified. As I'm sure many people who booked their all-inclusives with me to the Dominican would be.

"Listen, is there a point to this, Malone? Because if there isn't I have a date with my pillow."

"Yes, there is a point," she says. "There's been a development."

"What sort of development?" I say, twisting my hair out of the way. It was getting caught up in the phone cord.

"The Corrigans' house has been broken into. They ransacked Alice's room. I want you to have a look at it with me." Oh, man. That's the last place I want to go today. Or any bloody day. "I'll come pick you up," she says.

"That, Malone, is something you won't do."

I tell her where to meet me. Another street corner. I go upstairs and find something clean to wear. The starched underwear chafes at my crotch as I brush my teeth. When I spit, there's blood mixed in with the toothpaste. I probably just brushed them too hard, but I'll make an appointment with Dr. Davidson, my dentist, just in case. He takes care of my teeth, and I take care not to mention he supplies laughing gas for swinger parties. I hope it's not gum disease or a cavity. I'd really like to avoid that damn drill. I never should have watched *Marathon Man* with my dad at such an impressionable age.

The underwear isn't the only thing irritating me, as I put on my sunglasses and pile my tumble of hair up under a New York Yankees baseball cap. I'm getting tired of being at Malone's beck and call. This thing better wrap up soon, or I'll have to do some of my own drilling.

★ ★ ★ ★ ★

Kristina answers the door again, this time looking like a wasp flew into her yoga pants. As if Malone and I were the ones who broke into her house and tossed Alice's room, inconveniencing the hell out of her. Turns out she actually does.

"Are you responsible for this? Because if you are, my lawyer will eat your badge for breakfast."

"I assure you, Mrs. Corrigan, we are not responsible." Kristina looks at me, none too sure of my lack of responsibility when it comes to a break and enter, but lets us inside anyway.

"Take your shoes off," she says. Malone removes her Doc Martens. I keep my shit kickers on. She notices, but she doesn't say anything.

"They got in over here," she says, leading us into a kitchen bigger than four of my apartments put together. Recovered barnboard counters — where the barn must have housed a sacred cow — gleam in the track lighting. Pots and pans hang from a wooden ladder in the ceiling. I look at the name on the bottom of one. Jamie Oliver. They look like they've never been used. Kristina walks over to a sliding door leading out to a deck with a well-swept outdoor fireplace and a built-in barbecue.

"They broke the lock," she says, flicking the useless latch with a polished red fingernail.

Malone inspects the lock. Really, what did the Corrigans expect from such pathetic protection of their home? Most of those latches will pop open if you jiggle the glass door up and down a few times. And forget the security bar. With a crowbar you can lift the one frame of glass off the runners entirely. My advice to people with sliding doors is to brick them up and use a window to get in the backyard.

"Anything missing?" Malone asks.

"Not that I could determine. My jewellery is all there. We keep the finer pieces in the safe and it hasn't been compromised."

"But you mentioned Alice's room was out of sorts," Malone says.

"Out of sorts?" Kristina shouts. The wasp must be cruising right up her butt crack now. "They tore the place apart. Her duvet, her vintage beanbag chair, the hand-painted abalone-inlay jewellery box her father brought back from Japan."

"What the hell is abalone inlay?" I say. Then I remember I don't want to talk to this woman.

"It's made from the spiral shells of abalone, or sea snails," she says, turning to Malone. "I thought you could have told her that." Kristina the WASP has decided that Malone should know about anything that comes from Japan because of the shape of her eyes. Despite her being born here. And despite her mother being from China and not Japan.

"We really should have a look," Malone says with a sour face.

"You'll just use it as an excuse to go through Alice's things. For your investigation," she says, getting all snippy.

"Someone has already gone through her things," I say. Krisitna gives me a questioning look. I reply with an imperceptible nod. Might as well give Malone what she wants. She'll be easier to handle that way. Besides, the blonde isn't stupid. She isn't about to leave anything around that could link the two of us.

"Fine," she says, making it clear that it's anything but. "Make sure you don't make more of a mess. I have Consuela coming in at three to clean it all up."

* ★ * ★ *

Malone and I sift through the levelled contents of Alice Corrigan's room. It looks like a bomb hit it, but a bomb wouldn't have this kind of precision. Someone has sliced open the mattress of the canopied bed and pried off the velvet lid insert of the abalone-inlaid jewellery box. All the drawers of the white lacquered desk and matching dresser have been thrown out on the floor and emptied. A stack of stuffed animals with the guts ripped out of them lie on the floor like plush toy victims of Freddie Krueger.

"Wow, they really worked this place over," Malone says, picking up a Care Bear with his rainbow belly hanging open like a stupefied lip. We both have our latex gloves on again. Malone starts laying down some aluminum flake to dust for prints, but I know she won't find anything of interest.

"The only prints you're going to find are the Corrigans', and maybe Consuela's. This is a professional toss, Malone. They would have worn gloves."

"I know that," she says. "But the public gets pissed if you don't dust for prints after a break-in. I'll do just the desk and the sliding door downstairs to get Kristina the shrew off my back."

"Don't you use one of those fancy lights to find fingerprints nowadays?" I pick through a drawer of jumbled tank tops.

"Only the forensic team gets to use those. Lowly detectives have to do it the old-fashioned way." When she's concentrating on lifting one of the prints with adhesive tape, I grab a nice pink tank top from a drawer and stuff it into my jacket.

"Just wondering, why didn't you show that letter Alice wrote Tyler to her parents?" I've been meaning to ask since we interviewed the power couple.

"I'm holding that back," Malone says. "If anything is going to get me an extradition order from Spain, it'll be that letter. Let me know if you see anything with Alice's writing on it. We can get the lab to compare the handwriting."

I half-heartedly start looking through the other rifled drawers, which are all lying right side up. That means whatever the intruder was looking for, it wasn't flat or small enough to be taped to the bottom of one.

"What exactly are we looking for besides that, Malone? That the person who did this didn't find already."

"You never know," she says, still lifting prints. "Sometimes people don't know what they're looking for, even when they find it." She sees a shoe on the floor, one of those German sandals that are supposed to mould to your feet. I guess they were too sensible to take to Spain. "Pick that up and tell me what size it is," Malone says, concentrating on the dusting.

"It's got that weird European sizing," I say, turning it over in my hand.

"What's the number?"

"Thirty-nine."

"That's size nine U.S."

"For a small girl, she's got pretty big fucking feet."

"I'm size nine," says Malone, bristling a little. Jesus, try having canoes the size of mine and you can earn the right to be sensitive about the size of your shoes.

"Well, it's still not the same as the tracks you found in the zip line shack. Those were a seven."

"You never know. I've managed to cram my feet into a friend's seven and a half when I needed high heels for a party," says Malone. "Keep looking."

I inspect some more shoes. They're all size nine. When I get bored with that, I decide to look through Alice's jewellery box. Maybe I'll find something else in there I'd like to take with me. The design on the outside reminds me of my pink kimono, cranes and pagodas and other stereotypical stuff. There are some beads inside and a ring with a skull on it the size of a golf ball. I pull at the velvet-covered insert and tug it away from the lid. Little specks of white powder line the hidden side.

"What's that?" Malone says, looking over my shoulder. Shit. She reaches out with her gloved hand, dabs a gloved finger into the powder, and starts to bring it to her mouth to taste it. I grab her by the wrist so fast she winces a little.

"Don't do that, Malone."

"Why the hell not? It's quicker than the lab. I know what cocaine and heroin taste like."

"It's heroin," I say. "And my guess is it's probably laced with W-18. So unless you want to be a hundred times deader than Tyler Brent, I'd give it a pass."

* ★ ★ ★ ★

We didn't find anything with Alice Corrigan's writing on it. Which I thought was strange. Young girls are always writing things down in diaries or in the margins of notebooks. But there weren't any notebooks in Alice's bedroom. Her mother had said she had taken all her schoolwork to Spain so she could continue her studies online. That also explained why when Malone searched Alice's locker at school she didn't find anything but a granola bar wrapper and a copy of Isben's *A Doll's House* that didn't even have a drawing of a penis in it. We're at the lab now, talking with the technician who is going to analyze the white powder we found in Alice's jewellery box. He's also the one who told us the orange threads on Tyler's neck matched the chest harness provided by Daisy Chain Adventures. The boy had been hanged with it, he said.

"It's a very small sample," the short guy in the lab coat says. His hair is in a deep buzz cut. You'd think he'd use the clipper on a higher setting to give himself a little more height. Maybe he's afraid he might contaminate the things he's analyzing with a strand of hair. Severe brush cuts rarely look good. The average head is damn unattractive, often asymmetrical, and sporting a few birthmarks nobody normally notices when enough hair covers them up. This guy has a mole right on top of his head that looks like a brown, misshapen cherry. Marcus's fade is different. It has enough texture to cover up any imperfections. As if that man has any.

"Is there enough to figure out if it's heroin, or laced with anything?" Malone looks over at me as if I'm the one who laced it. She's still mad at me for grabbing her so hard. Even if I did it for a good reason. She said her wrist still hurts. I never figured her for such a crybaby.

"Should be," the short guy says. He walks across the room and places a bag containing Alice's jewellery box lining in a box behind a whole lot of other, similar boxes. When he moves past me I get a closer look at the mole on top of his head. It's raised and irregular and totally grosses me out. The man really should have a doctor check that thing out. "But I have a lot of other stuff to look at first. We had a raid on a tractor-trailer full of cows last night smuggling OxyContin over the Canada-U.S. border."

"I thought Canadians only exported weed," I say. It's not legal there yet. Although that piece of eye candy they have running the country says it's coming soon. Canada has one of the highest percentages of pot smokers in the world, plus lots of remote, empty spaces to covertly grow the stuff. They export it mostly to us Americans who smoke leaf even fucking more than they do.

"We see a lot of the illegal prescription drugs come over the border," the technician says. "Canada has national health care. A person can go to the doctor as much as they want and pester them for opioids."

"Don't we have national health care here as well?" Malone says. She and the lab tech look at each other and laugh. Even I manage to let out an amused snort.

"But what about the cows?" Malone says, after we've finished chuckling about the inadequacy of the U.S. health care system.

"We got a tip-off that they'd fed the animals balloons full of the pills just before they went over the Rainbow Bridge."

Malone and I look over at the other boxes holding samples waiting to be tested. Each plastic bag inside is smeared brown and speckled with straw.

"No way," Malone says.

"At least I don't have to collect it," the lab tech says. "Right now we have some of the city's finest either sifting through cow paddies or waiting for them to be made."

"Poor animals," Malone says.

"Yeah, it gives you a whole new appreciation for the term *drug mule*."

"They were cows, not donkeys," I say.

"Either way," the little lab guy says, "their shit stinks just as bad."

"When do you think you'll get to our sample?" Malone asks.

"Maybe tomorrow morning," he says. "Or the next day. I've got to try and lift fingerprints off the balloons."

"Won't that be, uh, difficult?" I say.

"Fingerprints are made mostly with the oil from your skin. Wash the cow crap off, and they'll still be there."

"Okay," Malone says, shaking her head with impatience. After the initial comedy of the situation, I guess she's a little miffed her case is now last in the queue behind a bunch of cow shit. "But tell me," she asks the guy while turning to look at me again. "If there is W-18 in there, would a little bit on your finger be enough to kill you?"

"If the purity is high enough, and you haven't built up a tolerance, it can take only a few grains," the lab technician says. Then he picks up a box from the front of the line and places it at his work station. Malone and I get out of there before he opens the plastic bag.

I'm smiling smugly as we walk down the hallway. Malone ignores me, but she quits rubbing her wrist to try to make me feel bad. Her phone buzzes in her pocket, and she takes the call in another room, making me sit outside on a chair like a kid in trouble with Principal Cutter.

"Let's go," she says when she comes back into the hallway.

"Where to this time?"

"Back to the Mendlers' house," she says. "That was Hawk Security. Jessica's father wasn't working the night Tyler Brent was killed."

CHAPTER 15

THE MENDLERS' HOUSE IS DARK when we pull up to the curb, but there's a double-cab Ford pickup in the driveway. It looks like it's seen a few too many winters; judging by the bald tires, it probably shouldn't see another one. It hadn't been there when we first interviewed Jessica and her mother. I guess they can only afford the one vehicle with the father's work being so sporadic. I wonder if the mother has a job. It hadn't seemed like it. Too much hassle trying to explain the state of her face to co-workers. A woman can only walk into so many doors.

"Doesn't look like he's here," I say, even though the pickup says otherwise. But it's cloudy and almost dinnertime. Most people would have turned on a light or two by now at this time of year with the sun still setting on the early side.

Malone and I had stopped at a hot dog cart after the lab; a late lunch. But I couldn't stop thinking about those poor bovines stuffed full of Oxy balloons. You never know what the hell goes into those wieners. A girl I knew in prison swore she bit into one once and found a vein. I'd tossed bun and all into a streetside garbage can without eating any.

"Well, we'll just have to see about that," Malone says.

"Come on, Malone," I say. It's been a long day, at least for someone like me who isn't exactly a nine to fiver. I really just want to relax with a drink somewhere. Maybe see if Marcus is still around so he can help me relax even more. "Why don't we try back tomorrow? The guy's a veteran. We shouldn't be hassling him anyway."

"His military experience just makes him a more likely suspect, Candace. He may have learned a few tricks about how to break a kid's neck."

"Correct me if I'm wrong, but I don't think they have zip lines in Afghanistan." But I think about my dad and know she's probably right.

"And the wife lied about where he was," she says. "There's that."

"Whatever," I say. "Let's get it over with."

Malone takes a deep breath and gets out of the car. Almost forgets to let me out of where I'm stranded in the back seat without door handles. "You know this is just getting silly," she says.

★ ★ ★ ★ ★

We ring the bell. No answer. Malone rings it again, more insistently. We stand waiting for the sound of footsteps on the stairs or the kerfuffle of someone trying to apply heavy pancake makeup around their eyes before answering the door.

"They're not home, Malone," I say, a stiff drink and perhaps something stiffer seeming within my grasp tonight after all.

"I heard something," she says. And then I hear it, too. A grunt, or maybe a sigh.

"Maybe you should call for backup," I say.

"I don't need backup," she says. "I have you." She puts her ear against the door and listens. Then steps away. Nothing.

"Did you hear that?" she says. I have very good hearing. There hadn't been another sound from inside since the grunt. "I'm quite sure it was a scream," she says, tilting her bobbed head at me. She tries the door; it's unlocked. "I don't think we have any choice. We have to go in. Someone may be in danger."

"You are so fucked up, Malone."

She opens the door to the house where no one has screamed, and we both step inside.

★ ★ ★ ★

We stand on the mat directly inside the door, and Malone calls out, "Hello! Mrs. Mendler? Jessica?" And then finally, "Mr. Mendler?"

"In here," a voice says from the kitchen. I can smell the smoke from here. Shit, I can take anything, dead bodies, cow manure, but I cannot stand the stink of bloody cigarettes right now.

We walk down the hall. Mr. Mendler is sitting at the kitchen table with his back to us. He's a mountain of a man, but he's hunched over like his glacial peaks are melting. A beer sits in front of him and it doesn't look like it's his first. But you'd probably need a full case to put a dent in this guy. Malone walks to the opposite side of the table, pulls out a chair, and sits down. I lean against the counter, away from the lit butt he has in his hand.

"Mr. Mendler," Malone says gently. Mendler looks up. He has a boy's round face on a man's body. He'd probably have bright eyes if they weren't so dull from the booze. His hair is cut in a poorly chopped mullet. He gives us a crooked grin, as if it is totally normal to have strange women come walking into his kitchen. I suspect he thinks we're a mirage. Behind the twisted smile, though, you can still see the good-natured big guy he used to be, a redneck for sure, but the nice one on the football team you called Moose. He could put the lead quarterback in traction, but he wouldn't punch a drunk at a party, even if he was breaking his balls. Of course, they all have their snapping points, these big, sweet guys. And the problem is that when they snap, someone usually ends up half-dead. So they learn young to exercise restraint.

Guys like Mendler are too obvious to use in my line of work and too dangerous to use for enforcement, accidentally killing people when they're only supposed to beat the shit out of them. Mostly they get jobs as bodyguards. They rarely have to touch anyone, just look imposing all day, and then go home to their mom's place where they watch *This Is Us* with her before eating through half the refrigerator. But Mr. Mendler had a stopover on that trajectory. Something dark took away his good nature. He never really wanted to hurt anyone, but he couldn't help it. Something broke him, I'm thinking, to a point where he doesn't care who he hurts anymore.

"Who are you?" he says, looking at Malone then slowly bobbing his face over to look at me. He can barely keep his head up, and when he puts the butt out in the overflowing metal ashtray, I'm relieved on a variety of counts. He's like one of those toy birds with the top hat that keeps tipping over to take a drink of imaginary water. Not a good candidate for holding a burning cigarette.

"I'm Detective Malone, and this is my associate, Carrie Fisher."

"You're missing those big buns on the sides of your head," he says, taking another drink of his beer. Honestly, Malone has to come up with another alias. This joke is getting old.

"What do you want?" he says, his head bobbing down toward the table again, looking for that elusive top-hatted bird drink.

"We want to talk to you about Tyler Brent," Malone says.

That brings his head back up with a vengeance. His eyes clear a bit, and he wills himself to focus. "That worthless piece of shit," he says.

"Looks like he knows him, Malone." She shushes me. I stay leaning against the counter but keep my guard up. This guy is a powder keg, and talk of Tyler Brent might ignite him.

"You've probably heard Tyler was found dead in Riverside Park last week," Malone says, pushing forward with the fire she's lighting. "We're hoping you can help us with our investigation, Mr. Mendler."

"And why the fuck would I do that?" The fog of his semi-consciousness is clearing. He looks at Malone straight on, no more bobbing.

"Well, if you don't want to answer our questions here, we could always bring this down to the station," Malone says. I know she can't make him go without having something to arrest him for. She's probably wagering his knowledge of citizen's rights comes from *Law and Order* reruns and the empty threat of being parted from his kitchen table with its readily available beer and smokes will intimidate him. She's wrong.

"Get out of my house," Mendler says. His voice is so low and threatening it makes me reach down the front of my pants for the gun that isn't there. His eyes are sharper now. He's reached into whatever training he had in Afghanistan to override the alcohol in his system and put him on full alert. I remember a guy in the Marines telling me how they made him and the rest of his platoon dig holes in the pouring rain for forty-eight hours straight, ordering them every five hours to lie down and sleep for twenty minutes. He lay down with his cheek in the mud in the hole he'd dug and slept, and when the Sargent woke him, he got up and dug again. The soldier learns to seal off the reality of his body and force his mind not to listen to it. All so he can do what he's ordered to do.

"We just need to ask a few questions," Malone says, trying to talk him down. She impresses me by not backing down. But if I were her I might put a little more distance between the mountain and myself.

"Get out of my fucking house," he says again.

"I'm sorry, Mr. Mendler, but if you won't answer our questions here, you'll have to come down to the station." I guess she really is going to arrest him. Although I'm not sure for what. Suspicion of being a drunken psychopath? If that were a crime, the joint wouldn't be big enough to hold everyone. Malone stands up from the table and starts fishing for the cuffs she had clapped on me earlier. I wonder whether they'll hold a guy like this.

He's quick. I'll give him that, particularly for a big guy with at least a dozen Budweiser in him. Mendler jumps up from his chair and grabs Malone by the London Fog lapels and throws her up against the stove. "I said get the fuck out of my house," he roars in her face.

I walk over, grab him by the long hair of his mullet, and kick out both his knees. I have him down on the floor so fast Malone doesn't have time to reach for her service revolver. The heel of one of my shit-kicker boots is wedged so firmly against a vulnerable part of the spine that an unanaesthetized root canal would feel like child's play in comparison. He groans, his cheek pressed into the floor. A little bit of blood trickles down his ear from where I pulled a clump of long hair out, just below where it abruptly changes to a short crop on top. Someone really needs to tell him that hairstyle went out with acid-wash — the '80s bleached jean fad, not the stuff you use to dissolve dead bodies in the bathtub. That acid's always in.

"Let's all just calm down here," Malone says, righting herself from the stove.

"What do you know about Tyler?" I say, grinding the toe of my boot in a little farther between the vertebrae. I really hope I don't have to slip this guy's disc to get him to talk. He's a veteran after all.

"I don't know anything. Except what that little fucker did to my daughter," he says, snarling through the pain.

"Where were you last Saturday night?" Malone says, going for her handcuffs again.

"He took her to those fucking animals," Mendler says, ignoring her question. "As an initiation. Let them do whatever they wanted to her." Now he's crying. "I'm glad the fucker's dead. He deserved it." Same as I suggested to Malone in the bar. The boy really was a poster boy for aggravated assault. "But I didn't kill him. I just wish that I had. Oh God, stop whatever you're doing. Jesus! This is fucking police brutality."

"I'm not with the police," I say, removing my boot. Malone hurriedly straddles him to put the cuffs on. She could have taken her time. It'll be a few minutes before he will be able to get up again.

She stands and asks him again, "Where were you last Saturday night, Mr. Mendler?"

The fight's gone out of him. The dullness has come back into his eyes. Then he shuts them. "I don't remember," he says faintly. Like the Marine in the trench full of rain, he starts to fall asleep. Within minutes he's snoring. By the time Malone and I have secured the house, he walks pliantly to the unmarked and gets in the back, following orders like a good soldier.

★ ★ ★ ★ ★

Apparently, you can't legally interview a person who has consumed a ridiculous amount of alcohol and make anything they say stick. If that's the case, they should throw out every statement I ever made to police. Although there have only been a few and they were always bullshit. Like I said, never admit to anything.

So, we've dropped Mr. Mendler in the drunk tank with the rest of the poor-decision-makers and gone to get a late bite at a sushi place Malone knows. The cops will interview him tomorrow when he's sober.

"It's Japanese, you know, not Chinese, if that's what you're thinking," Malone says, talking about the sushi.

"I'm a felon, Malone, not a fucking cultural moron."

"Sorry, I didn't mean to offend you," she says, as she pulls out the restaurant iPad from under the table that's used for ordering off the all-you-can-eat menu. Its white plastic frame is covered with pink lotus flowers.

"These places are all run by Koreans anyway," I say, looking around. A rotund, white porcelain cat with red and gold overalls sits on the ledge of the hostess station. The obligatory Happy Cat. I don't know what that cat has to be so happy about. At his weight he's a massive kitty coronary waiting to happen.

"What do you want?" Malone asks as she scrolls and taps out her picks of specialty rolls and nigiri.

"I like the spicy stuff," I say.

"Wasabi?" Malone says.

"I mean the spicy rolls," I say. I like wasabi well enough but had a bad experience with it. The one and only time my dad took me for sushi as a kid, he had gone to the can, and when they put out that little mound of lime-green liquid nitrogen from hell on the table with the ginger, I had thought it was guacamole. I fucking love guacamole. I think my dad had a worse cleanup on his hands that night than the cops waiting for those cows to crap in the tractor-trailer.

She orders a few more items off the menu then presses send. You don't even get a dedicated waiter anymore. Just a flurry of different Korean youngsters flying by your table with whatever order is ready. All of whom nod when I say the words *sake* and *Sapporo* to them but don't bring me either. I think Malone has gotten to them already.

"Well, hello, Chien-Shiung." A not-unattractive woman in her late fifties is standing at the table. She's well kept, but not in the way of Kristina Corrigan, with her ironed face and balayage highlights. More like she started off beautiful, and while the beauty has faded, you can still see it, as if her younger self is hiding behind a net curtain.

"Hi, Shelley," Malone says, with a plastered-on smile. I'm not sure what the reason is for the Polyfilla. The lady seems harmless.

"I haven't seen you since the Christmas party a few years back," Shelley says. "How are you?"

"Oh, pretty much the same," says Malone. She's not introducing me, as Carrie Fisher or anyone else. "I didn't know you liked sushi," Malone says, having exhausted what seems like a very limited repertoire in small talk.

"I'm just waiting for some takeout for my book club," she says. "We just read *When the Cherry Blossoms Fall* and I'm trying to stay on theme."

Malone still doesn't introduce me.

"Oh," she says instead. "Is that the memoir about the English teacher who works in Japan or the one that follows the history of World War Two?"

"I have no damn idea," Shelley says. "Most of us never read the book." She turns and smiles at me and then turns back to Malone. "Do you mind giving your friend and me some time to talk alone?"

"I don't know, Shelley ..."

"Just a moment," Shelley says, and the young woman behind the curtain appears at once very sad and determined. Malone looks across the table at me, and I give her the nod. She excuses herself to the restroom. Shelley slides herself into the booth, to sit across the table from me.

"You have your father's eyes," she says. She's right. I do.

"And his impatience with bullshit," I say. "Why did you want to talk to me?"

She moves one finger along the smooth surface of the table then looks up. "I knew your father when I was young. He was ..." She pauses, looking for the right word. Seems to find it in the surface of the table and looks up. "He was an exceptional man."

I look at the wedding ring on her finger, plain but solid. Remember Malone's reference to the cop Christmas party, something I would guess is also attended by the people they're married to.

"You're Doug Wolfe's wife," I say. "Or you were."

"Still am," she says, twisting the gold band around in endless circles.

"Not sure if you want to hear it, but I think you could have done better."

She laughs with her whole face, and I can see why my father liked her. The laugh is faded, like the beauty, but at one time it would probably have been a rip-snorting guffaw. My father loved women who laughed like nobody was looking. He said that was the one time you really got to see their true selves.

"Yes, well, I guess we all end up getting what we sign up for regardless." She bites her lip. "I had always wanted to talk to you, Candace, and when Doug came home ranting about you working with Detective Malone, I thought I finally had my chance."

"Okay," I say, wondering where this is going, and also how long Malone will be in the restroom. The spider roll has arrived, and it actually has eight legs.

"I felt very bad," she says. "When your mother left." Someone pours her a cup of tea from a decorated bamboo pot. I hold my hand over my own cup and make another attempt to request sake. "I was young, and when you're young, you don't always think about the repercussions of your actions."

I nod my head in agreement, thinking of Tyler and Lachlan. Alice. Even myself. Ah, to be young. So many repercussions. So little time.

"If it makes you feel any better, I think she would have left whether you were doing my dad or not," I say. "She wasn't exactly the maternal type." I remember her sending me with a note and a fiver to the store for smokes when I was four. The man behind the cash used to try to get me to come behind the counter and sit on his knee, but I always told him that my dad was outside waiting in the car. Maybe that's why I hate cigarettes so damn much.

"Oh, I don't think so," Shelley says, obviously never having had to evade child molesters in order to maintain her mother's nicotine habit. "A mother is bound to her daughter. She must have been very unhappy in order to leave you." Shelley wipes away a tear I didn't see coming.

"Is that why you stayed?" I ask her, looking around her shoulder to see if Malone is on her way back. I'm not good at dealing with the emotionally vulnerable. But in this case, at least I've asked the right question and not offended her, like I usually do when someone's upset.

"Yes," she says.

I look again for Malone, this time hoping not to see her. I've got an opportunity here. "How mad was your husband at my dad?"

"Pretty damn mad," she says with a laugh that's very different from the one that lit up her face earlier.

"Do you think he might have, you know, tried to get back at my dad?" I'm trying hard to keep my voice level and even. The surest way of not getting an answer is to let someone know how important the question is.

"You're wondering about Mike's death," she says. "No, Candace. Doug wouldn't have the passion for something like that. He always assumed your father would eventually get his comeuppance, given his lifestyle. Besides," she says, after the rainbow roll comes with its spectrum of multicoloured raw fish, "your father gave him an excuse to hate me all these years. As long as Mike Starr was alive and well, so was his shame. He wouldn't have wanted to give that up. Without your dad, he lost the living reason for his anger. Since his death, he's had to settle with just ignoring me instead."

"How come you stay?" I say, finally accepting the fucking tea. It doesn't look like I'm going to get served anything else. "Your daughter must be grown by now."

A man motions to Shelley from the front counter. He has a tower of Styrofoam boxes wrapped up in three white plastic bags. She must have a big book club.

"Leaving marriages is for the young, Candace. When you get older, marriage provides its own comforts."

"Even ones where you're hated?" I say, arching an eyebrow. This woman has many layers. My dad would have liked that, too.

"Yes," she says, getting up from the table. "Sometimes there's even comfort in that."

CHAPTER 16

"WE HAVE TO LOOK FOR LACHLAN."

"Oh, c'mon, Malone, haven't we done enough looking for today?"

When Malone returned from the restroom, we ate our sushi in relative silence. Neither one of us wanted to comment on the Wolfe in the room. Although Shelley was no longer in the room, having left to go discuss the controversial literary elements of *When the Cherry Blossoms Fall* over a couple of good bottles of Shiraz and a selection of raw fish.

· Women came and went in my father's life, but she is the first one I ever had a decent conversation with. Most of the time I scowled at them as they tried to make nice, pretending they could be the mother I never had. I had a mother. She just sucked as a parent. And I wasn't interested in having another woman slip into that role. But Shelley Wolfe was different than those other women, who all seemed to be cut from the same frosted-hair and honey-voiced cloth. She was made from material that had more texture than that. I'm sorry that she and my dad split. Even sorrier that she ended up tied to her sense of duty and a punishing bastard of a husband instead. She may think Doug Wolfe didn't have it in him to hurt my father, but a man who can hold on to his hatred for that many years doesn't do it for nothing. The whole point of keeping a full tank of anger is to provide fuel for the hope of revenge.

I'm thinking my own thoughts of revenge as Malone and I go about hitting some of the hot spots for teenagers with more time on their hands than sense. You can't see through the dirty window of the Gigabytes Internet Café on account of it being plastered with images from the online battle arena video game *League of Legends*. There's a knight, a Viking, and a monster that appears to be a cross between an armadillo and a jack-o'-lantern. Ahri, the nine-tailed fox, gazes wantonly at them all, with a deeply cut bustier and two black ears that look more like a cat's than a fox's.

Malone opens the door and we walk in. The place smells like the inside of a gym bag.

"Can I help you?" a young skinny guy with serious acne asks us, getting up from the reception desk. Behind him, half a dozen zombies sit in padded office chairs with the arms almost worn off. Their eyes are fastened to computer screens by an invisible tracking beam. Fingers tap nervously on keyboards and mouses, the only movement made by their otherwise-paralyzed bodies. Most of them are teenage boys, except for one fat, middle-aged guy dressed in a well-used bear outfit and sucking on a pacifier. He's one of those furries that dress up like woodland animals and have sex. I had to take out a moose once who was cheating on his wife with a porcupine.

"You see this kid around?" Malone asks, flashing a picture on her phone of Lachlan Reid. It must be from Facebook, a grinning selfie taken beside a fish aquarium in the shape of a woman's balloon-like breasts.

"Who's asking?"

Malone takes out her badge with her other hand. The guy scratches his face and one of his juicier zits bursts.

"He comes here," he says. "But I haven't seen him in a few days."

"When did you last see him?" Malone asks, putting away her badge and her phone.

"I don't know, maybe Thursday?" he says. He looks at Malone. "Wednesday?"

"Don't you keep records?"

"They have to set up an account. It has a time limit based on how much they've paid."

"Can you pull up Lachlan Reid's account?" Malone asks.

"No, the computers get wiped each night. If someone doesn't use up all their time before that they lose it." He adds as an afterthought, "We don't allow anything illegal."

"How the hell would you know if they were doing anything illegal if you wipe the history every night?" I ask, eyeing the furry with the pacifier.

"I walk down the aisles. Anyone looking at prohibited pornography, I isolate."

"Isolate?"

"I turn their screen around to all the others and we laugh at him. They don't usually come back after that."

"Anyone here now who might remember when Lachlan was last here?" Malone asks. She's not interested in pornography.

He turns around and reviews the zombies. "Maybe that one in the corner. The one with the Axl Rose bandana."

Malone and I walk over and stand behind the Guns N' Roses enthusiast. He doesn't even seem to notice we're there. I pull his headphones off and he snaps his head around. "What the fuck?"

"I'm Officer Malone." She shows him her badge. "Do you know Lachlan Reid?"

"Yeah," he says. He looks up at me with a face that says he thinks I could take out both Ahri the nine-tailed fox and the gleaming-eyed armadillo. "I guess so."

"You guess so, or you know so, kid?" I'm starting to get woozy from the smell of teen spirit in here. I want to finish this up for the night.

He looks anxiously at the screen, afraid he's going to miss an epic battle and lose his battle ostrich or something.

"I know him."

"When did you last see him?"

"Here. He's suspended, so I didn't see him at school." His fingers beat convulsively on the armrests. He's like an addict with a full hit dangling in front of him that he just can't reach.

"So when did you see him?" Malone asks.

"Couple of nights ago."

"And when did he leave a couple of nights ago?"

"I don't know," he says, turning back to the screen and making a few mouse clicks before swearing. He must have lost his battle ostrich.

"We close at eleven," the skinny attendant calls over from the reception desk, eavesdropping and trying to be useful.

"Any idea where he might have been going after that?" Malone says, swivelling the kid's office chair around to face us.

"Maybe the river?" he volunteers. He grasps both battered arms of the chair and tries to turn his head to look at the screen. Best interrogation technique I've ever seen. He'd give up his grandmother as Tyler Brent's killer if he thought it would get him back to that keyboard.

"Whereabouts?" Malone asks.

"Riverside Park," he says. Where Tyler was found. "Some of the kids hang out there."

"Anywhere else?"

"Home?" he suggests, his fingers still itching to get back to the game.

"No, he didn't go there. He's been missing since Thursday night."

"Wow," the boy says. "He was friends with Tyler Brent."

"Yes, we know that. Thus, our interest." Malone hands him her card. "Call us if you see him or you know anyone who has."

"Okay," he says.

Malone releases his chair and he swivels it hurriedly back to the computer. He puts the headphones back on after dropping her card on the desk. Then his expression goes flat again. From zero to zombie in ten seconds flat.

Malone drops a card with the pimply guy at reception as well. "You, too," she says, placing the card on the counter. "And, by the way, the bear in the corner is masturbating in public. That's illegal, in case you wondered."

We walk out the door.

"Takes all kinds, doesn't it, Malone?" I say when we get outside.

"Tell me about it," she says. She opens the door to the unmarked. "Now let's go see what kind is down by the river."

★ ★ ★ ★ ★

"Jesus, Malone, it's as cold as a witch's tit out here." The balmy early spring weather we were having in the morning has disappeared, much like Lachlan Reid. The sun is starting to set, and we are beating around in the bushes of Riverside Park again with flashlights. We checked where Tyler was found. Nada. Now we've expanded our search to the rest of the park.

"We've got to find that boy, Candace. The first few days of an investigation …"

"Yeah, yeah, I know. They are the most important," I say in a sing-song voice. It's not like me. I wonder if hanging out with Malone is having a negative effect on my usually biting sarcasm.

"Why don't you have a partner, Malone?" I ask, flashing my light in a garbage can, as if Lachlan is playing hide-and-seek with half-eaten sandwiches and empty juice boxes in there.

She stiffens a little, doesn't answer.

"I mean, Selena has a partner." Another perceptible stiffness, for what is most probably a different reason.

"I had a partner," she says. "But it didn't work out."

"What exactly didn't work?"

She shines her light in a small forest of birch trees. It bounces off the white bone of the tree trunks. "I caught him taking a bribe." I know what cops make and that bribes are considered the incentive bonus their boss never gave them.

"So, you were a good Girl Scout and reported him and he got sacked. Why didn't they get you someone else?"

"No."

"No?"

"I reported him, and they didn't do anything other than accept my partner's request for reassignment." She kicks at some low-lying brush. "Nobody wanted to work with me after that."

"Shit, that sucks, Malone." Sounds like the cops have their own code about squealers. But it doesn't seem fair. Malone is police. It's her duty to squeal.

"Yeah, it did. It does." She smirks at me. "I guess you're my partner now."

"Now, don't get all excited, Malone," I say. "Them's fightin' words." But I'm laughing. I kick at a few bushes myself, still chuckling. Not many people can make me laugh.

We're losing the light now and have to split up to cover more ground.

"You look over by the playground. I'll check Lover's Leap," Malone says. Lover's Leap is a sappy lookout on the river where a Native American princess is supposed to have leapt to her death in order to avoid marrying her father's choice, or because of the death of her father's choice, depending on what cultural appropriation bullshit you believe. You can see right down the gorge from there.

Malone walks down the trail that leads to the lookout. I walk up the grass to a field with a fenced enclosure. I open up the rusty gate to the playground and it makes a loud cry for oil in the silence of the empty park. The fence is quite high. Probably a good idea when there's a hundred-foot-deep gorge not far away.

The climber is more of a work of art than something a kid could play on. Pieces of treated timber are thrown like pick-up sticks, with rope webbing between them. Some are so far apart I'd have trouble spanning them with my own long legs. I stand up on a mostly level balance beam and zip up my jacket, but only after I've taken a couple of sips from the silver flask that I filled with Jack Daniel's from behind the bar at The Goon when Linda was busy with a male customer in the gents'. The last of the sun is setting on the other side of the river. My flashlight goes out. Great.

A bush rustles just at the edge of the open area, outside of the fenced playground. I can see someone but can't make out who it is in the dusk. I feel a bit trapped in here behind the fence, although I know I could climb out if I had to. It would slow me down, though. I jump down from the balance beam onto the ground. It's covered in that rubbery mulch that smells like old tires, and the soles of my shit kickers bounce a bit on the surface. I don't have my gun with me. I never carry it when I'm with Malone on account of my parole. That's why I didn't have it with me when we had the run-in with Mendler.

The figure moves closer, and I clench and unclench my fists. I'm wound tight and ready to spring.

A flashlight comes on. "Candace?" Malone says, blinding me with its beam.

"What?" I say, slowly relaxing my fists, unwinding the coil.

"We need to go over to the other side of the river."

"Why?"

"I saw a light come on in the zip line shack."

★ ★ ★ ★ ★

Malone replaces the batteries in my flashlight when we get back to the unmarked. There were extras in the glove compartment. A well-prepared Girl Scout no matter what she says otherwise. We drive rather than walk to the other side of the river. The bridge is about half a mile down and whoever is in the shack might be gone if we took the time to walk there, even if we hoofed it.

We park in the lot that services that side of the park and the zip line crowd. Malone douses the headlights as we creep in. Even though we can't see the shack from here and from that perspective they shouldn't be able to see us. There is one other car in the parking lot. A blue Hyundai Sonata with a nasty scrape on the front left fender. Looks like the damage has been there for a while. As I pass by, I run my gloved finger over the dents and feel the rust come away on my fingers.

"Cover your flashlight," Malone says. But I already have my hand cupped over the beam. The skin showing through my thin latex gloves tinges the light red, like when you're a kid hiding under the bedsheets with a friend telling ghost stories. Something I've seen in the movies but never actually done. Although I once woke up under a pile of sheets so disoriented I had to light a match to figure out where I was. I burned a hole in a guy's Ralph Lauren duvet cover that way. Man, was he pissed.

A wide gravel trail leads down from the parking lot with a sign posted for Daisy Chain Adventures.

"Why does it have such a candy-ass name?" I ask.

"Shh," Malone says, turning back to whisper to me. "They do rock climbing as well. A daisy chain is a type of strap used for securing yourself on a cliff." I wonder if Malone learned this from the zip line folk or if she rock climbs as well as plays hockey and runs. Which, quite frankly, is just way too much activity.

We have to watch ourselves, as the path turns rocky. Shale steps lead down a hill to the shack. Just like Malone said, a light glows from inside.

"Okay, we'll have to be quiet," Malone says in my ear, then thinks about it. "You're probably already good at that."

I nod.

"When we get down there, I'll cover you." She points to her holster. "I'll count to three, and you kick the door down." There's a loud thump from below inside the shack. A moan.

"How about I cover you, and you break the fucking door down," I shout-whisper into her ear.

"Non-negotiable."

We turn off our flashlights and move down the steps like we're the same person, keeping our bodies pressed together for support in case one of us falls. A more elegant form of what Uncle Rod used to call "the tepee," when two drunks coming home from the bar would lean into one another's shoulders in an inverted V to stay upright.

We reach the door. The window is high up in the apex of the roof, so we can't see inside. And whoever is inside can't see us.

"One," Malone mouths. "Two." She gets her gun ready. Another thump sounds from inside, and I'm not waiting for three. I put the full force of my right shit-kicker boot into the door. It flies open and one of the hinges falls off.

Just before I dive away from the entranceway I see on the floor a tangle of limbs, exposed skin, and long hair. Malone steps into the vacuum I've left, her gun held up with both hands.

"What the fuck?" A boy screams so loud I think he's going to wet himself.

"Goddamn it," Malone says, dropping her gun. "Come on out, Candace, it's just a couple of kids."

I take a quick look around the corner. So much for the Daisy Chain zip line's sophisticated locks. The boy is hiding behind a girl with her discarded shirt held up to cover her nipples. When I go to stand beside Malone in the doorway, I see yet another girl with her leggings peeled off hiding behind him.

"A couple?" I say.

"Okay, a thrupple," she says, shoving her weapon back into its holster. Her green eyes reflect the light of the camp lantern the kids brought as she turns to me, and we both start laughing. We laugh for a long while. It feels good. Like giggling under a bedsheet telling ghost stories with a friend.

CHAPTER 17

IT'S SUNDAY, AND I'M WORKING in the E-Zee Market again for Majd. This is the day he visits his mother, who lives on her own in a stronghold of an apartment on the other side of town. She speaks English, even majored in it at university in Homs, the modern city in Syria where they had lived. But Majd has to do her weekly shopping and pick up her meds. She hasn't left the apartment since he moved her there. After which she had three heavy-duty locks put on the door and bars installed on the windows. PTSD. Back in Syria, soldiers broke into her home and shot her husband and all of her sons one fine morning. All except Majd, who was out lining up for water. The city had been under siege for a while and all the infrastructure had broken down. Even now, Majd seems to breathe a sign of relief every time water flows out of the tap.

The little bell on the door jingles and Charlotte walks in, shaking out a polka-dot umbrella on the mat. I'm reading the paper. It's been a slow morning because of the heavy rain. Some woman has killed her husband with the heel of her Jimmy Choo stiletto, according to the headline. A messy but somewhat original form of murder. I wonder if she'll ever wear them again. Those puppies are expensive.

"Hi, Candace," Charlotte says, reaching into her tote bag purse. "I brought you some leftover meatloaf." She hands me a tinfoil-wrapped block in a Ziploc bag. It's got a few raindrops on it that run down the plastic.

"Thanks," I say, slipping the bag into the fridge behind the Beaver Buzz, an energy drink with twice as much caffeine as Jolt cola.

"How are things?" she says.

"Same old, same old," I say, returning to my stool. Honestly, the woman only saw me on Friday night. How much does she think a life like mine changes in less than two days? But then again, the last week hasn't been that typical for me.

She picks up one of the candy bars that line the front of the cash. Then looks through the glass at an elaborate hookah that's on display with various hash pipes and other drug paraphernalia. You're not allowed to display cigarettes where the kids can see them, but it's okay to put a bong front and centre above the freezer where they're picking out popsicles.

"Rod's really worried about you," she says. "This whole business with the police." So that's why she's here. She's my uncle's envoy. He's hoping the woman who took care of me for two months after I got out of the hospital might have more sway than he does.

"I want to find out about my dad, Charlotte."

"Your dad loved you, Candace."

"That's why I want to find out."

"He wouldn't have wanted anything to happen to you."

"I'm being careful, Charlotte."

"It's just that I don't know if this is what he would have wanted." She puts the candy bar down. "You don't know how broken up that man was when you got arrested. He was beside himself. The idea that you might do time. That you might end up, you know, exposed in jail." We both know what she means by exposed. There are inmates who would love to take down someone like me in jail, add it as a significant notch on their bolted-steel bunk bed post. You never knew when someone might shove a shiv in you at breakfast lineup or throw acid on you in the shower. It's not as bad as the male prisons, but it's bad enough.

"I took care of myself," I say. The rain is coming in on a slant, hitting the glass door and making the bell shake faintly.

"He would have done anything to keep you out of danger. Anything, Candace. And I just think …"

The phone on the wall rings. I pick it up.

"E-Zee Market," I say, like Majd has taught me, instead of a perturbed "What?" like I used to do.

"Candace?" I recognize the voice by now.

"For Christ's sake, Malone, it's Sunday."

"What, like you're off to mass or something?"

"Or something," I say.

"Well, I need you to come down to the morgue again." Shit.

"I hate that place. That pathologist, Layton, she creeps me out."

"It's Peyton."

"Whatever." Charlotte has moved over to the chip aisle, probably looking for something that pairs well with Girls' Night Out wine. I cup my hand over the receiver and turn away. "Besides, haven't we already learned everything we have to know about Tyler Brent?"

"It's not Tyler Brent. It's about Lachlan Reid."

I stretch the phone cord to stand behind the display with the hookah and the bongs. "You found him?" Then I remember that she's calling from the morgue. "Is he dead?"

"Well, sort of," she says.

"Sort of?" Being a little bit dead is like being a little bit pregnant. Either you're breathing or you're not.

"Just meet me at the morgue right away." She hangs up the phone.

I put down the receiver just as Charlotte is coming to the counter with a bag of popcorn covered in cheese dust. I'm interested in how Lachlan can be only sort of dead. So interested that I grab my leather jacket from the hook, slipping the shiny flask I had behind the counter into the pocket.

"Anyway, like I was saying, about your dad ..." Charlotte says, trying once again to complete the task that my uncle Rod has assigned her — to get me to drop everything and let it slide.

"What are you doing today, Charlotte?" I ask, using my winning smile. I really do have impressive teeth. I grab the keys for the cash register and put them in her hand. Then I pull my hoodie up and ready myself for the rain.

★ ★ ★ ★ ★

After leaving Charlotte in charge of the E-Zee Market, I head out to the morgue. The Nazi receptionist doesn't work on Sundays; Malone lets me in when I bang on the door. We walk down the hall and into the formaldehyde stink of the mortuary. There's a small lump sitting under the white sheet of the autopsy table that's about the size of a dead cat. Peyton, the undernourished pathologist, pulls back the sheet as we stand in front of it.

I turn to Malone, pissed off. "A fucking foot, Malone?" I look back at the roughly severed foot with the sneaker still attached. A beat up, used-to-be-white high-top Jordan. "You brought me all the way down here for a goddamn mystery appendage?"

"Not a total mystery," Malone says, nodding to Peyton, the pathologist. She turns down the top corner of the shoe, and written inside in blue pen is a name. Lachlan Reid. Really, the kid is seventeen years old and his parents still label his clothes. Kids today can't even wipe their own noses anymore. I'm surprised they don't make teenagers wear those idiot mittens on a string.

"That doesn't prove anything," I say. "Someone could have stolen his shoes."

Malone nods to the pathologist again, who turns the foot over and pulls the other side of the high-top down. There's a stick-and-poke tattoo on the outer ankle with a small blob of a heart and a first name. *Jessica*. Above that you can see the remnants of the professional tat that went up the leg, a thumb and finger of one of the hands that encircled the wolf.

"I asked for a rush on the DNA," Malone says. "Lachlan's dad provided us with a sample from the boy's hairbrush."

"Where's the rest of him?" I ask.

"Probably still at the bottom of the harbour," the pathologist says. "Feet wash up from time to time. The ankle is a weak spot, and it often breaks off as the body decomposes. The air in the sneaker provides buoyancy. Feet will float when the rest of the body doesn't."

"The kid wouldn't have had much time to decompose," I point out.

"I'm thinking perhaps there was a chain wrapped around the ankle with something heavy to weigh him down. Might have been wrenched off when he got dumped in the water. I have to examine the striations on the bone more." Maybe that's what happened to my dad's watch. Maybe the bastard chained him down by one hand and it pulled it off when he broke free, its moon face falling to the bottom of the lake to be buried in silt.

"You find his phone in the vicinity?" Malone asks.

The pathologist consults a clipboard. "No," she says. "But those aren't very buoyant." Tell me about it. I dropped a burner off a dock once and that thing sunk like a circuit-boarded stone.

"How long you think he might have been down there?" Malone asks.

"Hard to tell. Like I said, I have to examine it more."

"If you had to guess," Malone presses.

"Given the temperature of the water and the number of bacteria present, maybe late Thursday, early Friday morning?" She replaces the sheet. "Now, I have two suicides and a retirement home death to go over." This is our cue to leave, I guess. Dr. Peyton Kolberg snaps off a glove and walks us out, keeping her hawk eyes on me and my sticky fingers. I notice her own fingers as she holds open the door for us. They're so skeletal they rival those of a partially disintegrated hand dangling from beneath one of the white sheets. Someone needs to do an intervention with this woman.

"Well, I guess that rules Alice Corrigan out. She was in Spain by the time Lachlan hit the water. Although I'd still like to talk to her about the night of Tyler's death."

"You're assuming they're related," I say, interested.

"Of course I'm assuming they're related," she says. "Two best friends with gang tattoos end up dead in the same week."

"You know what they say about assuming, Malone."

"And what's that?" she says all sarcastic-like, expecting me to give the usual breakdown of the word with "u" and "me."

"It's just a fucking excuse for a wild-ass guess."

★ ★ ★ ★ ★

Once we're in the hallway, I ask about Mendler.

"A couple of detectives interviewed him earlier today," she says. "Apparently, he was at a strip club with a bunch of army buddies on Saturday night. We woke them up calling at six this morning to confirm. It checked out. Although I'd like to talk to some of the girls themselves. They'd remember a guy that size."

I've seen some pretty big apes in peeler bars. Even in the nice ones. If there is such a thing. Just because you have to wear a suit to get in doesn't mean you might not lose your shit when Miss Behavin' comes on and starts up her remote control car with the dildo attached.

"Do you think he knows anything about Lachlan?" I'm starting to really get into this detective crap. It's like hassling people for a living. I could get my head around that.

"He doesn't seem to have had him on his radar. Although he knew he was a friend of Tyler's. He was picked up on a domestic Thursday night but was let out in the early morning."

"Surprise, surprise."

"Jessica and her mother are staying at a halfway house. I talked to Jessica on the phone. I'm trying to get her some counselling for now. Maybe someday down the road she'll press charges."

I'm impressed that between dealing with Tyler's foot, Mendler, and a pain in the ass like me that Malone has had time to follow up with the girl. But I guess a cop like Malone probably makes the time for things like that. I bet she's a natural with the emotionally vulnerable.

"We're not booking him with anything to do with the boys, but I haven't dropped the assault on a police officer yet."

"Will you drop it?" I ask.

"Probably," she says, checking her watch so she can write the exit time down next to our names in the log book at the empty receptionist's desk. "But for now, I want him where I can see him. I'm not fully convinced he didn't have anything to do with either Tyler or Lachlan." She finishes writing in the log and puts the pen down. "Or maybe knows someone who does."

When we turn around from the desk, Selena is tapping the entry code into the keypad outside the front door. She and Danny Anderson walk out of the rain and through the glass double doors. Malone gets antsy the moment she sees them.

"We heard about the foot," Selena says.

"And the connection to the Daybreak Boys," Danny says. "Why didn't you tell us about this before, Malone?" I guess Selena doesn't share everything with her partner.

"Yes, well …" Malone says, trying to look all business, but still messing with her hair. "We're still in the preliminary part of our investigation. We weren't sure what their involvement was with the gang."

"And when you found the foot?" he asks.

"Well, yes, then we thought maybe there might be a gang connection."

Danny runs a hand through his wavy ginger hair. "I thought *you* would at least put it together," he says, looking at me. "You're a PI. Don't you all keep up with what's going on out there on the street?"

"It's nice to see you again, too, Danny," I say, raising one eyebrow at him. He clears his throat and looks away.

"In any case, we're here now," says Selena. "The pathologist ready to brief us?"

"Yes," Malone says, looking like she's just been told off, which she has.

"Listen, Malone, just keep us in the loop, okay?" Danny puts a hand on her shoulder and smiles. "You know you're our favourite girl in homicide. Don't hold out on us if you think you've caught a dirty one." Malone looks up at him and lets out a nervous titter. The sound of it makes me cringe.

"No, Danny," she says. "I mean, I won't."

"Hey," Selena says, as they start down the hall. "And don't miss practice tonight at the Lakeshore Arena. We missed you the other night at the game."

"I'll be there," says Malone, smiling. She watches the two vice cops walk away until they're out of sight. Or perhaps she just watches Danny. That boy has an ass to be reckoned with.

"Yes, Danny. No, Danny," I mimic. "Honestly, Malone, you need to grow a pair."

Her eyes throw sparks again, but this time they don't make me smile. "Why do people always say that? Like you have to be a man to be assertive."

"It's just an expression, Malone."

"Well, it's a stupid one."

"Not as stupid as you acted around Danny."

"Fuck off, Candace."

"Not many people tell me to fuck off and get away with it," I remind her, stepping over and looking down to emphasize the difference in our heights. But as usual, she doesn't back off.

"Where were you on Thursday night, early Friday morning, Candace?" she asks tightly.

"At a bar, where else?"

"What bar?" she says.

"Oh, for fuck's sake, Malone," I say, standing down.

"I'll need the name of that bar, Candace. And the names of people who can vouch for you being there."

She's dead serious. We are no longer under a blanket with our flashlights.

I shake my head. "I don't need this bullshit."

I go to the door to walk out, but you also need the code to exit.

"Open the door, Malone," I say. She just stands there.

"You've got to understand, Candace. It's my job."

"We've all got a job to do. Now open the goddamn door."

"I have to take you down to the station, get you to make a statement."

"You're arresting me?"

"No, of course not," she says, looking sheepish, her earlier tough-cop persona dropped. "Listen, we just need to get a statement so I can clear you. You were one of the last ones to see Lachlan alive. And with your history, I just want to make sure nobody comes bothering you about this." She thinks she's protecting me.

I bang my fist on the door then turn around and put out my wrists to her.

"Oh, come on, Candace."

"If you are going to do a job, Malone, you might as well do it right."

★ ★ ★ ★ ★

Malone leaves me in an interrogation room for someone else to come and take my statement. She needs to go down to the beach where the foot washed up, and she doesn't want me contaminating the scene. She brings me a coffee, and I pour some of my flask into the cup after she leaves.

I wait about fifteen minutes, and then Saunders walks in. He sits down at the table with his stupid-ass tattered notebook and a bottle of water. Trying to improve his shitty health by drinking eight glasses a day, I suppose. Doesn't he know that those bastards are ruining the environment with their plastic-encased tap water?

"We meet again, Candy." Oh man, if we weren't in a cop shop, I'd deck him. "I understand you've been very co-operative with Detective Malone's investigation," he says with a smirk. "I hadn't pegged you for an informant."

"I'm not a fucking informant," I say. I haven't informed on anyone. I'm starting to think I might deck him regardless.

"Whatever you say." He leans across the table. "You know, the tech crew have been going over those security tapes you gave us."

"Really," I say, sitting back and yawning. But it does concern me a little.

"How long do you think it'll take them to figure out they're a load of horseshit?" he says with a smile.

"I don't know, Saunders. How long did it take for your old lady to figure out you were?" The smile disappears. "Listen, you going to ask me where I was on Thursday night or what?"

He sits back in his chair and starts flipping through the pages of the notebook.

"You know I don't buy this crap from Malone that you're doing all this out of the kindness of your heart."

"You don't think I have a heart, Saunders? Come on, I wear it on my sleeve."

"You're wearing my patience, is what you're wearing," he says, looking up. "What's in it for you, Candace? Has she got something on you? Promised she'd go easy if you help her out? Because if you are involved in Tyler Brent's death, I don't care what she says, I'm coming down on you. Hard."

"Hanging kids from zip lines isn't my style."

"You'll use any style if it gets the job done." He puts his pen and notebook down. He must have been caught in the rain. The fine wisps of hair he has left are plastered to his head. They look like dark pinworms stuck to his scalp.

"I'm on to you, Candy. You may have that little Asian girl snowed, but you can't fool me. You wriggled out of twenty-five to life last time. You won't do it again. I'm taking you down. Just like I would have taken your low-life father down if he hadn't done us all a favour by getting himself killed."

I stand up from my seat and reach across the table. Saunders jumps back in his chair, almost falling over. But I'm only reaching for the filthy notebook. I write down the name of a bar and the name of a man and throw it across the table at him.

"Here's all you need to know, you bloated prick. Now do me a favour and stay the hell out of my way." I throw open the door to the interview room, and a dozen cop heads turn around when it bangs against the wall.

CHAPTER 18

WHEN RORY GETS HOME TO HIS SQUAT, I'm holding Bubba the turtle upside down above his tank.

"What the hell, Candace?" he says, dropping the dolly he uses to cart around his huge battery for recharging. That must be a bugger to lug up the stairs.

"What did you find out about those kids, Rory?" Bubba squirms in my hand. I'll need a bucket of hand sanitizer after this.

"Come on, Candace, he's still traumatized from that thing with the filter. Put him down."

I pinch one of the wet leathery legs. Bubba squirms more insistently. The messed-up turtle doesn't even have the sense to retreat to his shell. "No, we're going to talk about it now. You've had days to find out something. Were they prospects for the Daybreak Boys or what?"

"Not prospects," he says, still too nervous about his turtle to sit down. "Just ran some chemical on the street for them."

"And?" I say, knowing by his shifty eyes there's more.

"They might have gotten into some trouble at one of the safe houses." Now we're getting somewhere.

"Where's the safe house?" I ask, knowing I have leverage with the turtle dangling.

"They move them around. They have a few hotel rooms around the city. They rotate them with their bill-counting machines and the naked girls that measure and bag the product."

"What sort of trouble?"

"You know, stupid shit, like taking selfies with the girls and playing the elevator game in the hotel."

"What the hell is the elevator game?"

"You push a bunch of buttons in a special sequence but don't get off when you come to them. Supposed to send you into another dimension."

"That is the stupidest fucking thing I have ever heard."

"There was a girl who did it and no one heard from her again," says Rory.

"You better tell me what else they did, or no one's going to be hearing from Bubba again."

"That's it, Candace."

"They'd have to do more than that to get themselves killed, Rory, and you know it."

"I don't know, Candace," he says, running his hand through his greasy hair. "If anyone finds out I told someone about it …"

I reach out with the other hand and grab Bubba by the tail. "How fast you think this turtle's tail will snap off if I hold him upside down by it? I hear they can't swim without those things; it's like a rudder."

"No, don't!" he shouts. His voice echoes off the peeling walls of the squat. He really is attached to his turtle.

"Okay, okay, word is they lifted some stuff. Some smack and some cash."

"How much cash?" I roll the little tail back and forth in my fingers and the turtle's eyes start to bug out on each side of his head. I'd never really hurt Bubba, but I got to make this look good.

"Fifty K, all right. Now please put my turtle down, Candace."

"That's chicken feed to the Daybreak Boys." I hear they sometimes count a million a week on those machines. The money isn't just from the drugs, of course, but from all the pies the gang has their dirty fingers in. The Daybreak Boys might have put Tyler and Lachlan in the hospital for stealing that amount from them then recovered the cash and the drugs. But the monetary expense and the attention brought on by taking a hit out on two high-school kids shouldn't have been worth it to the club, just like Selena had said. The Daybreak Boys would know Tyler and Lachlan would never rat to the cops if they roughed them up. The kids would only end up implicating themselves.

"Maybe they were trying to send a message," he says, wiping a bead of sweat from his forehead. "Now please, Candace, that's all I know."

I drop the turtle into the tank. He makes a loud plop as he hits the water.

"It better be," I say, making my way out the open door. "Or next time, you'll be cleaning Bubba up with a pool skimmer."

★ ★ ★ ★ ★

I run through the E-Zee Market on the way to my apartment. Majd observes me but says nothing. I guess Charlotte did okay running the store. I go upstairs and grab the douche bag from the bathroom and cut open the seam I glued shut. My ID is all there, along with a chunk of cash for a rainy day. I have a feeling the weather may change.

"You okay, Miss Candace?" Majd asks when I come down the stairs in a hurry.

"You didn't see me," I say, then I jingle out the door.

When I arrive at Uncle Rod's place, he's just getting out of the shower. A faded tan towel is wrapped around his waist. He's wearing an old-style shower cap that makes him look like a cooked bag of Jiffy Pop popcorn.

"I need you to stash a few things for a while."

He shakes his head. "I knew no good would come of this."

I drop the bag of ID and cash on the coffee table. "Come on, Rod. Just for a few days. If you can hold on to a gun for a pumpkin terrorist, you can hide some of my shit."

"My concern is not with what I'm hiding, but what I'm hiding it for, girlie."

"There've been some developments," I say. Now I even sound like Malone.

"And what might those be?"

"That Lachlan kid has taken a permanent swim in the harbour. And it looks like these boys were on the wrong side of the Daybreak Boys."

"Jesus, Candace. You should have been an old dog for the hard road there, known what could happen. Didn't you see this coming?"

"Maybe."

"For God's sake, girl. Let me get my kit on and we can talk about this."

"Will you hide the stuff for me or not?"

"Of course I'll hide it for you. What's got your knickers in such a twist? Besides these boys playing with your dad's old customers."

"I've got to go to a hockey game," I say as I fly through the door and down the street. Like I said before, I'm good at remembering things.

Rod stands on the stoop in his towel and shower cap.

"The door's not an arsehole, Candace. It doesn't shut itself," he shouts after me.

Now that one I don't think he made up.

★ ★ ★ ★ ★

The Lakeshore Arena is colder than the other night at the zip line shack. I sit down on a splintered bench in the viewing area and try not to think about the icy chill seeping through my jeans to my ass. Two women next to me are cheering and raising a big red foam fist with the pointer finger in the air, even though it's just a practice. If this were a men's hockey game, Uncle Rod would have called them puck bunnies, hockey's version of groupies. They have the same enthusiasm for the players on and off the ice as girls do for musicians, but wear fewer tube tops, on account of the cold.

About a dozen women fly back and forth on the ice, practising passes, trying their slap shots on the goalie. The team name is written on their jerseys in neon pink:

Chicks with Sticks. Malone is number twelve. It takes me a minute to pick her out under the helmet and bulky equipment. She looks so much taller on the skates. Selena is playing net, which is ridiculous given her size. She's like a dwarf star trying to guard a netted black hole. *I could do better*, I think. You don't need to be able to skate, I figure, and I can cripple anyone who gets too near with my goalie stick. But if I remember correctly, that might be against the rules.

"Would you like some hot cocoa?" the girl beside me asks, holding out a steaming thermos. I pull out my own flask and tip it to my lips, indicating to her that I brought my own beverage. A stray hockey puck flies up from the ice and hits the seat next to me, splintering it some more. I throw it back on the ice and it hits the goal post, knocking it off its moorings. The puck bunnies get up and move to another seat after that. This is also when Malone notices me. She skates up to the boards and takes off one of her hockey gloves to unfasten the clasp on her helmet. I walk down from the bench and meet her there.

"What are you doing here?" she says.

"Looking for you."

"Why?" She pulls off the helmet and shakes her hair out.

"You left me with that bastard Saunders," I say.

"Shit, Candace. I hadn't meant for that to happen. I asked Bonnie Berry to take your statement."

"Bonnie Berry? Is that her real name?"

"According to her, it is."

"He fucking worked me over in the interview room." I make it sound worse than it was. I want her to feel guilty.

"Shit," she says again, casting her green eyes down at the helmet in her hand. I don't need to look at the dot matrix scoreboard in the rafters to know I've gained a point in the blame game.

Selena skates over, leaving the goal unattended. The huge pads on her legs practically come up to her chest.

"Is there a problem here?"

"No," Malone and I say together.

The buzzer sounds and the rest of the players start to skate off the ice. Selena eyes me suspiciously. Like I might reach across the board divider and do some damage. As if I could when they're wearing all that goddamn equipment. It would be like trying to put a dent in the Stay Puft Marshmallow Man.

"You coming for a beer, Chien-Shiung?" Selena asks tightly.

Malone looks up at me. Even with her skates on, I'm still taller than her.

"Not tonight. I'll catch up with you next time."

We all stand there awkwardly for a while. Then Selena leans in to her friend and says, "I hope you know what you're doing," and skates away.

"Want to go for a drink?"

"I'm still pissed at you, Malone."

"Want to come for a drink anyway?" she says, brushing a strand of sweaty hair out of her eyes.

I let her sweat some more before I answer.

"Okay, but this time I pick the place."

★ ★ ★ ★ ★

We're in a back booth at the Albion, a joint halfway between the Vodka Bar and the dives where I usually hang out. That way both Malone and I won't feel out of place. Or perhaps we both will, but at least that makes us even. That's the beauty of compromise; you each get to have the pleasure of the other person not getting what they want. It's Sunday, so the real action happened here last night when the college kids came for the "buck-a-draft" beer. The floorboards reek of all the dollars they spilled, and there's a hole in the wall that the busboy is trying to repair with Polyfilla in between clearing tables.

"What are these?" Malone says. "They taste like mocha smoothies." She sucks hard on the straw to vacuum up the last of the frothy caramel-coloured liquid in the bottom. It's her second. She had wanted to order a vodka cooler, the same kind Shannon the body shot girl had left at my place, but I had convinced her to try something different.

"They're called Paralyzers," I tell her, sipping on my Jack Daniel's with ice. "Made with milk and cola." Truthfully, the milk and cola make up only half of the drink. The other half is pure liquor. But I don't tell Malone that. She's having too much fun.

We're playing the drunk girls' version of Would You Rather.

"Okay," she says. "That guy over there with the bike shorts that leave nothing to the imagination or the bartender with the harelip?"

I look over at the two men. The bartender's harelip is a bit of a turn on, but the guy in the bike shorts seems to be packing a considerable unit. "The biker boy," I say.

"Eww," says Malone and motions the waiter for another drink.

"Okay, my turn," I say. "The college boy who looks like he'd wet his pants if you talked to him or the three-piece suit with the hula-girl tie and cocaine on his upper lip?"

"Hmm," Malone says. "Is there a third choice?"

"No, Malone. There isn't."

She squints her eyes, like she's concentrating real hard and it's not easy.

"The hula-girl tie."

"Are you kidding me? Isn't he a felon in your eyes?"

"I don't know," she says, burping with no apparent shame. "He's cute in a rumpled bed sort of way." Her third Paralyzer hasn't come yet, so she reaches over, grabs my drink, and takes a long sip. I motion the waiter to bring me another as well. Malone is paying again.

"So, tell me, Candace, how did you get into, you know, your line of business?"

"I don't know what you're talking about, Malone."

"Oh c'mon, Candace, we're off the record here."

"How do I know you're not wearing a wire?"

She reaches down and undoes a few buttons on her shirt, not without difficulty. Then she pulls the lapels out and exposes a red lacy bra. "See," she says, smiling. "No wire." The waiter places her Paralyzer in front of her and hands me my Jack. He looks down at the lacy bra and smirks.

"Happens to them every time," he says, then walks away. Malone does up the buttons again.

"Okay, so now tell me."

"It was a bit of a family business, Malone. As you know."

"Hmm," she says. "Did you ever want to be anything else?"

"Well, I did go to fucking university."

"I forgot," she says, taking a long draw on the straw. Then she blows into the drink and makes bubbles with the milk. "What did you study?"

"Criminology," I say.

"No shit?"

"Of course, shit," I say, laughing. "I was a psych major."

"No shit?"

"This conversation is starting to get a bit one-sided, Malone." I move the stir stick around in my drink, mixing the Jack Daniel's with the melting ice. "What about you? Did you always want to be a cop?"

"No," she says.

"Then what did you want to be?"

"A Spice Girl." She makes a mountain of frothy bubbles with her straw; they reach up and one pops on her smiling lips.

★ ★ ★ ★ ★

We give last call a pass, and the harelipped bartender shows us out the door. There's no one left in the bar, and he wants to close down for the night. I intercepted Malone's drinking at a certain point and switched her to coffee. She's still feeling it, but not like she would have if she'd ordered that fourth Paralyzer she'd wanted. When she gets outside, she breathes in the cold spring air nice and deep, like she's never tasted anything so fresh before. She doesn't want to drive, and I don't have a valid licence, so we stand on the deserted street and pray for cabs. It's dark and empty, the type of situation where most women have the sense to be nervous. But then again, we're not most women.

"You know, Malone," I say. "About these Daybreak Boys ..."

"What about them?"

"I'm thinking maybe you should back off."

She leans against a lamppost and closes her eyes. "Funny, that's what Selena said. Told me I should let vice handle it."

"That's advice you should fucking take, Malone," I say. "These guys play for keeps."

"I think the foot in the morgue kind of tipped me off to that," she says.

"The guy who heads them up. Pauly Strachan. He's a serious psychopath. They call him The Cubist."

"Why?"

"Because when he's finished with you, you'll look like a painting by Picasso. Seriously, Malone. You don't know these guys."

"But you do," she says. It is a statement, not a question. She opens her eyes. "I know your father used to work for them, Candace. I wouldn't have taken you on and not read your file." Just then her phone makes one of those notification noises that sound like an angel getting their wings. Shit, if I knew she had her phone with her I would have told her to call a goddamn cab.

She pulls out the phone and squints at the screen. "It's about your alibi," she says, trying to read the text. Then her relaxed face changes. I think I know why.

"Danny Anderson?" she shouts. "Danny Anderson was your bloody alibi?" She holds the phone tightly in her fist.

"He invited me to trivia night," I say. I'd done quite well, too. Not every girl can tell you that Dom Perignon was the Benedictine monk who invented champagne. But I can sense Malone is not aggravated by my superior knowledge of useless sparkling-wine facts.

She stares at me for a second and then throws up her hands and starts walking away. I follow her. It's not safe for her walking alone in this neighbourhood. Not that I care, or anything, but I'd have a hard time explaining another person disappearing after they'd been around me.

"It wasn't anything, Malone."

She whips around to face me. "Did you sleep with him?"

"I'm not one to kiss and tell."

"Quit the bullshit," she says.

"Does it matter?"

"Of course it matters," she says. "Danny doesn't know who you are. He can't be consorting with a known criminal."

"Why not?" I say. "You are."

The truth is, I didn't bang the guy. That ginger hair and hot bod were tempting, but he's way too much of a candy striper for me. I mean, the man has a stamp collection. He said he'd show it to me when he invited me back to his apartment and I think he actually meant it. I could seriously hurt a boy like that.

"I just can't believe you," she says, her hands on her hips. "You know what, this whole thing is over." She starts walking away again.

"What do you mean?" I haven't invested this much time and energy not to come away with the goods.

"I'm done with this whole arrangement," she says over her shoulder. "Fuck Tyler Brent. Fuck the Daybreak Boys. Fuck ..." She doesn't finish. I'm not sure if she was going to say 'Fuck you' or 'Fuck Lachlan's foot.' In any case, she is seriously pissed. I need to throw her a bone. I catch up and grab her by the shoulder, which doesn't do anything to improve her pissiness.

"I've got some information about Tyler and Lachlan," I say. "And what they might have done that made them targets for the Daybreak Boys."

That gets her attention. "I'm listening," she says, still walking, but a little more slowly. My long legs have to take unnaturally short steps in order to match the pace.

I tell her about my meeting with Rory. About how the boys were already in trouble for playing stupid games, and then the money and the horse went missing. I leave the part about me threatening the turtle out. She listens. She listens real good.

"We're going in there," she says.

"What do you mean, we're going in there?" I stop on the sidewalk, but Malone continues on. She does a little half-pirouette to face me, calling back words I don't want to hear.

"We're going to the Daybreak Boys' clubhouse," she says, then turns around again and keeps walking. A lonely cab comes around the corner. She raises an arm to hail it.

"That place is like a goddamn fortress, Malone. It's reinforced with cement blocks a yard thick. About a dozen bikers with Uzis sit by the front door ready to mow down anyone without patches who comes over the welcome mat." The cab stops at the curb. "Who the hell is going to get us in there?"

Malone opens the door of the cab. "You are," she says before climbing inside. "Wait for my call tomorrow." She closes the taxi's door and taps the driver on the shoulder. The cab takes off around another corner, leaving me alone on the street wishing I'd let Malone have that fourth Paralyzer.

CHAPTER 19

"THIS IS SO RACIST," MALONE SAYS.

"You got to play the part." I'm using black liner to emphasize the shape of her eyes. I've put her in a tight black *The World of Suzie Wong* dress with distracting cleavage. You can see the red lacy bra poking through.

"Like everyone who's Asian belongs to the triads," she says.

"It's the only way those white supremacist bastards will let you through the door."

I've set up a meeting with the Daybreak Boys. Told them I have a "Straw Slipper" from the Red Dragons from out east in town who's interested in finding a distribution cell for Hong Kong heroin. The triads have names and numbers attached to every level of their organization. Straw Slippers act as liaisons and have the number 432. White Paper Fans are administrators. Their number is 415. If I worked for them I'd be a Red Pole and 426. The numbers are supposed to be lucky. I hope some of that numbered luck rubs off on Malone and me.

"It just irks me," she says.

"Immigrants get a bad rap," I tell her, drawing the black lines up into the outside corners of her eyes. It would annoy me, too. Particularly since new immigrants are about as likely to commit a crime as hack off their own genitals. I learned that in school, but I've also observed it. Freshly minted U.S. citizens are too damn happy about being here to do anything to jeopardize it. It's the people already in the country who feel entitled enough to break the rules.

"I was born here," she says, trying to pull down the high slits on either side of the black wrap dress sprinkled with silver dragons. We finally found one in Macy's after a search through Chinatown came up empty.

"To people like the Daybreak Boys, you'll always be a foreigner trespassing in their country."

"Are they really that bad?"

"Tuning in to ten minutes of *Fresh off the Boat* by accident when they're looking for *Dexter* is about as left wing as they get."

"Wow."

I step back to inspect my handiwork. She looks damn good, even as a stereotype. "We don't have to do this, Malone," I tell her.

"Yes," she says, blinking her eyes now that I'm done with the liner. "We do."

"What about Jessica Mendler's dad? You said you still weren't convinced he didn't take out the little shit."

"We don't refer to murder victims as little shits, Candace. Every life is valuable." She smacks her lips together to distribute the red lip gloss she's applied.

"Besides, the dad's out. I talked to the strippers. I talked to the bartenders. He was at the Doll's House all that Saturday night and into Sunday morning. That place is open twenty-four-seven, can you believe it?" Malone doesn't seem to realize that the appetite for women bent over naked doesn't know how to tell time. "And when he was let out for that domestic on Thursday, Lachlan was probably already at the bottom of the lake. Between the evidence and my gut, I'm thinking he's not our man."

She walks over to the mirror, checks her face, adds a little powder. Maybe she's thinking a lighter skin tone will make her more appealing to guys with swastikas on their helmets. I look out the floor-to-ceiling window of her apartment. The twentieth-storey apartment looks out on the east side of the city and the lake. I don't think her cop salary pays for this. There must be some family money backing her up. There's a soft grey sectional couch in the middle of the room, with muted charcoal-and-white accent pillows. It would be a nice place to watch the sunrise. But right now the sun is on the other side of the building.

"What do you think you're going to learn there?" I say. "You can't wear a wire. They'll be on to that in a second." I can't believe I'm helping Malone with this. But she said if I didn't she'd try going undercover alone, which would definitely stir the shit up and probably get her killed. She doesn't know the landscape. I'd be left to Saunders and his tough-guy interrogations about Tyler Brent's death and I'd never find out what bastard took my dad's watch after slitting his throat.

"If I can find out which members were involved with Tyler and Lachlan, I can use it to get warrants later to search the clubhouse or their homes for something incriminating."

"I told you, they don't do their own hits. If you toss their homes, you'll just find their old ladies and a bunch of bike tools in the garage." The Daybreak Boys know better than to soil their own nests. You wouldn't be able to tell an MC member's house from an average midlevel businessman's. Which, after all, is what they are. They say half the time their wives don't even know what they're up to. Although I think that's a crock of shit. Where do they think the money comes from, selling fucking Girl Scout cookies?

"We always find something," says Malone.

"If you ask too many questions, they're going to waste us right there in the clubhouse," I say.

"I'm not stupid, Candace." I figure she's right about that. But I'm risking a lot here. Of course, if things go south, I can lie and say that I didn't know that Malone was a cop. That I was taken in as well. Maybe even get Danny Anderson to arrest me to make it look good. I'm not patched, of course, being a woman. But I'm an Official Friend, which should buy me some protection and trust. Bikers have their own terminology for roles within the club: Full Member, Prospect, Hangaround. They don't assign numbers like the triads, though. But Official Friend or not, there'll be nothing I can do to save Malone's ass if they figure her out. Her foot will never wash up on any beach. They'll sink her cubed-and-bagged body in the deepest part of the lake.

"I don't like this," I say. "I just want to go on the record as saying that."

"So noted," she says, putting on a pair of black stilettos. I hope she's as good at wielding those as the cheated-on wife in the newspaper. She's not taking her gun. There's nowhere to hide it in that tight dress. "What time is it?" she says.

"Eight o'clock." We're meeting them at nine. I check my own reflection in the mirror. There's a tiny black hair between my brows that I missed when I was tweezing. Malone's mirror must be better than mine.

"Okay then," Malone says, putting on her London Fog and taking a deep breath. Her eyes pop with all the liner and mascara. She looks like one of the girls down at the Happy Ending Massage Parlour, except her right bicep isn't overdeveloped from hundreds of hand jobs and no one is holding her passport.

She turns off the lights, and we walk out the door and down the hallway to the elevator. The gun in my pants rubs against my last pair of starched underwear.

"You ever do an undercover op before, Malone?" I ask as we step inside the elevator.

"Nope," she says, pushing the button for the ground floor.

As the doors close, I wonder if they will open again on another dimension. I also wonder if Malone will ever get to watch another sunrise. Hell, I wonder if I will.

★ ★ ★ ★ ★

If the sun were rising, we wouldn't know. The Daybreak Boys' clubhouse used to be a tavern, but now all the windows are bricked up or covered with steel plates. We're in the foyer, getting frisked. There's a moose head on the wall opposite, and I briefly wonder if the rest of the moose is on the other side.

A fully patched member goes over Malone, lingering on the hot spots, as you can imagine. They assign a prospect to me. No one wanting to be the one to do the job. Malone is escorted by the others into the main room, and I'm left alone with a pasty kid with a barbed, tangerine-tipped mohawk. His Fu Manchu mustache hangs off his face like two furry saddlebags strapped around the chin. Despite the badass grooming, his cut-off leather jacket looks shiny and new. He really should roll it in the dirt a bit to make it look more like the rest.

I can't see a visible gang tat on him. They probably won't let him get one until he's fully patched. MCs will rip the skin right off you if you try to put one on before you've earned it. Tyler and Lachlan must have thought they could get around this by hiding their ink under their pant legs, making sure the wolf was encircled with only four arms instead of the official five. But the truth is, if the Daybreak Boys had found out, they would have taken a blow torch to their calves just the same.

The prospect rubs his hands together and then starts walking toward me. I don't move from where I'm standing under the watchful glass eyes of the moose.

"Touch me and I'll cut your nuts off."

He stops a few feet away. The orange spikes of his mohawk gleam under the overhead light, so sharp they could probably cut glass. I wonder how he fits that 'do under a motorcycle helmet. Looking over his shoulder, he sees that all his buddies are gone. When he turns and looks back at me, I lift one side of my lip and give him my best snarl. After a moment of consideration, he and his punk haircut do an about-face, leaving the foyer to join the others. I follow, just close enough behind to let him know his nuts are still not out of danger.

A fully stocked bar runs the length of wall where I go to stand beside Malone. I saw it as soon as I walked in, being the type to notice such things. Then again, I've been here before, with my father, when I was much younger. There's a full casino in the basement. I'm not sure who gets roughed up if someone doesn't make good on their markers, since the house and the members inside are one and the same. A large chalkboard is set up on an easel in one corner; the bikers use it to communicate if they think they might be bugged. The walls have posters of Harley Davidsons and naked women, mostly in some form of bondage. The girls, not the bikes. A carved wooden plaque bolted to the wall reads NO RATS, NO FAT CHICKS, NO GUNS in black embossed letters.

"So, Candace, long time no see," says Pauly Strachan, sprawled on a leather sofa with deeply riveted brass studs. The rest of his crew are similarly reclined in armchairs and other couches, except for the soldiers standing guard at the exits. All of them are dressed the biker part in their motor-oil-stained jeans and black jackets. The Daybreak Boys don't have the class of the more well-known MC that controls them, with their three-piece suits and well-managed hedge funds. They're just a bunch of nasty street thugs who like hitting people and who saw *The Wild One* too many goddamn times.

"Well, you know I was on the inside for a while," I say. Heads on thick necks nod around the room. Doing time is a mark of prestige to be acknowledged.

Pauly sits alone on the leather sofa, either a testament to his rank or how much he stinks. His long, greasy black hair is held back with a faded gold bandana. He wears two wide copper bracelets on each wrist and a tight T-shirt with the stars and stripes across the chest. Give him a pair of thigh-high black boots and he'd look like an incredibly ugly Wonder Woman. The black wolf head etched on his right bicep has all five disembodied arms surrounding it. Each inked hand sports a tattoo of its own, a small dagger. This symbolizes how many people he's killed, and I think the number might be understated, despite his orders from head office to farm the murders out. This is, after all, the guy they call The Cubist. Not many people who mess with him are left alive in much more than an abstract way.

"I heard about that," he says. He pulls a fat cigar out of his pocket. A lackey jumps up and cuts it for him before he lights up. Jesus, hasn't anyone heard of nicotine gum or the goddamn patch? "Also heard your dad went for a swim while you were in the pen. That's a shame. He was a good friend to the club."

Once the orders came from the larger syndicate that runs this puppet gang that they should distance themselves from hits, my father did a fair bit of work for these goons. Those higher up in the food chain were sick of the vicious shits getting caught for their crimes and then selling their souls and their superiors' identities in order to get murder reduced to manslaughter. I remember one Daybreak Boy walked up in broad daylight and took out a prosecutor waiting in line for a hot dog at the beach with his kids. By turning in one of the big boys, he got off with homicide by misadventure. As if he accidentally lifted his thirty-eight and shot the man between the eyes, blowing brain matter onto the ice cream of his two daughters like red and white sprinkles. My dad would never take a target out in front of his children. He also would never get caught. A combination that well suited a group that didn't need the liability of amateurs or the outrage of the public. It was bad for PR.

"But as much as your father did for us, I can't let you carry a gun in my club, Candace." He takes a good pull on the stogie. The end is wet and twisted from his lips. "I can see it at the front of your pants."

I look down at my crotch. I'd worn the baggiest boyfriend jeans I could find to hide it both from the gang and Malone. But Pauly knows me too well. "I dress left," I offer.

"Not without a dick you don't." He points with his cigar at the plaque. "Didn't you read the sign, Starr?"

"I guess I missed that memo."

He motions to one of the soldiers to reach in and remove the gun. I keep my gaze trained on Pauly as the assigned biker slips his filthy hand in my pants and roams around unnecessarily for a while before pulling out my piece. I can't let them think I care, despite the fact that the next time I see this bastard I'll be breaking every finger in his grimy fist. The prospect in the corner tries to hide behind one of the others but his tangerine-tipped spikes stick out above like an orange-ombré stegosaurus. They'll deal with his failure later.

"So, tell us about your little friend," Pauly says, leaning back with his cigar, nice and comfortable now that he's made it clear who's in charge.

"This is Amy Tan," I say. I'm getting Malone back for Carrie Fisher. And the chances of any of these louts having ever read a book without pictures is nil. "She's with the Red Dragons."

"That much you told us." Pauly turns to Malone. "You speak English, China Doll?"

"I speak English," she says.

"So, what do you want with my boys?"

"I want you to move some product for us locally," Malone says, faking a slight Asian accent. She doesn't want to overdo it and end up sounding like Long Duk Dong from *Sixteen Candles*.

"Some H, I understand," drawls Pauly. "With or without the apache?" He doesn't use the street term, China White, for heroin mixed with fentanyl. His Aryan Nations sensibilities won't allow him to credit the Asians with anything he's into. "I thought all you Chinks were about straight opium. Rolling them into little sugar balls with white rice and shit." Damn, maybe he did read *The Joy Luck Club*. In any case, he's wrong about the sugar. Pure opium is sickly sweet on its own. You don't have to add sugar.

"Not since the nineteenth century," Malone says, smoothing down the skirt of her short dress. She had complained about the length all the way over in the taxi. "My organization doesn't want to offend you, Mr. Strachan. We don't want to set up any kind of competition with your current business."

"You bet your yellow ass, you don't." I wonder how Malone is handling all these racial slurs. They're even making my skin crawl, and I've been exposed to a lot of hard-core bigots. Though not in a while. My tolerance for intolerance is sliding these days. But Malone doesn't let on that it bugs her any more than I let on when the creep put his hand in my pants. Besides, people are pigs. She probably heard worse in the playground as a kid or while driving her car with the window down when some road-raged asshole decides she's at fault.

"We have excellent and reliable suppliers," Malone says. "The opium comes from the Golden Triangle and gets synthesized into heroin at our facilities in Shanghai before being shipped through Hong Kong. It is of the highest quality."

"What about meth?" Pauly asks her.

"As I'm sure you are well aware, China has unrestricted access to all the precursor chemicals used to make crystal methamphetamine." Malone knows her stuff. "We could offer that as part of the agreement, if it suits."

"And why would we want an agreement?" Pauly says, turning his head and blowing a smoke ring. I can see his disgusting tongue poke out between his lips to put the hole in the middle. "We've got our own suppliers."

"My understanding is that those suppliers can be a bit hit and miss, leading to costly dry spells in merchandise.

Our production can be counted on. And the higher quality will increase your sales. Edge out other competitors. We only ask for a nominal percentage and some other assurances."

"Assurances," Pauly laughs. "She wants some assurances, boys." All the other bikers chuckle on cue. When Pauly speaks again they get cut off faster than a badly edited laugh track. "And what assurances might those be?"

"I told you these guys were legit," I break in, even though I had meant to just stand here and say nothing. But I don't like where Malone is going with this. She doesn't get the hint.

"We've had some concerns about your on-the-ground distributors," she says. "There have been rumours you've been compromised."

"Compromised?" he says, coughing on his cigar smoke. "Who the fuck said that?" Jesus, I know this is what we came for, but cutting so quickly to the chase could get us carved up into little pieces. I'm sure she's got her brothers and sisters in arms supporting her out there somewhere, a well-positioned SWAT team hidden close by watching the place. But that false sense of security is making her reckless. If she gets in trouble, I don't understand how she's supposed to signal anyone from behind these bricked-up windows.

"We were told that two teenagers had managed to appropriate some of your product and revenue without permission. These two teenagers are now dead. I assume you took care of this issue yourselves, but I am concerned about future incidences." Oh man, I hope this doesn't get back to Rory, or he's going to pack up his turtle and move to Shanghai himself.

"We manage our people," Pauly says. "And anyone else we need to manage."

"And what about people outside your organization?" Malone says. This wasn't part of the script.

"Like who?"

"Political friends who protect your interests. Or law enforcement who make sure your business is not interfered with." The beady eyes of the wolf tattoos around the room seem to stop and stare at her. So do I, in disbelief.

"Nobody interferes with us," Pauly says, stubbing out the cigar in a vintage marble and chrome ashtray standing next to the leather couch. "If they know what's good for them."

"Nonetheless, we would have to know where you have loyalties. We do not have our own connections in this city and cannot access their assistance ourselves. For instance, if a raid is imminent, how are you notified? We would need to know this information to feel confident of our safety." What the hell is she doing? I may not know what the signal is to release the SWAT guys, but I'm ready to light Malone's hair on fire with the smouldering stogie in the ashtray just to alert someone.

"You know, Chinkerbell, I think before I fill you in on that I'd like to get some assurances of my own." It's time to get us out of here. I look over at the guys guarding the foyer door. Try to figure out if I could incapacitate them fast enough to make a run for it. I probably could, but the three deadbolts on the reinforced, bulletproof front door might slow me down a bit.

Pauly makes eye contact with a couple of soldiers in the group, the one who stuck his slimy hand down my pants and a bigger one wearing a T-shirt that says I HATE YOU.

"I'd like you to be our guest in the meantime. While I check out your credentials." The two selected members move away from the crowd.

"C'mon, Pauly, don't be like that," I say. "You think I'd bring you yellow grass?" I use the common term for a snitch combined with the racial slur to make him think I'm one of them.

"Tell me, Starr," he says, ignoring my protests as he gets up from the leather sofa to stand between the two soldiers, who now flank me and Malone. "When are you going to start working for us?" I look behind him and see the indent his butt left in the sofa cushion slowly shrinking away.

"I'm retired," I say. And it feels as dumb coming out of my mouth as it sounds.

"That's too bad," Pauly says. "You know, we always preferred your work to your old man's. He was good at what he did, but he could be ..." He nods to the biker next to me and then faces me again. "Unpredictable."

"I think you have the wrong guy," I say. My dad was spot-on.

"And I think maybe you should join your friend while we check things out." The biker who got the nod pulls out a semi-automatic and gestures with it toward the basement stairs, while the other prods Malone in the same direction, the heel of his hand to her back.

Something tells me they aren't taking the two of us down there to play blackjack.

"Aren't you breaking the rule about guns?" I say as we're both led away.

Pauly looks over at the plaque on the wall and then back at me. "Well, you know, sometimes we let fat chicks in, too."

CHAPTER 20

"WHERE DO YOU GET YOUR EYEBROWS DONE, MALONE?"

She's sitting on the cement floor of the furnace room with her arms clasped around her knees but still free to move around. They'd taken her purse with her phone and anything else that might have helped us before they locked us up. I'm chained by one handcuff to a pipe halfway up the wall. They aren't taking any chances with someone like me. The room has an air cleaner attached to the aging furnace and a water softener in the corner. I suppose those tough bikers don't like to get their dainty hands chapped when they wash up after taking a crap.

Malone ignores my question. Instead, gives me one of her own. "Tell me, Candace, why choose this kind of life?" She rests her chin on her knees in abject defeat.

I pull with the handcuff on the pipe for the hundredth time, trying to loosen it. It doesn't budge. "You might as well ask a dog why he licks his balls," I tell her.

"Because he can?"

"Because it's in his nature, Malone." And probably because he can, but that's not the point. "Besides, getting locked up by the Daybreak Boys is not my kind of life. My kind of life is smarter than that."

"It's like that story about the scorpion and the frog," she says dreamily, resting her head on her knees.

"No, not like that." I hate that goddamn story. About how the scorpion convinces the numbnuts frog to carry him across the river but ends up stinging the frog to death when he gets to the other side. "That scorpion was a total shithead. What did he need to get on the other side of the river for anyway? He should have just stung the damn frog to begin with and skipped the boat ride."

Malone sighs. She gets up and looks through the crack in the door again, also for about the hundredth time. She's already told me the two bikers who brought us down are still out there. The rest have gone out to the Freaker's Ball, an annual event that is well attended by several MCs, not all of them friendly to one another. It usually involves a lot of hookers, enough booze to fill Lake Michigan, and at least one moron sucker-punching a rival gang member and starting a biker war. Honestly, I don't know who hosts the thing, but you think they'd have more sense than to invite sworn enemies and get them shit-faced. The guys at the door are pissed for missing the event. I heard the one guy bitch about it to the other when he was locking my cuffs. They wouldn't have dared complain to Pauly. Unconditional acceptance may be a fiction of the loving family, but in a biker gang, it's the real deal.

Malone sits back down on the floor. I assume the situation on the other side of the door has not changed.

"Well, this is a fine kettle of fish," she says, wrapping her arms around her knees again. I can hear rain starting outside, coming down heavy on the steel fortifications of the clubhouse like machine-gun fire. The boys are going to have trouble getting around in their Harleys in that. I hope they all get soaked and die of pneumonia.

"Is that all you can come up with?" I say to Malone. "A fucking fish reference." I've had enough of this waiting around, hoping we can find a way out of this mess. I got Malone to check the furnace and the other equipment earlier to see if there was anything we could use to bust open the door or break the pipe. Two things that, even if we managed them, might result in nothing more than annoying the hell out of the guys with the guns in the hallway. I'm sick of this crap. "Quit the bullshit and call in the cavalry, Malone. We're out of our depth here."

"Well," she says, "there's a problem with that."

"And the problem is?" Don't tell me she forgot to arrange a signal. Who knows how long we'll sit here before the cops finally decide something's gone wrong and storm the place. In the meantime, the damp is screwing with my hair.

"There is no cavalry," she says. "Nobody knows we're here."

"Tell me you're shitting me, Malone."

"I'm not shitting you." She's lucky she's out of range of my free arm, or I'd reach over and slap her silly. "I couldn't risk it," she says.

"So, getting the two of us locked up while the Daybreak Boys figure out we're a couple of goddamn liars was a risk you were willing to take, but making sure you had backup wasn't?" I pull at the handcuff on my wrist a few more times. The attached end clanks loudly against the pipe. Still no joy.

"I'd never have gotten approval for it." Her chin sinks lower between her knees like she's trying to hide.

"Then for fuck's sake, why did you take so many chances with those questions you were asking?"

"I was trying to gather information."

"Well, it looks like that's what the Daybreak Boys thought, too, putting us in our current shit-show position." I can't believe Malone pushed so hard asking about Tyler and Lachlan. And then that stuff about connections and how they got their tip-offs from law enforcement. Malone's been around the block enough to know that you shouldn't get into that sort of stuff at a first meeting. Unless you're running out of time, or it's something you already know. I turn and look at Malone.

"You know there's a mole," I say.

She looks down at her stilettoed feet but doesn't say anything.

"You knew all along." She lowers her head more, and then it all fully dawns on me. "Fuck, you knew right from the beginning. That's why you asked me to help you. It had nothing to do with Tyler Brent. You knew he was involved with the Daybreak Boys and you needed me to get closer to them and find out who they had on the force."

"I'm sorry, Candace."

"You're sorry?" I shout then keep it down so the soldiers outside don't hear. "I'm sorry is for a dog pissing on the carpet or a prick coming too fast. Not for lying your goddamn face off and getting us both killed."

"We won't get killed," she says, but I can hear her voice waver.

"Perhaps you don't understand our situation here, Malone. Those maladjusted freaks are going to ask around if there is an Amy Tan with the triads, and once they find out that you are not, in fact, the author of *The Kitchen God's Wife* we will be completely and royally screwed."

"We'll find a way out."

"How, Malone? The walls are reinforced with steel. The windows are either bricked up or covered with bulletproof plating. There are alarms all over the god-damn place. And there's an electromagnetic door with a key code to get in and out." She knows these things, but I'm on a roll. "You aren't going to break us out with a hairpin or a call for help with two coconuts you made into a radio like the Professor on *Gilligan's Island*."

I kick a wall with my shit-kicker boots a few times. All it gets me is a sore fucking toe. "Tell me," I say to Malone, turning away from the wall, "Did that asshole Saunders know what you were up to with me? Selena? That fat fuck Wolfe? Did you all get together in the break room and have a good laugh about it?"

"Candace …"

"Maybe it *was* the Mob that called in the hit on my dad, and you have some Scarpello snitch bastard set up in a cushy witness protection scheme you'll never give up. Not in a million years." I'm not about to let my mother's family off the hook. They could have decided to make an example of the man who defiled one of their daughters all those years ago. Hell, even Uncle Rod is still a possibility, despite my call with Agnes. Old ladies forget things. Although she appeared to still have all her marbles. At this point, I'm not discounting anyone. Hell, I'm half-ready to believe Malone did it.

"Candace, it wasn't like that," she says. "I never meant for you to get hurt."

"Yeah, you just meant to use me to find a bent cop," I say, blowing a piece of hair out of my face.

"No, I mean, in the beginning maybe," she corrects herself, looking up from her knees. "In the beginning maybe I didn't care about lying to you, but later on I felt terrible. After I got to know you." She doesn't fucking know me. Nobody knows me. "After that I thought, well, I thought …" she says, wiping some soot off one cheek that she got inspecting the furnace.

"You thought we were fucking friends, Malone?" I turn away and laugh. It's not a nice, under-the-blankets-with-a-flashlight laugh. More menacing sarcasm, less pillows with Ballerina Barbie on them. "You thought someone like you and someone like me could be friends? I'm the scorpion. You're the goddamn frog," I tell her, throwing back my wildly frizzed hair. "And there's a little detail you missed in my file. I don't have any friends."

We don't talk to each other after that. The old furnace gears up, so loud and laboured it sounds like the launching of the *Queen Mary*. It must be getting cold outside. The two of us sit and think about the nature of scorpions and frogs. I reach into my jacket and take the last belt of the burning liquid left in my silver-plated flask. I hate that fucking story.

★ ★ ★ ★ ★

Malone gets up and looks through the crack in the door again. I've been passing the time trying to snap off split ends with one hand.

"There's only one guard out there now," she says.

"The other one probably went to take a whiz." Perhaps he's washing his precious hands with the softened water right now, his Walther P99 pistol parked on the basin.

"You could create a diversion. Yell out that you're sick and need the washroom."

"I don't get sick."

"Well, then yell out that you've got to have a bourbon or you're going to rip the handcuffs out of the wall. Come on, Candace, work with me here."

"And then what, Malone? What are you going to do? Strangle him with your pantyhose?"

"There has to be something here we can use," she says, pacing around the room. She looks in the water softener, but it's only full of salt. Then she tries to unscrew the intake pipe for the water heater, but she's not strong enough. I am, but I can't reach that far.

"What about your flask?" she says. "I could hit him in the face with it."

"Be my guest," I say, throwing her the flask. "But I'm not creating a diversion. All this caper is going to gain us is a load of lead in our bellies. And I already ate."

Just then we hear something fall to the floor with a slump on the other side of the door. Malone runs over and stands behind it against the wall with the flask raised. I stand up as well as I can with my wrist handcuffed halfway up the wall. We hear the sound of a key in the door, and when it opens I'm blinded by the light that pours in. I almost don't see him in time to warn Malone.

"Well, you took your sweet time," I say. My smile is warning enough for her. She lowers the flask. Marcus stands in the doorway and runs one hand through his fade, the fallen biker guard sprawled on the floor behind him.

"I told you, Candace," he says, stepping into the furnace room, his deeply delicious brown eyes melting me for a moment. "I'm not one to leave a lady behind."

★ ★ ★ ★ ★

Marcus has been trying for a while to get me free, but he can't budge the pipe any more than I could. Malone is frantic.

"Can't we use the gun and shoot off the handcuffs?" she says. She has the guard's snub-nosed Ruger in her hand, having relieved him of it as he lay dozing on the floor. Marcus doesn't use firearms. He said he had enough of them in the army. He just uses a sleeper hold to incapacitate his targets for a minute or two while he jabs them with a tranquilizer dart. It puts them out for at least an hour. After all, you don't get the bounty if you bring a bail jumper back in a coffin.

"You've been watching too much TV, Malone. The bullet will just ricochet off the metal and I'll end up with a slug in me. Are you sure there aren't any handcuff keys in Sleeping Beauty's pockets?"

"I checked them three times. Even stuck my hands down his pants."

"Do you see, Marcus? There's nothing this woman won't do for me." I smile sweetly at Malone then spit on the floor. "And there was nothing on the dude upstairs?" Marcus took him out first. He's lying on the linoleum floor in the shitter.

"Sorry, Candace," Marcus says.

"How did you know I was here?" I ask, after he's booted the pipe with his tan hiking boots a few more times.

"I track people for a living, Candace," he says, taking one last kick. "With all the stuff you had going on, you think I wouldn't keep tabs on my best girl?" Shit, I'd blush if I wasn't so worried about being shot at any moment. Marcus is good, but there are security-alarm booby traps all over this bunker of a clubhouse. Chances are pretty high that one has remotely alerted a biker at the Freaker's Ball, and they're on their way back right now, cursing at all the girls and beer they'll miss.

"You got to leave me, Marcus," I say, looking deep into those fabulous eyes. I hope he doesn't notice the stray hair between my brows.

"We can't leave her here," Malone says. "We just can't." But Malone understands as well as Marcus and I do that staying would be a losing game for everyone involved.

"The faster you bring the reserves in, the better chances we all have. Including me, Malone."

Marcus leans into me with one hand braced against the wall and kisses me on the lips like a gentleman. No tongue. "I'll see you soon, Candace." And I hear the promise in that.

"Not if I see you first," I say and lick him behind the ear. The wiry bristles of his fade feel rough and reassuring, like a cat's tongue.

★ ★ ★ ★

The shot rings out less than a minute after Malone and Marcus have taken off up the stairs. I try my hardest to pull away from the pipe, hoping that Marcus may have loosened it a bit, but I'm just as trapped as ever. When the guy in the heavily creased biker jacket comes down the steps, I'm still yanking on it.

"Looking for these?" he says, dangling the handcuff keys from his right hand. They jingle a bit, like Majd's door at the E-Zee Market, but not really. More like a wind chime made out of bones. In his other hand he has the Ruger revolver that Malone took off the guy in the hall.

"I'm sorry if you thought your friends would find a way to get you out. They've been detained. My buddy's upstairs with them. Or at least one of them. The other's permanently incapacitated."

"I'm surprised you know such big words, Chuck." His name is stitched on his biker jacket. "I figured a guy like you wouldn't have made it much beyond the vocabulary in *See Dick Run*."

"Oh, you're a funny one, aren't you, Candace?"

"Fucking hysterical," I say. He takes the gun and clocks me hard across the face with it. I can feel the hot blood start to leak from my nose.

"You weren't laughing that other night." I don't know what night he means. I've never seen this fucker before today.

"I tell you what. You want these keys, funny girl, you come and get them." He unzips his pants, drops the ring inside, and pushes me down to my knees.

When he pulls his filthy junk out, I do what I'm supposed to do. He has a gun to my head, after all. I try to pretend it's Marcus, but it's difficult because he's not as well hung or as clean. I gag more than once. The keys are so close I could grab them with my bottom teeth.

"Oh yeah, you weren't laughing that night after the party."

After the party.

He leans against the wall with his free hand and grabs my head with the other. The gun hangs off his thumb. "No one had you pegged for a virgin, Starr. Figured your daddy or that Newfie uncle would have had you as a kid. But we broke you in good, didn't we, the boys and I."

If I thought I was going to throw up before, I'm definitely going to now. I can taste what I drank from the flask coming up in my throat, and it's burning worse than it did on the way down. I'm crying, too, something I never do. The Daybreak Boys. It was those bastards all along who cracked my head open and took turns. That's why no one was talking. Not because they didn't know anything. But because they were too fucking scared.

I think about the fact that I was a virgin. And about how I lost the year at universtiy and just about everything else after that. How a bottle became my only friend, just like my dad, who was trying to heal his own wounds he couldn't talk about. I think about what my life might have been like if it all never happened.

And then I bite down so hard I chip two of my perfectly even teeth, although I don't realize it until later. I spit out his junk on the cement floor like a limp worm.

Chuck staggers and turns around, a reflex of the body when it's confronted with a lethal force it needs to distance itself from. He's spurting blood like one of those baking-soda volcanoes in science class they used to make erupt by adding vinegar. He's in shock from both the loss of blood and the loss of his shaft. I stand and pull him in close to me from behind, whispering in his ear, before I use both the handcuffed arm and my free one to yank his head around and snap his neck, going for a lower vertebra. Then I drop him to the floor. He lies there staring straight up, paralyzed and unable to breathe, but still alive. I reach down into his crimson-soaked underpants and pull out the keys. They work just fine despite being coated with Chuck's hemorrhage.

The gun is on the floor. I put on the black leather gloves in my pocket and then pick it up, spitting a few more times, before stepping over the guy in the hallway and making my way silently up the stairs.

I hope as that rapist prick runs out of breath, unable to move on the floor of the furnace room, that he hears over and over again in his head the words I whispered in his ear.

"Who's laughing now, Chuck? Who the fuck's laughing now?"

CHAPTER 21

THE MAIN AREA OF THE CLUBHOUSE is dark when I get to the top of the stairs. The only light is coming from a neon sign behind the bar that reads GIRLS, GIRLS, GIRLS. It casts a yellow glow across the empty club room. They are in the foyer, where the spiky-haired Fu Manchu prospect was supposed to frisk me. I can hear Pauly Strachan's voice, low and threatening. I can't hear anyone else.

I flatten myself against the side wall and creep along it slowly toward the sound of Pauly's voice, inching my way around the corner until I stand flush behind the door to the foyer, the gun raised in my hands. Blood trickles out of my nose and onto my T-shirt, which is already soaked with the gore from Chuck's groin. I don't think Charlotte will ever be able to get the stains out.

"Tell me who sent you," Pauly says.

No answer.

"You know, you're not getting out of here," he says. "Nobody leaves my clubhouse until I'm ready for them to leave. But you, you're not going anywhere. This place is like fucking Hotel California for you."

There's a sickening crack as he pistol-whips whoever he's talking to. A woman cries out. It's Malone.

"But I can make your stay last a long time if I want. So long you'll be begging for your hotel bill, sweetheart. When the rest of the boys get back from the party, we could have a lot of fun with you." I bring my eye up to a crack in the door jamb where the frame's a bit splintered at the hinge. Probably the result of a friendly bar brawl where someone slammed the door a few times into a fellow biker's face. I can see that Pauly has the drop on Malone. She's on her knees on the floor, her head down. The pretty dark-brown bob hangs over her face. Marcus is on the rug by the front door, not moving. Pauly reaches down and lifts Malone's chin, forcing her to look up at him. Her face is streaked with blood and her left cheek is already beginning to swell like an overgrown tumour where he hit her with the gun.

"Now tell me why you and that little slut Candace came into my club. And I'll do you a favour and shoot you right here."

The space in the door jamb is probably big enough to fire through. If it isn't, I'll just get massive kickback and splinter it more. The bullet's trajectory will get messed up and the shot will angle away. I could hit Pauly. I could hit Malone. I could hit the moose head on the wall. But if I take a shot from the open doorway, I expose both myself and Malone. Pauly'll have that split second to shoot her, and even if he doesn't, we'll end up in a Mexican standoff until the rest of his buddies get home and call it off.

I'll only have the one chance. I lift the pistol to the opening by the hinge, trying to take my aim through the slim crack. Squeezing the trigger, I ready myself for either the death of Pauly Strachan or the splintering of wood that might mean my own.

The gun fires. Wood does splinter. When I come into the doorway with the Ruger trained on him, Pauly stands there holding his neck, where his carotid artery is spurting fluid. He's still holding his own gun, but now it hangs at his side. When I shoot him between the eyes, he finally drops it. Malone dodges his beefy body as it slumps to the floor.

"Candace," she says.

I run over to the front door and look through the crack it's been left open. The street is empty. Then I kneel beside Marcus and roll him over, but there's no reason to try to take a pulse. His brown eyes stare blankly up at me, and there's a bullet hole behind his ear where I licked him. I close the heavy lids with the long lashes and turn to Malone, raising my gun.

"Okay, Malone, we're done."

She sees the snub-nosed revolver in my hands. The liner and mascara I applied have smudged, making her look like she has two black eyes. Or maybe Pauly did that.

"What are you doing, Candace?"

"I'm doing what I should have done right from the beginning." I walk over and stand towering above her, the gun trained on one of her green eyes. "Tell me who killed my dad, Malone. Tell me now."

She doesn't lower her head. Doesn't look as frightened as she should. She just looks sad. Sad and tired.

"I can't," she says.

"It was that bastard Wolfe, wasn't it? You and your homicide buddies covered it up, protecting one of your own." We're wasting precious time with this. The rest of the Daybreak Boys will be showing up any minute. But I've got to know. "That's why you won't tell me," I say.

"No, Candace."

"Then why? I've done what you wanted. It's obvious the club took out those kids. I've solved your case. Now tell me."

"I can't," she says. I think I can hear the roar of bikes in the distance. I move the gun lower, so it's aimed at her heart.

"Why the hell not?"

"Because I know what you'll do," she says. "You'll kill them."

"Well, of course I'll kill them," I say. She must have known that all along.

"And then I'd have to arrest you," she says, then spits some blood from her busted lip onto the floor.

So, there you have the crux of it. I'm the one who kills, and she's the one who arrests killers. We're the damn fable played out in the foyer of a biker gang's clubhouse with a moose head looking on — imprisoned by our own natures as much as we'd been imprisoned in the furnace room.

"You were never going to tell me, were you?" I say. "You were playing me for a fool all along." My finger twitches on the trigger of the gun.

"I was going to, in the beginning. But now, Candace, I care about what happens to you." She spits again, runs her tongue along her teeth to see if she's missing any. "I didn't before. But I do now."

"You're a bitch of the highest order, Malone." I put the gun level with her gorgeous eyebrows, right in the middle, where there's not one stray hair. She lowers her head.

"I'm sorry, Candace." The sound of bikes is getting louder. I need to get this over with. Do what has to be done. So I do.

I go over to Marcus's body and put the biker's gun in his hand.

"We're done here, Malone," I tell her.

Then I run out the door and into the night, leaving Malone to her nature.

★ ★ ★ ★ ★

Shots ring out soon after I take off down the street. One rockets past my cheek so close it takes care of a couple of split ends I missed. The sun will be coming up soon, but for now it's too dark for me to see where the gunfire is coming from. I run down an alley, use a skip to climb up on a fire escape. It's greasy from the rain, and I slip and bang my knee on the slick metal so hard it makes me wince. But I keep going. I can hear a clang as someone else jumps onto the fire escape from below.

Once I reach the roof, I can see down into the street. The one-eyed lights of the Harley Davidsons are advancing in the dark. I can hear boots on the fire escape. The next few buildings are either on level or slightly below the roof of this one, with gaps between of only twelve feet or so. The real estate is too expensive even in this shitty part of the city to leave even a few square feet not built up. We used to jump across these as kids, back when we were too young and stupid to understand death could catch us, even if we could run like the wind in our Keds.

I take a running start and leap from the one roof to the next. My long legs and experience as a child playing deadly games serve me well. I make it across three buildings, each time with a running start. The last one I barely make, scrambling my way up the ledge, my injured knee throbbing like a bugger. After I pull myself up, I turn around and see the faint figure of the shooter come up onto the roof of the first building in the grey light of pre-dawn. I deke around the far side of the apartment roof and down the fire escape, jumping the last few feet onto a parked Subaru. It makes a nasty dent in the hood. Then I'm using those long legs my mother gave me to run toward the rising sun. To the side of town that Malone's living-room windows look out on in the distance.

I run like I couldn't that night the Daybreak Boys knocked me unconscious and ripped my new life away from me. So I couldn't fight back. So I couldn't see their faces. But I've seen their faces now. And whether Malone arrests me or not, I'm going to fight back. I'll fight back long and hard, with the vengeance of a scorpion.

★ ★ ★ ★ ★

Rory is asleep in his bed when I break in the door. He jumps up when he sees me. Then runs protectively over to Bubba's aquarium.

"I swear, Candace, I told you everything," he says, pleading.

"I don't care about that," I say. "I need firepower. Serious firepower, Rory."

"What the hell for, Candace?" He knows I don't normally use guns, even though my dad taught me how to use all of them. The semi-automatics, the high-powered rifles, even a sawed-off shotgun he took off a target expressly for my lesson. He felt a girl needed to be schooled in such things, just in case the need arises. And the need is arising big time.

"You don't need to know what for, Rory." I grab him by the collar of his T-shirt. "You just need to get me some artillery." I notice he isn't wearing any pants. His limp unit dangles as I raise him off the floor by his shirt. Seeing it gives me a nauseous feeling deep in my belly, reminding me of Chuck. I lower him to the ground. "Get some fucking pants on," I say.

He scrambles in the corner, grabbing and yanking on a pair of track pants. I start to feel bad. Rory is a nice guy. He was a friend of my dad's. And here I am threatening his turtle and breaking down his door all in the same forty-eight hours. This is a new thing for me, feeling bad about my behaviour. I decide to go for a different approach.

"Listen, Rory." I sit on his bed, patting the mattress to indicate he should sit beside me. "There's a job I need to do, and I need some special tools to do it." Rory stays in the corner beside the aquarium. He's not going to leave Bubba unattended.

"What kind of job?" he says warily.

"You know I can't tell you that." It's easier if I tell him it's for a job, instead of revenge against the Daybreak Boys. A professional hit is clean and untraceable if you know how to do it. Revenge is messy and has a habit of returning to its owner.

"What kind of stuff do you need?"

"Whatever you can get on short notice. I need it by tonight." If Malone got out in time, she'll be bringing the wrath of the entire police force down on the club. I won't be able to touch those guys in jail. If she didn't get out, they'll be looking for me. I can't give them the time to get organized.

"That's a tight timeline, Candace."

"Can you do it or not?"

He doesn't say anything.

"Listen, I'm sorry about Bubba." This is possibly the first time I've said sorry in my life. "But I need your help." Another thing I don't think I've ever said before.

Rory lets his guard down a bit. Turns on the lamp on the table. I can see the suffering kid my dad locked in the basement behind his tired eyes.

"Geez, Candace, you look like shit."

"I've had a rough night." I gather up some of the bedsheet to staunch the blood flow from my nose.

Rory comes over and sits down beside me. "Okay, Candace, I'll see what I can do."

With that settled, I've got a call to make. "You got a phone I can use, Rory?" He reaches under his pillow where an old flip phone has been charging. You'd think with all his technological skills he'd have something better. I punch in Uncle Rod's number. No answer. I try again, but the phone just rings and rings. Charlotte's number and the E-Zee Market are the only other numbers I have memorized. I call the one most likely to produce my uncle.

"Hello," a half-asleep voice says on the other end.

"Hi, Charlotte."

"Candace, is that you?"

"Yes."

"Is something wrong?" She's coming more awake now. Must have looked at the time on her alarm clock and realized I'm usually horizontal at this hour and not making phone calls.

"I'm trying to get a hold of Uncle Rod," I say. "Did he sleep over there last night?"

"No, Candace. He didn't. I don't know where he is."

"I really need to get a hold of him," I say. I watch Rory go over to the aquarium. He reaches into a Styrofoam cup and drops in some fresh worms for Bubba. "I've run into some trouble. With the Daybreak Boys."

Charlotte doesn't say anything, but I can hear her intake of breath through the phone line. "You found out," she finally says.

"Yes, I did." Shit, did Charlotte know it was the Daybreak Boys who jumped me all those years ago? Did Uncle Rod?

"Why didn't you tell me?" I expect her to start sputtering lame excuses, but she doesn't.

"Your father loved you so much, Candace."

"Of course he did." What's this got to do with my dad?

"When you were on trial, he was absolutely destroyed. When the wife was going to testify, it looked like you'd be doing a life sentence. He would have done anything to stop that from happening. You've got to understand."

"Understand what?" None of this is making sense.

"Understand why he was going to give himself up. Admit to everything he'd done. Well, most of it. He knew if he gave the police the right information they'd reduce the charges against you. Take it down to a lesser charge than murder, which they did anyway when the wife disappeared. But it was too late for Mike. The Daybreak Boys had him killed when they heard he was going to talk. He'd done so much work for them. It would have all come back." I can hear her sniffle through the phone. "I'm so sorry we didn't tell you, Candace. But Rod said not to. He said this would happen. He said you'd go after them. It's suicide to take on that gang, Candace. We were only trying to protect you."

Your father could be unpredictable, I hear Pauly Strachan say again. It wasn't about the rape. It was about my father. It had always been about him. Even what they did to me was just a sick act of bravado against Mike Starr, the infamous hitman. They wanted to prove they could brutalize his daughter and get away with it.

"I've got to go," I say, still stunned. "Tell Uncle Rod I'm looking for him."

"Please, Candace, please don't do this," Charlotte says.

But I've flipped the phone shut, cutting her off in mid-sniffle.

"I need to get out of here, Rory."

He turns his attention away from the turtle. Bubba doesn't go for the worms, just starts smacking his head on an aquarium rock. "Okay, Candace," Rory says. "Where are you going?"

"You don't need to know that," I say, getting up from the bed. I toss the flip phone to him. He catches it with one hand, his reflexes undamaged despite years of being a junkie. "But I'll be back tonight. Don't let me down." I walk through the busted open door and then take the stairs two at a time. I don't have long. I need my uncle's help if I'm going to do what I'm planning. Charlotte's right. It would be suicide to go after the entire gang myself, even with their leader out of the way. I need a partner. But I'm not paying attention now. I don't check out the perimeter before I exit. When I burst out of the front door of the building there are two cop cars parked sideways blocking the street in both directions.

"Hi, Candy." The muzzle of Saunder's gun presses hard into the small of my back. A couple of uniforms get out of the cars and train their own guns on me. "Guess what, sweetheart? The tech boys came back with your E-Zee Market security tapes. You're a lying bitch."

He frog marches me to the closest cop car, throws me over the hood to put on the cuffs. The one on my left wrist bites into the swelling and bruised skin of where I was chained for so many hours back in the clubhouse. Saunders yanks me up by my trussed hands and opens the door to the police cruiser.

"I'm going to enjoy this, Candy," he sneers. A bit of his spittle hits me on the cheek. Then he pushes me headfirst into the back seat and slams the door.

As the cop car pulls away, I lie back on the torn-up vinyl upholstery and close my eyes. Too tired to put up a fight.

CHAPTER 22

IT'S NOT JUST THE TAPES. While I sit in the same interview room where Saunders badgered me last time, I hear the rest of the evidence against me. Danny Anderson can only account for my whereabouts until eleven thirty on Thursday, the night of Lachlan's disappearance. I tell them I was at The Goon until last call, but that doesn't fully cover the window of opportunity. No one spent the night with me in my apartment above the E-Zee Market. I had turned Marcus down at the bar. Not that he could vouch for me even if he had. Only the Scarpellos' envoy had seen me by my apartment, and something tells me mentioning that guy won't get me anywhere. No one says anything about Malone. I don't know whether she made it out of the clubhouse alive or not.

"You're going down, Starr," Saunders hisses at me. "Just like I said you would." He doesn't even have his tattered black notebook with him. His evidence is documented properly and ready to go to the prosecutor for arraignment. But there's more.

"We had an anonymous call, Candy. What do you think they told us?"

"That you have the fashion sense of a colour-blind used-car salesman?"

Saunders presses his lips together then goes on. Bonnie Berry, the cop who was supposed to take my statement before, is also in the room. She doesn't say much, just makes sure the video camera in the corner is on. Although I did catch her smirking a bit when I insulted Saunders with the used-car-salesman joke.

"That you were seen in a bar with Alice Corrigan's mother, Kristina. Not long before her daughter's boyfriend, Tyler Brent, was executed. Everybody knows the broad hated him." He wets his lips. He's loving this. Even his few wispy strands of hair are tensed with anticipation. "We're looking for her right now. And this time, we'll make sure none of your friends get to her before she testifies against you."

"I don't have any friends," I say to him. That fucking blonde. I wish I never saw her surgically enhanced face. Or gotten involved with her teenage daughter's loser of a boyfriend. The video keeps rolling. But I say nothing. If Saunders thinks I'm going to confess, he's as dumb as the Walmart loafers he's wearing.

There's a knock at the door. Bonnie goes to answer. There's some murmured exchange. Then she comes over to Saunders and whispers something annoying in his ear. He stands up from the table, the chair making an angry scrape across the floor.

"We're not done here, Starr." He and Bonnie leave the room. I hear someone step in behind me. Probably Saunders's boss or that fucker Wolfe come to gloat. I'm a spectacle here in the squad room now that everyone knows who I am. My Princess Leia cover has been blown.

A cop walks over to the corner and turns the camera off. When she turns to me I can see her swollen cheek is taped up. I think the bastard might have broken her cheekbone. My nose is taped, too, but I don't think it's broken. She sits down at the table.

"How you doing, Malone?"

"I've felt better," she says with a sigh.

"Tell me about it."

"Things don't look good for you, Candace."

"I didn't do it." She cocks one eyebrow but lets my denial stand.

"I didn't tell them about the bikers," she says.

"What bikers?" I say, leaning back in my chair. Even if the recorder is off, she could be hiding a wire in her lacy red bra. Or maybe she's wearing a blue one now. She probably does her own laundry.

"The one whose dick you bit off before you broke his neck," she says. "And the one you shot to save me. They assume Marcus did it. Well, not the biting off part, but the rest. And I didn't correct them."

I'm not surprised by the police's conclusions. After all, that's why I'd left the gun in Marcus's hand. A move I know he forgives me for, wherever he is now. Not his corpse. That's in the morgue. But the rest of him. The part of him with the strong and gentle hands. The part that called me his girl. Whenever the police are looking for someone to blame, they always look for the darkest skin in the room.

"How did you explain the state of Chuck's dick?" I say.

"I told them I did it."

"No shit?" I actually laugh, despite the circumstances. How does Malone do it? She can make me laugh even when I'm cuffed to a table waiting to be arraigned.

"It's given me a certain amount of street cred," she says, smiling. "I'll have to put up with a few nicknames for a while, I guess, but it'll eventually die down." I doubt it. There was a kid in my class who shit his pants once in circle time when the teacher wouldn't let him go to the restroom. He's still called Crapper to this day.

"Once they find Kristina Corrigan, they're going to arraign you, Candace. There's nothing I can do about that. Right now, they don't have much, just their suspicions about the tapes and the anonymous tip."

"If there's nothing you can do, why the hell are you here?"

"Because, like I said, I care about what happens to you, Candace." She reaches into her tailored black pants. She must have a closet of them. I can visualize them all hung up in a row like a battalion of half Malones. When does she get the time to iron? She unlocks the cuff from the table and puts it around my other wrist.

"I'll take you out by the back door," she says, standing up. "You've got twenty-four hours to clear yourself, Candace. I don't care what you do, but be back here the same time tomorrow with something I can use to get you out of this." She walks over to the door. You could knock me over with a wisp of Saunders's hair, but I don't need to be told twice. I get up and join her at the door.

When she walks me through the squad room, a few people look up. But they turn their heads back to their screens just as quickly. They figure Malone is taking me to a holding cell or somewhere else. She takes me down the stairwell and unlocks the cuffs when we get to the fire exit.

"Twenty-four hours, Candace," she says, as I rub at my wrists.

"Twenty-four hours, Malone," I tell her. And then I saunter down the alleyway and climb the fence at the end. When I drop down the other side of it, Malone is still in the doorway.

As I walk away, I wonder if she really believes I'll come back.

★ ★ ★ ★ ★

I only stop once to make a call from a pay phone to a burner. Guess there's one more number I remember. I leave a message after the tone with an address where to meet me. It's a risk, but I need to take it.

When I get to Rod's, the door's locked. But I've got the key. I open it quickly, step inside, then shut the door behind me just as fast.

"Uncle Rod!" My voice echoes through the empty house. No response. Where the hell is he? The blank TV screen reflects my image. I'm a mess, just like Rory said. My hair looks like a rat's nest. And although I can't make out the colour of my swollen nose, I can guess it's purple. I call out again for my uncle then check the basement to see if he's working at his tool bench down there. I come back up into the living room and realize I can't wait for him. I've got to get out of the city and find someplace to lay low. The Daybreak Boys will have to wait. I can't get at them from a cell anyway. But I will get them. That you can bet on as surely as the roulette wheel in their clubhouse basement.

I've got to find where Rod's hidden my stash. I pick up the land line on the hall table, checking with Charlotte again to see if he showed up there. But there's no answer. It goes to her voicemail. I slam the phone down. I'm going to have to find where he put my IDs and cash myself.

"Hide contraband in plain sight, Candace," I remember my dad saying again. He and Rod were cut from the same cloth, just like Charlotte said, so I start with the fridge. Not tucked into the package behind the bologna. Not in the carton of eggs that's a few months old. There's nothing in the freezer but mojito mix Charlotte brought over and some more bologna, furry with frost.

I start to tear the rest of the kitchen apart. If Mrs. Boddis is home next door, she'll be calling the cops about the noise instead of a peeper this time. I try to place the pots and pans and cutlery down more gently, but it slows me down. Looking for an obvious place where no one would look is harder than I thought it would be.

I start in on Rod's bedroom after that, giving up on the obvious places. Getting a screwdriver from the basement, I remove the light switch and electrical outlet covers. Nothing is hidden inside. I pull all the clothes out of his closet and rip open the soles of his shoes with the screwdriver. Nothing. I even dig to the bottom of his clothes hamper but only find the pilled green cardigan he's owned for over twenty years. Agnes knit it for him.

The bathroom is a similar story. I unscrew the outlets. I look in the toilet tank. Check under the sink and in the medicine cabinet. There's nothing big enough to house my stuff. Then I run down to the basement and get a wrench to go at the pipes. It's a long shot, but I'm running out of ideas. The elbow pipe comes away with nothing inside but a spidery clump of my uncle Rod's hair.

I sit on the floor of the tiny bachelor bathroom, my legs sticking out the door. There is no way I'm ever going to find my stash without Rod's help. I'll just have to cool my jets until he gets back. Malone said I had twenty-four hours. And the Daybreak Boys are all on the run now from the cops since the thing with Malone. I'm safe for now.

I go to the fridge and grab a beer left over from the hockey game then sit down on the couch and crack it open. The cold, hoppy liquid races down my throat, soothing it. I haven't had a drink since my flask ran out in the Daybreak Boys' furnace room. The cops wouldn't even let me have water after I was arrested. Oh, they kept saying they'd bring me something to drink, but they never did. A tactic designed to break me. I slam the beer bottle down on the coffee table. It causes a thick head to form that I have to down quickly so it doesn't spill over the lip. The force of my frustration has knocked the cupboard door in the coffee table open and a couple of the Stanley Cup playoff tapes spill out. I stare at them on the carpet for a few moments before it dawns on me: This is where Rod hid the gun, the one he was holding for the pumpkin bomber. I can't believe I forgot. I write off my stupidity to alcohol withdrawal and not having slept in the last thirty-six hours.

Pushing the coffee table away from the couch, I start yanking the tapes out while I kneel on the carpet. I pull each cover off, the tape and box both labelled with Rod's careful handwriting, then I throw it on the floor beside me and fetch another. When I've gone through them all, I search around in the back of the cupboard with my hand, even stick my head in there looking for a panel or something. Then I cross the room and pry apart the dinosaur of a VCR. No stash, no gun. And now Rod is going to kill me when he gets home. You can't buy those ancient pieces of crap anymore.

I sit back on the couch, put my face in my hands. Then pull away quickly when I realize how much it hurts my nose. I grab the beer and almost finish it off. I'm going to have to go out for supplies if I have to wait much longer for Rod. He doesn't keep liquor in the house.

In the discarded pile of tapes and their covers beside me, one label catches my eye: *Stanley Cup Playoffs 2015*. He'd written the title as well as the year on each tape and box. Like the year wouldn't be enough. He only ever tapes the playoffs. But there's something odd about this particular label. Something that's making my spidey senses tingle when I look at it. Then it comes to me, what makes this one tape different from the rest.

"The label's on the wrong side," I say aloud, even though I don't usually talk to myself. Normally, you stick the label for a VHS tape on the side with the window or you block the little grooved circles that fit into the player and turn the tape around. I pick up the tape and look through the window to the inside where the spools with the black tape are wound around. When you look close like this, it is obvious. But if you were just sorting through the tapes, you'd never notice. It's just a picture of spools and black tape pushed up against the see-through plastic window, a Photoshopped internal decoy meant to hide what is really inside.

I can't be bothered to remove the five screws that hold the tape together. Instead, I lift the tape above my head and crack it on the edge of the coffee table. My ID spills out wrapped in a wad of cotton batting that was used to keep the contents from rattling around. When I pull that out, I find my cash hidden at the bottom. He's a crafty old bugger, my uncle Rod. Jesus, how I admire him.

Then I remember the Diamondback pistol Rod was holding for the guy who blew up the pumpkin patch. It was small enough to fit in one of the tapes. I could use a gun to replace the one the Daybreak Boys took off me. I search through the pile of tapes and find another one with the label on the wrong side. When I crack it against the coffee table the Diamondback doesn't fall out, but a phone does.

I pick it up and press the power button. It takes a little while to boot up, but at least it's not dead. When the screensaver comes on, the battery icon reads 59 percent. The screensaver is a picture of a girl with Tyler Brent. I run my thumb against the glass, and all the icons come up. The kid didn't have a password, the cocky bastard. I scroll through his recent emails and texts to see if I can find anything incriminating, but there's nothing in the email but spam. And the texts are mostly graphic photos sent between him and Alice. Sexting. Don't they know that's how Andrew Weiner got caught?

I scroll through all the pictures stored on the phone. Just like Rory said, there are selfies of Tyler and Lachlan posing with the naked girls who sort and bag the Daybreak Boys' drugs. They even took pictures next to the cash-counting machine and the precision digital scales with little mountains of snow on them. These two kids were too stupid to live.

The last photo isn't a selfie. It's a shot Tyler has taken of Lachlan with one of the girls in his lap. I guess they wanted to get the full frame on that one. Standing behind her are Chuck and the biker with the I HATE YOU shirt. And one other person, not patched or dressed in the colours of the gang. He doesn't even have a leather jacket on. Just a sensible navy-blue windbreaker.

I drop the phone onto the coffee table like it's burnt me. This is more than I bargained for. I pick up the broken VHS tape and look inside. More cotton batting. I pluck it out with my fingers and something rattles at the bottom. I'm hoping for more bills tucked into Rod's brass money clip. I'm going to need to get farther away from here than I thought. But when I dump the final contents of the tape out on the coffee table, no cash falls out. Something else does. Something else entirely.

I grab the phone and start calling Charlotte's number, but before I can get in all the numbers a voice calls to me from the direction of the kitchen.

"Put the phone down, Candace." He's still wearing the navy-blue windbreaker he was wearing in the photo

Tyler had taken. He must have come in through the back door. His red wavy hair is the colour of my beer with drops of blood mixed in.

I put the phone down on the coffee table.

"Now push it across the floor to me," he says, his Glock held casually in front of him. "No sudden moves."

I push the phone across the worn carpet toward him. He picks it up, never taking his eyes or the gun off me.

"So, you're the bent cop Malone was looking for," I say.

"I take offence at the word *bent*, Candace," Danny says. "I'm just a guy trying to make a living. And it's not like you're without your secrets. Carrie Fisher, for God's sake. How stupid does Malone think I am?"

"You sent my uncle Rod after the boys to get the phone." I pick up the beer bottle and take a delicate sip.

"Yes, and I have to thank you for finding it, Candace. I thought Rod was holding out on me. Guess I was right." He looks around at the trashed room, the broken VHS cases on the floor, the VCR with its guts hanging out. "Looks like you've saved me a lot of hassle."

"How did you know Tyler had the picture of you?" I ask, still holding the bottle in my hand. I plan to whack it on the coffee table like I did the tapes and use it as a weapon. All he needs to do is give me an opportunity.

"Can you believe it?" Danny says, running a hand through his curly locks. His hair remains unchanged afterward, still sticking up in wonderful waves. The guy must use a hell of a lot of product. "The little bastard was trying to blackmail me. Selena and I did a talk at his high school during Drug Awareness Week. He recognized me and tried to get me to cough up fifty K for the picture."

"So, the drugs and the money the kids took wasn't the reason you sent in Rod. You wanted the phone." I take another sip of the beer to camouflage my true intent. Also, I need it.

"Oh, I would have loved to recover the money and the heroin, Candace, believe me. But unless Rod was lying to me about recovering that, as well, I have to assume Alice Corrigan has it stashed somewhere. You didn't find a big bag of horse and a wad of cash in one of those tapes, did you?"

I just stare at him. Like I would tell him if I did.

"Now stand up slowly and step away from the couch," he says. "Oh, and roll that beer bottle over to me first, very slowly, or I'll make sure your next drink will drain out through the holes in your abdomen." I do as I'm told. I don't have much choice. Like back in the furnace room. Although if Danny knew how that ended, he might decide to take his chances and put those holes in my abdomen now.

He throws the bottle down the hallway. I hear it crash against the lithograph Charlotte had framed of the spaghetti scene in *Lady and the Tramp*. Then Danny comes in behind me and motions with the gun. "Out through the kitchen, Candace." We step over the pots and pans on the floor, and he opens the back door.

"Where are we going?" I ask, still looking around for anything I can use as a weapon. The only thing I can reach is a kitchen witch doll hung next to the door, also compliments of Charlotte. I don't think I could do much damage with it. Maybe if Rod hadn't put her wooden-spoon broom in a drawer.

"We're going for a drive, Candace. Just for a little drive."

I walk out into the failing light with him, and he shuts the back door. The *something else* is left gleaming on the coffee table. I had to leave it behind.

CHAPTER 23

DANNY HAS ME IN THE BACK of the unmarked, but there's a metal mesh barrier between us so I can't get at him. I sit in the middle and look at his face in the rear-view mirror.

"I'm sorry about this, Candace, really I am. I think if you and I had had a chance to get to know each other we could have really had some fun times."

"This isn't my idea of a fun time."

"Agreed, but didn't we have a great time on trivia night? You were pretty good with the questions. Even I didn't remember what was written on the walls of the Overlook Hotel in *The Shining*."

"Redrum," I say, looking out the window of the car. There's no point in trying to bring attention to myself in the back seat of the car, to scream or bash on the glass. The other motorists will take one look at the thinly painted-over police force insignia on the door, the mesh running between the back and front seats, and assume I'm some jacked-up hooker being taken to the station for processing.

"That's right. It's murder spelled backward, isn't it?" He chuckles a bit, his hands held firmly at ten and two o'clock. "But you had a bit of an unfair advantage there. What with you having committed so many."

"Do you even own a stamp collection?" I ask.

"Yes, I do. It's a shame you won't get to see it. I have a 1930 Graf Zeppelin in mint condition. I'll sell it someday when I retire. Which I'll be able to do a whole lot earlier than I planned, due to the generosity of the Daybreak Boys and others like them."

We pull into a familiar parking lot. The floodlights make long shadows on the pavement. It is full-on dark now. Danny parks then opens up the door to the back seat. I don't get out.

"I'll shoot you right here in the car if I have to, Candace. You're an escaped prisoner after all. I'd only be doing my duty." He's probably right about that. The cops won't care if I'm found dead in the back of the unmarked. The daughter of Mike Starr, a notorious killer. Good riddance to hardened criminal rubbish, they'll say, and pat themselves on the back. I get out of the car.

Danny motions at me with the gun again, and I walk in front of him, going where he tells me. He's too smart to stick the gun in my back, where I could possibly reach behind and disarm him before he has a chance to pull the trigger. I'm my father's daughter after all.

He takes me past the fenced-in playground, through the forest of birch trees, then finally down the slippery stone steps to the lookout, Lover's Leap, the highest point facing out on the gorge. The river is still running high, and he has to speak up when he tells me to turn around at the ledge to be heard over the rushing water.

"I really am sorry about this, Candace. But you're just too much of a liability now."

"Just like Tyler and Lachlan," I say.

"Well, those two were just way more trouble than the money they brought in selling Molly for prom after-parties, weren't they? Just imagine the two of them thinking they could blackmail me. Me, Danny Anderson, the wonder boy of vice." He starts laughing again. "Like anyone would have believed them. If it weren't for that picture they took of me and the boys." The moon's out tonight, the cloudy weather replaced by clear skies. The first of the stars are beginning to show themselves, despite the urban glow. I can see Danny's teeth. Unlike the rest of him, they're not pristine. He hasn't seen a dentist in a while.

"Now, come on, sweetheart. Be a good girl and jump. There's so much damn paperwork in a police shooting. I'd really rather be at the gym."

I don't move. This time he'll have to shoot me. At least it'll be quicker than lying for hours in broken pieces on the sharp rocks before I die.

He looks around, getting impatient. "I don't have all night, Candace."

"I'm not jumping," I say. "Go ahead and shoot me." His mouth forms a tight line. A guy who looks like him isn't used to women saying no. But he wasn't joking when he said he really didn't want to have to shoot me. I can tell from his delay. Too much to explain to Malone and the others when they find out I was helping her find a mole in the force. Even if I didn't know I had been.

"I'm not jumping," I tell him. I stuff my hands in the pockets of my leather jacket, partly for warmth, partly for the stance.

He exhales impatiently and then takes out Tyler Brent's phone from his pocket to make a call. Probably trying to raise one of the Daybreak Boys who hasn't been arrested to come help toss me off the cliff. He wouldn't risk taking me on by himself. He squints at the virtual keyboard like he's trying to remember the number of someone as dirty as him who owes him a favour. It'll probably be my only opportunity. I lunge at him.

I'm quick but not quick enough. He drops the phone when I grab him, but the gun goes off. It's so close and so loud the vibration of the impact moves through both our bodies as one. We hold on to each other in a tight bear hug like the fighting hockey players holding each other up on the ice. I hear the shot echo off the dripping limestone of the gorge, and wonder if that will be the last sound I ever hear.

But it's Danny who slumps in my arms and then to the ground when I release him to run my hands all over my own body. I move along my jeans, and my leather jacket zipped up tight against the cold, checking for blood, for a gaping wound. It isn't until Malone starts down the steps that I realize the shot didn't come from Danny's gun; it came from hers.

"Are you okay?" she says, rushing toward me.

"I am," I say, trying to regain my composure now that I know I don't have a hole in me for the beer to run out.

"But only due to a hell of a lot of luck. I'm surprised you didn't shoot me instead of him with your fucking hands shaking like that." Malone looks down at her still-quaking hands holding her service revolver.

"It was Danny all along," she says, looking down at the dead vice cop. She got him right in the back of the head. His ginger hair is stained now with a different kind of red.

"How did you know we were here?"

"I was tailing you all the way from the station," she says, holstering her weapon. She hadn't believed I'd come back after all. "When I saw Danny come out with you, I thought he was arresting you. But when he brought you here, I knew something was wrong."

"He killed both boys," I tell her. "They had a picture on Tyler's phone of him with the Daybreak Boys." I want to make sure she has the correct series of events. Or at least the version I want her to have. After all, it wasn't Danny who actually killed them. Regardless, the lie makes me walk over to the ledge and look out over the swirling water, to take a deep breath. I've never had problems facing a person when I was dishonest before.

That's why I don't see him come up from behind and smash her in the back of the head with the Diamondback pistol. I just hear the impact and the muffled gasp before I turn around and see Malone fall to the ground.

"My, my, young lady. You sure know how to look for trouble. That's for sure."

"Well, I am my father's daughter," I say to Uncle Rod, smiling my best winning smile, despite the chipped teeth. Rod keeps the pumpkin terrorist's Diamondback pointed in my direction as he walks toward me.

"What's with the gun, Uncle Rod?"

"Oh, I think you know what, Candace." He reaches down to Malone's inert body and pulls her service revolver from its holster. Then he pockets his gun and holds hers up in his gloved hands.

"I've been keeping tabs on you. You and your little cop friend here. I was watching from my yard when you came out of the back door with the red-haired fella. I went back in the house once you'd gone 'round the side. Then I followed you and her that was tailing ya." He edges down one step. "I saw what you found, Candace."

We both know what he means. What I had found at the bottom of the last VHS tape in the coffee table was so much more damning than Tyler Brent's phone. With Danny Anderson's gun at my back, I had to leave it behind even though it broke my heart in three places. The brilliant blue face of my father's Rolex, the silver stars still shining with the moon.

"You know, I don't rightly know why I kept it all this time," Rod says, scratching his head with the gun. "Such a right pretty thing, it was. I guess I just couldn't bring myself to throw it away."

"It was you who shot at me. Outside the Daybreak Boys' clubhouse." I'm putting it all together now.

"Well, things were getting a little too close for comfort there. I figured the boys would talk. Those kind always do. Tell you about your dad and what he was going to do to get you off of that murder charge."

"The Daybreak Boys didn't tell me. Charlotte did."

He shakes his head. "That woman wasn't born with a lick of sense that a skeeter could tell of." I'm amazed he can still come up with this colourful crap, given the circumstances.

Malone starts to groan on the ground. He backtracks up the stairs a bit to keep us both in his sights.

"Why did you do it?" I ask him, although I think I already know. "Why did you kill your best friend?"

"Best friend?" he says, spitting on the ground close to where Malone lies, just barely lifting her head up. "Now tell me, what kind of best friend is going to turn himself in and blab to the coppers about all and sundry? Your father and I worked for the Daybreak Boys together and even before that. It was only a matter of time when it would all come back on me. I told him that. But he wouldn't listen. I used the knife on him, figuring he wouldn't expect that from me. Nor would you."

"But I called Agnes. She said you were in St. John's."

He smiles and puts his free hand up to his ear to mimic a phone. "I'm sorry, ma, but I won't be coming in till the morning, eh. A nor'easter blew in and my plane's after being delayed." The goddamn weather again. I should have known.

"Now I see why you didn't want me working with Malone."

"Well, I couldn't have her telling you, now, could I? But you wouldn't keep away, would you, Candace? Even though your uncle Rod told you to steer clear. And I had enough on my hands trying to find that boy's phone."

"Where was it? Alice Corrigan's house?" I need to keep him talking.

"Ah, that was just smoke and mirrors, dear. I got the phone from that Lachlan boy before I took him for a walk on the pier. He showed me where they'd hidden it, in a knothole of one of the birches." He gestures toward the forest behind him. "I didn't want Danny here figuring out what I had." He gestures with the gun at Danny's body on the ground. "I was going to blackmail him using the email, so he wouldn't know it was me. Get the crooked son of a bitch to transfer some money to my bitcoin account." Rod doesn't own a remote garage door opener, let alone a computer. I didn't even think he knew what bitcoin was. He's probably been hanging out at the Gigabytes Internet Café with the furry.

"And you made the anonymous phone call to the cops about me and Kristina Corrigan." Malone is fully awake now, although still on the ground. I want her to hear all the facts straight.

"Yes, I figured that might slow you down a tad." He winks at me, like we've just shared an in-joke, then sighs. "Oh, Candace, how do we find ourselves here, child?" He shakes his head. "You know I have to kill you now, darling. I can't be looking over my shoulder for the rest of my life. And you never were one to let things slide."

"I thought Dad and you said to never use a gun. That they tell stories." I'm buying precious time. I can see the rustle in the bushes behind Rod, but his well-trained ears can't hear it on account of the rushing water below us.

"The only story this gun is going to tell," Rod says, holding up Malone's service revolver, "is that a poor lass of an officer died in the line of duty struggling with a known felon to retrieve her gun, which the assailant had just used to kill her comrade in arms." He spreads his arms out dramatically. "And with her last breath, she manages to get back the gun and squeeze out one last shot." He trains the gun back on me. "That shot will be for you, Candace."

"You always were good at making things up, Uncle Rod."

He narrows his eyes, not pleased with my sarcasm. "I loved your father like a brother and I loved you, particularly as a little mite." He smiles briefly at the memory. "But a man's got to take care of his own self. That's the first rule of the game." He begins crossing himself, using the hand with the gun in it, a plea for forgiveness before the fact.

I'm thinking that I didn't even know he was Catholic when the baseball bat strikes him strong and true on the side of the head. He falls hard, joining Danny on the ground. I run up and take the gun from his limp hand, plus the little Diamondback in his pocket.

Malone lifts her head, slowly bringing herself up to a seated position. She must have one monster of a headache. The figure with the baseball bat has already retreated into the trees.

"Who the hell was that?" she asks me.

I walk over and offer her my hand, pulling her up to standing. Then I hand her back her service revolver. She manages to put it in her holster even though she's still unsteady on her feet.

"That," I tell Malone, "was a purebred fucking scorpion."

EPILOGUE

IN THE END, they can't even pin the doctored security tapes on me. Majd showed them his circa-1980s system and told them the time stamp's been busted for some time. He also confirmed that I'd been working the cash register that day for him. There was an emergency with his mother. One of her three locks had come loose. He'd left me in charge of the store and stayed with her for a better part of the night. When he came back to the E-Zee Market at three in the morning, I was still manning my station. The E-Zee Market closes late on Saturday nights. None of the meth heads and bums who come into the store at that time of night could confirm or disavow his story, rarely knowing what day it is at the best of times.

Majd really is the most awesome of Syrian refugees.

Lovely Linda got called in to the cop shop. But she swore up and down that she'd never seen me with Kristina Corrigan at the bar. And she works there from open to close, she told them with a wink. Ask anyone.

Kristina's alibi held up for the night Tyler was killed, even if mine was a little sketchy. Her husband confirmed they were having family game night, though when pressed he couldn't remember what game. He mistakenly believes his wife and daughter are the ones providing him with an alibi. The truth is that he was at work, trying to get into the business-casual pants of a young intern. When Tyler was being killed, he was sending racy emails to her on the company server as she sat outside his office at her desk typing coy replies. Proving he's a guy who didn't learn much from either of the Clintons.

And it doesn't really matter about my alibi, does it? Danny Anderson admitted to taking a contract out for both Tyler and Lachlan, and Uncle Rod admitted to being the guy Danny hired. I mean, Malone heard it all that night at Lover's Leap, didn't she?

After a safe amount of time has passed, Kristina and I meet in a secluded place to split the fifty K. She'd found it with the jacked-up heroin in Alice's jewellery box long before Rod got there. A mother knows her daughter's hiding places.

I count out the cash, making sure the extra is in there for Tyler. Then I shove it deep in the front pocket of my boyfriend jeans. "What are you going to do with the heroin?" I ask Kristina.

"I'm going to plant it on my best friend," she says. "She's screwing my husband."

I have no doubt that she will. It does not pay to get on this woman's bad side, as I learned that day in The Goon when she first approached me about killing Tyler Brent. He did deserve taking out when you think about it. For what he did to Lachlan, Alice, and especially Jessica Mendler, who never did press charges. She and her mom are still too afraid, but at least they're safely back home now after spending some time at the shelter. Mr. Mendler has entered an in-patient program for people who have messed-up heads from the war. Malone is trying to get Jessica into a similar program for civilian survivors. The battle is just the same.

In any case, these things were only the tip of the iceberg when it came to Tyler's twisted crimes. I checked him out after Kristina came asking for the hit. I could see how a mother wouldn't want her daughter mixed up with him. Why she would want such a boy to be taken care of. But I'm retired, like I said. In any case, there is not much chance of Alice Corrigan getting mixed up in anything these days. Her parents made her trade sunny Spain for an all-girls boarding school in Alaska.

"How did you get the kid to drink the beer?" I ask. I'd told Kristina to spike a couple of brews with Valium to make Tyler more pliant for what was to come. "I thought he'd smell a rat when you offered him free booze, what with you hating him and all."

Kristina smiles with perfectly veneered teeth. They seem to glow under the full moon that's come up over the gorge, peeking out between the balloon lips she's sporting from a recent collagen injection.

"I went to his house that night," she says. "The parents had taken their little girl along with them to a town hall meeting for Concerned Citizens for Feral Cats or something equally preposterous. I met Cynthia Brent at the grocery store that morning, and she couldn't stop going on about it."

Cynthia Winogrodzski-Brent — I almost correct her, but I stop myself. Good thing they took the little sister with them to the cat meeting. I guess they were afraid to leave her with Tyler after he shoved her head into the oven.

"I told him the drinks were a peace offering. That I wanted to bury the hatchet and find a way for us to all get along." She makes a quick brittle cough that I think might be a laugh.

"And he bought that?"

"People will buy anything when there is free alcohol involved," Kristina says. She's probably right about that.

"When he got dozy enough, I poured him into the passenger seat of my car and drove him there," she says, indicating the other side of the gorge where the zip line shack sits dark and tightly shut up for the night. "He was still able to walk, but I had to hold him up. I told him Alice was waiting for us inside."

I nod my head. This was all part of the plan. Kristina had doctored the harness and stored it in the shack that morning. I'd shown her how to take the webby material from the chest restraint and fashion it into a noose using a video from YouTube. Well, YouTube showed how to make a noose, not how to make one out of a zip line chest harness. Like I said, you can learn to do anything on the internet, but some creativity still comes from the offline world.

Kristina was supposed to throw the noose around Tyler's neck when he was blotto from the Valium and then push him off the landing deck. He'd be dead in the fifteen seconds it would take to get to the other side.

That night I'd watched from the top of the embankment on the other side of the river. That was the agreement. I wouldn't do the hit myself. But I'd show Kristina how to do it then stick around long enough to make sure she didn't run into any trouble. I also helped her with the locks at the zip line shack. I have some experience letting myself into places I have no business being.

"I'll be honest, I didn't think you'd have the stomach for it," I tell her.

Kristina considers me for a moment, her balloon lips held tightly together, before she speaks. "Tyler Brent was a menace," she says, saying his name like she's spitting out a rotten peach pit. "To my daughter. To society. That's the part I couldn't stomach."

"But he was still just a kid," I say, feeling the weight of the cash in my pocket. I must be developing a conscience or something.

"Teenage boys are men, Candace. Stupid with freshly minted testosterone and inexperienced, but *still* men. I don't subscribe to the 'boys will be boys' mentality. I don't think you do either."

She's right, I don't. But still I'm surprised at her venom, the deadliness of this society maven's sting. I had watched from the shadows that night on the other side of the gorge, thinking she'd never have what it took to actually murder the boy. After all, even I couldn't bring myself to do it — a kid that young, no matter what he'd done, or might do once he had a few years on him.

But then I saw the silhouette of Tyler's twitching body coming across attached to the pulleys of the static line, Kristina hanging on to him tightly from behind. She was making sure. Riding to the other side of the river like a mad dog into hell with the boy who was ruining her daughter. I don't know if I'll ever understand that part. How she clutched on to him while he died. Although I guess I can understand a parent's love for a daughter, and maybe that's enough to try to comprehend.

"You really screwed things up when you forgot to push him into the gorge afterward," I say, not a fan of a messy job. It was supposed to look like an accident. Just another wasted teenager who had broken into the zip line shack, gone for a joy ride, and ended up smashed on the rocks below. I had warned Kristina not to push him in while he was still alive. People were often lucky enough to survive such falls. When they found him halfway down the rapids with a broken neck and the harness on, they'd just decide he wasn't one of the lucky ones.

"I saw some lights down below in the gorge," she says. "By the river. People using their phones as flashlights. It spooked me."

"There's a trail down to the water's edge," I say. "The junkies go down there to shoot up. Wash the syringes in the rapids."

Kristina curls up her overblown upper lip in disgust. "How would junkies have phones?" she says with disdain.

"Everyone has a fucking phone these days." Except me, I suppose. Maybe I should do something about that.

"Anyway, I was concerned someone would see me push him off the edge," she says. "So I unhooked both our lanyards from the zip line pulley and dragged him just out of sight." I had missed all this, having hightailed it out of there as soon as I saw Tyler's head lolling to the side like a broken ragdoll once they reached my side of the gorge.

"Did you get rid of the evidence, like I told you?"

"I burned the harnesses at home in the outdoor fireplace." I remember now noticing the freshly swept stone hearth in the backyard when Malone and I went over to search Alice's room.

"What about the carabiners?" I ask, thinking she might have forgotten the metal coupling links that fasten the harness.

"I melted them down in my wire and metal jewellery class and made a necklace." Kristina reaches a hand toward her highly chiselled clavicle and pulls out a lumpy blue pendant shaped roughly like a heart. Guilt hidden in plain sight. Always the best plan. She could have been a pro. Maybe she will be after this. The woman continues to impress me.

Even Rod hadn't noticed her tailing him the night he followed Danny and me from his place. He really is losing his touch in middle age. I'd called Kristina from a pay phone near the cop shop after Malone let me go. She'd gotten a burner phone after we set up our little deal, so no one ever saw anything in the phone records. I told her the cops were onto us and to meet me at Rod's to get our stories straight. Kristina had come once she got the message. But when she saw Danny pull up in the unmarked, she had the sense to stay in her Ford Explorer. When he marched me out with the gun and drove me away, she had seen Malone follow behind.

And then Rod came out of the house and took off after her. I can just see Kristina's black SUV following all the others like a train's caboose.

"You always keep a baseball bat in your car?" I ask as she's getting ready to leave.

"My son is an all-star," she says proudly. I didn't even know she had another kid. "I'm late for his game now." She turns to me one last time before she walks away. I think I can see a faint movement in her cheek. She must be due for her next Botox shot. "I trust this is the end of our little arrangement," she says. "I don't want to hear from you again, Candace." She's thinking I might try to blackmail her, but I won't.

"I think we're square now," I tell her. And we are.

★ ★ ★ ★ ★

Uncle Rod is resting uncomfortably upstate, having survived Kristina's baseball bat. He's got the better part of the Daybreak Boys with him. The ones left in town don't trouble me. Rory put out the word that Malone had tricked me into bringing her to the clubhouse. A favour to me along with the cops that allowed him to remain in his squat with Bubba unmolested. And the new leader of the gang, the one who replaced Pauly, is glad the bastard is gone. He's ordered all the others to stand down.

Of course, while Rod has admitted to Lachlan's murder, as well as my dad's, he still insists to anyone who'll listen that he didn't rub out Tyler Brent. But no one believes him. Malone remembers everything he said as she lay on the ground at Lover's Leap, despite her concussion. And he had told Danny and the Daybreak Boys that he'd done it to collect the fee for both hits. Danny, being dead, can't confirm or deny this. But the gang members were happy to give up whoever they could to strike deals. So, all told, Uncle Rod is now serving three consecutive life sentences.

I think I'll leave him there, safe in his cell, for old time's sake. Not take advantage of my connections on the inside who could slice his throat open in the shower. Like I said, I have people who owe me. He'll probably suffer more serving the rest of his life locked away. Newfies weren't made for enclosed spaces; that's why they made the province so fucking big.

The old don of the Scarpello family has rallied. His cancer is in remission for now. But it's only a matter of time. There will be bloodshed when he does finally pop off. These things are rarely settled peacefully. I don't know if my mother is alive or dead, but she's the type of opportunistic termite who might come out of the woodwork when he does. In any case, I'll keep my distance, at least for the time being. A female don is out of the question right now. But things are changing in the world of women. The future is female, I'm told.

As for Saunders, he's been relegated to the ranks of those collecting police tape, that job being recently vacated by Doug Wolfe, who retired with a full pension. He's got a little trailer in Florida now. I saw a postcard from him tacked up on the squad room bulletin board. I think Shelley stayed behind with her book club.

Malone takes me to get my eyebrows done before I get on the plane. She goes to an experienced Indian girl who uses a taut thread to pull out the hairs. I lie back in the chair and enjoy the little tugs of the razor-sharp thread on my skin. Malone says it lasts even longer than waxing.

Selena drives us both to the airport to see me off, the behaviour of a friend — or maybe she just wanted to see me out of town. I walk up the ramp carrying my dad's army duffle, his Rolex tucked safely in an inner zippered pocket. The two detectives stand side by side and wave to me. They are partners now, Selena finding herself in need of one, with Danny the bent ginger in the morgue. Selena has told me she's getting tired of playing goalie. Maybe I'll join their hockey team after all.

Agnes is waiting for me at the St. John's airport. She still drives, she informs me, though not at night. I tell her I got Rod a job working on a Disney cruise ship, playing the Little Mermaid's dad. He'll have to get lost at sea eventually, but I spare her that for now. She's old.

When we get to her little blue house on Franklyn Avenue, the Céilí is in full swing. Charlotte is dancing in the living room, having come on an earlier flight. She's forgiven me for Rod after she found out what he did to my father. And besides, a lady of her age can't wait around for three consecutive life sentences to run out. Right now, she's bumping hips with the fiddle player. He has a full head of hair and kind sea-blue eyes. Agnes' pet hedgehog, Boris, is running loose and nabbing cheese doodles that fall on the floor when people dig into the bowl.

I'm introduced around. Everyone toasts my welcome with some Screech in plastic tumblers. Janet, the accordion player, starts up a song in honour of my arrival.

The familiar notes make me smile as I sit down on the couch and sip at my rum.

Charlotte starts to sing loudly and mercilessly off-key with the accordion music. It's the Spice Girls' "Wannabe."

I guess I still have family after all, I think, as Agnes brings me some fried bologna on a plate. I dip the processed meat in the ketchup and bring it to my mouth. It tastes at once both sweet and sour, like all good things do.

ACKNOWLEDGEMENTS

SO MANY WONDERFUL PEOPLE have contributed to bringing this book and Candace Starr to life. Please know that I would like to take all of you out to The Goon and buy you a beer. Failing that, there are these acknowledgements.

I'd like to thank my husband for being my beta reader and for giving encouragement and feedback within the minefield of a long-term relationship. Marcus, you are a trooper and, as always, my main muse.

Thanks also to my family and friends for listening, often repeatedly, to my ideas, my fears, and to my fears about my ideas. I couldn't have gotten here without you. And to Stacey Madden, who read my short story about a hitwoman hired to rub out a rotten boyfriend and said, "This would make a great novel."

To the talented folks at Dundurn, thank you for making this book a reality. Know that you possess a job that makes dreams come true. My sincere gratitude to Scott Fraser in particular, who waved his magic wand and turned a writer into an author. You get a chaser of

Writer's Tears with your beer. To Jenny McWha, many thanks for having my books' backs. When it comes to driving the editing process, I will always choose you to ride shotgun. I also appreciate the work of Dominic Farrell, and only partly because he laughed out loud at my initial manuscript (but in a good way).

The Algonquin Tavern, known as The Goon in my youth, no longer exists. But in the memory of this delicious Toronto dive bar, I toast you all.